PRAISE FOR *GIRL OUT OF WATER*

"*Girl Out of Water* swept me up in its wake and did a perfect kickflip on my heart. With a cast of characters worthy of every reader's love, Silverman explores the confusing depths of the teenage experience, and its ebbs and flows, with humor, grace, and savvy."

—John Corey Whaley, Printz winner and
author of *Where Things Come Back*

"*Girl Out of Water* is both thoughtful and fun. A perfect summer read!"

—*New York Times* bestselling author
Melissa Marr

"A touching and layered debut. Silverman offers a heartful exploration of love, friendship, family, home—and their upheaval."

—Adi Alsaid, author of *North of Happy*
and *Let's Get Lost*

"Readers looking for a warm coming-of-age story and a swoony summer romance will love *Girl Out of Water*!"

—Miranda Kenneally, author of *Defending Taylor* and *Catching Jordan*

LAURA SILVERMAN

sourcebooks
fire

Published by Sourcebooks Fire, an imprint of Sourcebooks, Inc.
P.O. Box 4410, Naperville, Illinois 60567-4410
(630) 961-3900
Fax: (630) 961-2168
www.sourcebooks.com

Library of Congress Cataloging-in-Publication data is on file with the publisher.

Printed and bound in the United States of America.
VP 10 9 8 7 6 5 4 3 2 1

For Grandma,
a steadfast lover of books and of me

ONE

I FLOAT IN the Pacific Ocean.

As I straddle my longboard, cool water lapping around me, I watch surfers up and down the coast take on baby waves, four-footers that will carry them a short distance before breaking into froth and foam.

I'm waiting for something better.

The sun beats down on the slip of my neck between my wet suit and hairline. The tender skin burns, but I don't dare move to massage it. Seagulls circle overhead, squawking over the swilling water. They dive to the surface, then soar back up, carrying scraps of seaweed and tiny fish.

And then I see it—in the distance, coming toward me, coming *for* me. My gaze flickers over the green-blue water as I watch the wave take shape. It's not a three-footer or even a four-footer. No, it's much better. My fingers drum against my thighs, and I lean forward, gnawing my sun-chapped lip.

As the water climbs, mounting higher and higher, my body thrums with anticipation. Waves are mild in Santa Cruz. It's rare to catch an overhead one, for me anything taller than five ten. But the wave coming for me now, the wave rattling toward me with unfettered determination, looks closer to ten feet, which would make it the tallest ride I've ever had.

I know I should feel fear—fear of a riptide dragging me under, fear of losing control and cracking my head against my board's sharp fin—but all I feel is overwhelming adrenaline. This is it. My miracle wave.

The water hurtles forward with growing fury. I slide from my sitting position onto my stomach, my lower body pressed firmly against the board, hips taut and feet pointed. With a practiced arm, I paddle to the right so that my board spins to face the shore. I take two short breaths and then a single deep one, a ritual I've been doing since I was a little kid. And then, before I have time to second-guess or readjust, the wave is right behind me. I jump to my feet. The cold spray is every-where, consuming and empowering. I'm riding the wave, a beautiful and terrifying barrel wave that arcs over my head so that I'm parallel to a wall of rushing water, the nose of my board just seconds ahead of the break.

But then my lead falters. The wall of water becomes a dome of water, surrounding me on all sides, and then I do the most reckless thing possible: I panic.

I should submit to the wave, dive under and wait for it to pass overhead. Instead, I try to keep going, which is basically impossible when ten feet of water crashes on top of you. The force slams into me, submerges me deep beneath the surface, cutting off all oxygen and any sense of up and down as I swirl like a helpless scrap of plankton. My board flips up behind me and knocks me hard in the side. I instinctively gasp and salt water rushes in, burning my throat.

Air. Air. Air.

I claw my way back to the choppy surface, gasping and wrestling onto my board for support. My heart pounds, my side throbs, and seawater clogs my ears. And in the distance, the remains of my miracle wave rocket toward shore without me.

I paddle back to the coast in defeat. Eric greets me. A sweatband pushes back his curly blond hair, so I can clearly see the amusement in his eyes. "Holy shit, Anise." He pats me on the back. "Rad fucking ride."

"Shut up." I lift my surfboard, then spear it into the sand. "Like you haven't been pitted a million times." I unzip the top portion of my wet suit and tug it off my shoulders, letting the fabric hang around my waist.

"Dude, that was a compliment. No need to get your bikini in a twist." He grins at me, and I bristle. "Seriously, though.

Chill. Wiping out on a ten-footer isn't going wreck your rep-
utation of most awesome surfer ever."

He's not just flattering me. I *am* an awesome surfer—the
best in our group of friends, a dozen or so of us who get
together almost every day during summer from low tide to
high. "I know," I finally say. "But it's still infuriating. That
was such a good wave, and I almost had it." I shift on my feet,
then glance back at the towering swells. "I'm going again."

I'm reaching for my surfboard when Eric places a hand
on my shoulder. "No, you're not," he says. "We promised
everyone we'd meet them at the Shak for lunch, and we're
already like an hour late."

His hand lingers for a moment, hot against my bare skin,
and I have to force myself not to lean into the touch—this is
Eric, my friend of seventeen years; the kid I took bubble baths
with as a toddler when his mom watched me overnight; the
absurd preteen who, when I first got my period, made a mini
surfboard out of my pads and tried to float it on shallow waves;
the person who has spent countless rainy afternoons on my
couch, in pajamas, watching surf competitions on ESPN2 and
stuffing down days' worth of junk food in one sitting.

This is also Eric, my recently single and unfairly attractive friend, whose six-pack is glistening at me like a fucking
Hollister billboard.

"Fine." I force myself to pull away from his touch. "Let's
go food."

I hate to leave the ocean on a sour note, especially when it's offering up glorious waves, but I have a bad habit of ditching my friends for surf. So Eric and I both grab our boards and head down the shore toward the Shak, which is technically called Suzie and Sal's Surf Shak, but all of the locals (and the yearly tourists who think they're locals) go with the shorthand version.

I watch the foamy water lap onto the coast as we walk, then notice a glint in the sun. I yelp and drop to my knees, scavenging through the sand.

"What?" Eric asks.

"I think I see one!" I dig, only to find a shard of a beer bottle. "Fail." I pick it up to throw away later, wondering if it's from a recent bonfire or washed up with the tide. Eric and I collect sea marbles—smooth, colorful glass orbs the ocean churns out, so rare we only find about one a year. We have a tradition: whenever one of us finds a sea marble, we give it to the other person.

"Bummer," Eric says.

"Definitely a bummer," I agree.

We continue down the beach and approach the Shak, with its familiar tin awning coated in green paint and smattering of wooden benches and umbrellas staked in the sand. The majority of the lunch crowd has already dispersed, but our friends are still planted at a table, chowing down on hot dogs slathered in pineapple chunks and hot sauce, fish tacos drizzled with wasabi balsamic vinaigrette, and my personal favorite, watermelon and papaya fruit salad mixed with cayenne pepper and crushed sugar.

"Hey there, strangers," Tess says. She's Samoan, and even though it's still the beginning of summer, her skin is already a deeper shade of bronze than usual. She holds a veggie dog in one hand and an almost-surely-not-virgin strawberry daiquiri in the other. Apparently day drinking during summer is perfectly appropriate and not at all a sign of early onset alcoholism. "How was…*surfing*?"

"Fine," I say, then shoot her a look that I hope conveys, *I love you, but shut the fuck up.*

Tess is my best friend. We've been attached at the hip since we could walk the half-mile distance to each other's house. Unfortunately, I made the mistake of telling her I've been thinking about Eric (or more precisely, the perfect planes of Eric's shoulders as he paddles out to catch a wave) as potentially more than a friend lately.

"Anise Sawyer ate it on a ten-footer," Eric says.

A chorus of "no ways" and "oh shits" erupts from the table, and I cross my arms and stare at Eric. "Really?" I ask. "You had to tell them?"

"Oh, come on." He puts an arm around my shoulder and pulls me into a half hug, which leaves me wondering how the hell he smells like spearmint after being soaked in briny water for five hours. "It makes us all feel better to know you're not infallible. Besides, you should be bragging, not hiding."

"Can you go into specific detail?" Marie asks. We've been buddies ever since we both brought surfboards to first grade show-and-tell. Her arm is wrapped around her girlfriend,

Cassie, who makes up for her five-two height with the most impressive set of abs and biceps on the West Coast. They'll come in handy when she heads off to boot camp for the navy at the end of summer.

"No, I can't," I say stiffly. I know I sound like an asshole. I know I should laugh with the rest of them, play off my fail like it's no big deal. But, well, surfing is the one thing in this world I'm good at. Like really good at. And I love it. So whenever I screw up a ride, it stabs hard, like how an argument with someone you love cuts deeper than an argument with a stranger.

"Okay, okay you guys," Tess says. "We actually have important details to discuss."

"We do?" I ask.

"Oh, yes. Surf Break."

Around the table, everyone cheers with variations of, "Fuck, yeah!"

I say it perhaps loudest of all because Surf Break is *fuck, yeah* amazing. It's a festival held at the end of every summer, a giant three-day party posted up right in our backyards. Professional surfers come in droves to perform demos, local bands and a few famous headliners play on temporary stages constructed on the beach, and dozens of food trucks flood the area. Not to mention the thousands of drunk, sunburned festival attendees.

My friends and I have been attending since we could toddle down the beach in plastic orange floaties. And as soon as we were old enough to ditch our parents, the festival got a lot more interesting.

"All right," Tess continues. She pulls a tattered notepad from her enormous yellow-striped beach bag. Since she prefers sunning over surfing, she always comes to the beach stocked with supplies: sunscreen, novels, her sketchbook, colored pencils, and more. "We have one weekend of nonstop partying to plan. First item on the agenda: Who wants to host the bonfire?"

"I'll do it," I say.

"Really?" Tess raises her eyebrows. Most years I keep my Surf Break schedule commitment-free, leaving plenty of time to go off on my own, watch the demos, learn some new moves from the visiting professionals and amateurs alike. But since so many of my friends are leaving for colleges all over the country at the end of summer—or, in Cassie's case, enlisting—this will be our last Surf Break all together. I don't want to miss a minute of it.

I nod. "Really."

"Awesome." She tips her drink in my direction, takes a sip, and then writes on her notepad while going on to discuss an absurdly long list of other details.

A few minutes into the discussion, I nudge Eric's shoulder. "Back to the waves?"

We haven't eaten yet, but I have a couple of power bars that will sustain us for a few more hours. And as much as I love Tess, the idea of surfing with Eric is infinitely more appealing than listening to her discuss the important advantages of Kraft *jumbo* marshmallows over regular Kraft marshmallows. He nudges me back with a playful smile. "If you insist."

"Oh, I do."

As we leave the Shak and head back to the surf, his fingers graze against mine.

This time I don't pull away.

———

Six hours later, I'm trailing up the sandy wooden walk to my house. My surfboard is damp and gritty under my tired arm, but the strain is good, the kind that tells me my muscles are growing, the kind that tells me this year I'll be able to paddle longer and harder than ever before. The sun is half-set, the Santa Cruz horizon a mess of orange and red with the faintest hint of violet. The ocean reflects the light and resembles a giant bowl of pink lemonade.

I'm late for dinner. Very late. If the sun has almost slipped away, it must be close to nine. But Dad won't mind. He understands the call of the water in the summer, when I can surf all day instead of cramming in a couple of measly hours before and after school. The few times he's lectured me for staying out too late, I calmly reminded him that he was the one who bought his little girl a surfboard when she was seven.

And besides, there was no chance I was going to come

home early tonight. Eric and I surfed together all day, catching wave after wave, taking breaks on the shore, digging our toes into the damp sand while discussing the details of each ride. As the day progressed, I felt him pulling closer. It wasn't my imagination—the way I'd catch him watching me out of the corner of his eye, the way he'd sit next to me so that his bare shoulder would press against mine. Maybe wanting my friend of seventeen years isn't so wild. Maybe I'm not the only one wanting it.

I readjust my grip on my board as I approach home, a ramshackle one-story house perched right behind the dunes. It's a fourth-generation inheritance from my great-great-grandparents, a small and crumbling structure sitting on about a million dollars' worth of prime beachfront property. Sometimes when the bills start stacking up, Dad considers selling and moving further inland, but then the construction company he owns will pick up a few extra jobs, and we're in the clear.

Before heading inside, I grab our mail because Dad never remembers to get it. I tuck the stack of letters under my free arm and head into my garage. Like a true beachfront family, we keep the vehicles in the driveway and the gear in the garage. The entire two-car space is packed with surfboards, kayaks, paddles, as well as buckets and boogie boards for when my younger cousins visit, not to mention decades' worth of beach chairs, umbrellas, and extra towels hardened from years of salt water.

After dropping off my surfboard, I enter the house through

the garage door, which is unlocked like always. I call out, "You home?"

"In here!" Dad calls back.

As I follow his voice to the kitchen, I pick through the mail to see if SURFER Magazine came. It's mostly bills and junk, but then I spot a postcard. The front side shows a picture of some bar called Kelsey's in Reno, Nevada. I flip it over. The backside reads *Dear Anise* in handwriting I haven't seen for years.

My mom's handwriting.

"You coming?" Dad calls.

"One second!" My voice cracks and I clear my throat with a quick, tight cough. I slip the postcard into the entryway table's junk drawer. I'll read it in private after dinner, away from Dad's prying eyes and questions: *Are you okay, sweetheart? Let's talk about it. I love you.*

I head into the kitchen with the rest of the mail and find Dad sitting at the small, round table. A two-person family doesn't need much eating space. When company comes over, we sit out on the deck, relaxing on the weathered patio furniture and watching the waves.

Instead of joining him at the table, I hoist myself up onto the kitchen counter, letting my feet dangle. I grab an apple from the fruit bowl and take a huge bite. Hunger never strikes in the water, but it sure as hell makes up for it later. I glance back at the entryway. My hand shakes—more of a tremor really, like my blood sugar is low. Hopefully Dad doesn't notice.

"What's up?" I ask and direct my attention back to him, taking another bite of the apple.

He looks more stressed than usual—the three lines on his forehead crunched a little deeper, his shoulders sagged a little lower. For forty-one, Dad's in great shape, mostly from working construction during the day and then running the beach and practicing yoga in the evenings. But that hasn't kept his hair from turning salt and pepper or the arthritis in his knees from kicking in. "Well…" he says slowly.

Fuck. My grip on the counter tightens. Dad is a come-right-out-and-say-it type of guy. For him, open and honest communication is the solution to just about every problem. He almost never picks his words carefully, and when he does, it's never to share good news.

He leans forward on the table and clasps his hands together. "Now I don't want you to worry," he says, "because she's going to be perfectly all right, but—"

My mouth goes dry. I struggle to swallow a bit of apple stuck in my throat. *She*. He must be talking about my mom. Something happened to my mom. I fight the urge to jump off the counter and grab her postcard. I will myself to not care. This is the woman who abandoned us and who still *repeatedly* abandons us. The woman who took off before I started walking to follow a band no one had ever heard of around the country. The woman who came back full of presents and apologies when I was three. The woman who left again weeks later because she wanted to work on some fucking riverboat casino in Louisiana. The woman who has been in and out of my life so many times that sometimes I wake up in the middle of the night wondering if she exists at all.

"—Aunt Jackie was in a car accident earlier today."

Oh. *Oh.* A confusing mixture of relief and anxiety floods through me. "Honey, are you okay?" Dad asks.

"Umm, yeah." My fingers tap rapid beats against my legs. I need out of my wet suit. The tight fabric constricts. I jump from the counter and peel it off. "What happened? Was it serious? Is she okay?"

"She'll be okay," Dad says. "But it was serious. Both her legs were crushed. Severely. She'll be in the hospital for weeks for surgery and recovery and then in a wheelchair when she comes home."

"*Fuck,*" I breathe out the word slowly. Dad doesn't mind when I curse. He says if his teenage daughter is going to have one vice, it might as well be a sailor's mouth. "That sucks. Shit, that sucks."

And it really does. I'm closer to Aunt Jackie, my shit-excuse-for-a-mom's sister, than I am to my actual shit-excuse-for-a-mom. I sure as hell see a lot more of her. She has three young kids—twin boys and a girl—and every summer they scavenge up the cheapest tickets they can find and come stay with us at the beach for a couple of weeks. Money is tight for them because Aunt Jackie's husband passed away about six years ago from a heart attack, but they always make the summer trip a priority.

Even though it interrupts my summer surf time, I love having my little cousins around. We trail up and down the beach, hunt for seashells, build sandcastles, and ride boogie boards. Since they only come once a year, the ocean is still magical to them. I love seeing it through their eyes as opposed to the eyes of Santa Cruz locals.

"Is she okay?" I ask. "Like awake and stuff? Can I call her or should I wait until tomorrow? How's Emery? And the boys? Do you have her number? I always forget to save it in my phone."

Dad doesn't answer right away. Oh god, what if the kids were involved? Dread knots my stomach. "Honey," he continues, "you know how I said Aunt Jackie will be in a hospital and then a wheelchair?"

"Yeah…"

"Well, it's summer, so your cousins are home. And Jacks will be in the hospital for a few weeks and then in a wheelchair for even longer. She won't be able to take care of them on her own."

"Oh," I say. "*Oh…*"

"We're going to spend the summer in Nebraska helping out your cousins and Aunt Jackie. I'm going to have to pick up some work while I'm there, so I'll need your help with the kids during the day."

Spend the summer in Nebraska? I've never left California, much less spent weeks away. Why would I, when everything I love—my friends, Dad, the ocean—are all within a half mile of my bedroom? But of course I want to help. Of course I want to be there for my aunt and little cousins, even if the idea of being that far away from home makes me wish I could take my wet suit off a second time.

"O-kay," I say slowly.

Dad clears his throat. "Sweetheart, when I say we're going to spend the summer in Nebraska, I mean…*all* summer."

"*All* summer?" I pause. "Like what part of *all* summer do you mean?"

He rushes out the next words. "We leave tomorrow, and we'll be back a week before school starts."

"A *week* before?"

He nods.

And then it hits me. Coming home a week before school starts means I'll miss the entire summer. It means I'll miss Surf Break, my last chance to spend three nonstop days with some of my closest friends. By the time I get back home to start my senior year, half of my friends will already be on their way out of town.

I stare down at my wet suit. It's crumpled in a pile on the kitchen floor. Tomorrow I'll yank it back on and head out to the surf with the sun rising behind me. Tomorrow I'll meet up with friends. Catch wave after wave. Make bets on the best ride. Eat veggie burgers and plantain chips at the Shak. Tomorrow I'll have salt in my hair and sand between my toes.

"You should probably pack tonight," Dad says, though I

can barely hear him. Through the open window, the ocean's amplified. It's calling to me. It won't let me leave. It won't let this happen. I cannot spend the entire summer in Nebraska. "Flight's tomorrow morning at eleven."

TWO

I SLUMP IN my chair at the kitchen table and stare out the window at the beach. The ocean looks distorted through the old and mottled glass. Before Dad left the room, he promised the summer would be okay—good, even. I want to believe him. After all, this was the man who promised there weren't any monsters hiding under my bed, and he was right. But the thought of being away from my friends for the entire summer is a lot scarier than hiding monsters.

I pull out my phone and send a mass text:

Code red. Being shipped out to Nebraska tomorrow for ENTIRE SUMMER. Meet at the Litchfield Dunes at midnight.

The Litchfield Dunes are half a mile from my house, behind

the Litchfield Estate, which has been empty for five years now due to a case of rich people spending money they don't have, making it a particularly excellent spot for us to gather late at night. My stomach twists with anxiety or hunger or both. I've only left Santa Cruz a handful of times, excursions including the *sorry your mom is trash, let's go to Disneyland* trip when I was eight and the *sorry your mom is still trash, let's go surfing in San Diego* trip when I was eleven. I didn't even go to my uncle's funeral because I had my first serious surfing injuries at the time—a broken arm and a sliced leg that needed a dozen stitches.

The idea that tomorrow I'll be boarding a plane to Nebraska for the entire summer seems so absurd, so far from reality, that I actually start to feel quite calm. After all, there's no reason to get upset about something that can't actually happen.

My stomach grumbles. Dad is an amateur chef and cooks dinner for us most nights, but he had something more important on his mind today. I stand up and scour the kitchen for food, finding a couple of cold slices of veggie pizza, another apple that I slather with chunky peanut butter, and a giant bag of trail mix I eat by the handful. All the M&M's are gone because Dad loves chocolate but doesn't buy junk food, which is how I always end up with a bag of just raisins and nuts. I finish everything off with a bowl of my favorite cereal combination: Cap'n Crunch, Lucky Charms, and Cocoa Puffs. It took years of hard cereal munching to concoct this perfection.

This is a typical evening for me: consuming an entire day's worth of food in about twenty minutes.

Then the text messages flood in, reminding me that today is anything but typical.

WHAT? DETAILS
I'll bring some brews
Dude. Not okay. Also I've got the lighter fluid.
Marshmallows. More marshmallows.
You are NOT allowed to go

I don't respond and put my phone on silent. I'll give everyone the full story when I see them. I spend another half hour scarfing down whatever other food I can find: carrots and hummus, turkey jerky, and a handful of grapes. Then I stuff my ragged tote bag with more snacks and water bottles, yank on my damp wet suit, leaving it half-unzipped, and head toward the garage for my surfboard. I pause by the junk drawer where my mom's postcard hides. It's a weird coincidence that the first time I've heard from her in almost two years also happens to be the day her sister gets into a car accident. Too weird. I yank open the drawer and pull out the card.

My heart thuds as I read it, ears alert in case Dad comes down the hallway. My hand shakes again, making the scrawled writing harder to read.

Dear Anise,

Hi, sweetie! I miss you, and I hope you and your dad are doing well! I'm thinking of swinging by for a visit this summer. I think we're due for some mother/daughter time, don't you? I'll probably be there in June. Or maybe July! We'll see!!!

Love,

Mom

As always, she hasn't included a phone number or address.

My mom will be here this summer, and I'll be in Nebraska. I tell myself this is good. I won't have to see her. I don't want to see her. I won't have to sit here like I did when I was eight, ticking off the days until her arrival on some off-brand My Little Pony calendar, wondering when she'd finally show up. It'll be a nice *fuck you* when she arrives with a mason jar of organic jam from some cooperative farm and three weeks of dirty laundry to find out that Dad and I aren't here. A taste of her own abandonment cocktail.

Dad never speaks badly of her, always makes excuses for her, and welcomes her back into our lives as if this behavior is normal. But as I've gotten older, I can see through his resilient act. I know he only does it for me. Every time she leaves it rips away at him too. Well, at least this summer we won't be around for her to hurt.

I take the card in both hands and start to rip it, but I hesitate half an inch in. Instead, I open the junk drawer, shift around spare keys and rubber bands and dead batteries, and bury her postcard at the bottom of it all.

―――

I'm the first one out at the dunes. It's nearing midnight, and the beach is silent, save the hum of the water lapping methodically against the craggy rocks and sand. The moon bathes the beach in a subdued glow more soothing than the piercing sun. I hug myself tight and close my eyes, breathing in the salted air, letting the familiar scents and sounds wrap around me.

The frustration and anxiety is still there, but the sound of the water, the glow of the moon, lulls the unease. For now, I'll pretend these problems aren't mine. For now, I'll let these few minutes of tranquility stretch out into an eternity. For now, the rest of the world can float away on the gently rocking water until nothing exists except the tide, the moon, and me.

I inhale deeply. Once. Twice.

And then my eyes flick open. A figure rushes down the beach, silhouetted legs pounding down the sand.

"Anise!"

Tess. My best friend who claims she never runs except when someone chases her. So unless there's a man with an ax behind her, she must have made an exception. For a second I think she's going to run into me and topple us both to the ground, but she stops short, bends over, and breathes with strained force.

I move toward her, but she lifts her hand. "Hold on." More panting. "Please don't put me—" More panting. "—in the same vicinity—" More panting. "—of your disgusting level of athleticism."

I wait patiently for a few more seconds. Then Tess stands

upright and says, "You are not allowed to leave me. I will hate you forever." And then she does, in fact, launch herself at me, tackling me to the ground, obstructing my air supply. But I don't care. I hug her back with the same ferocity.

"I'll hate me forever too."

Tess and I release each other but stay on the ground, backs against the coarse sand and eyes on the star-flecked sky. Our hands find each other and hold, like when we were little kids and always chained together. The feeling is reassuring.

As we wait for the others to arrive, I tell her everything—everything except for the postcard because if I don't tell her about it, then maybe it won't exist.

Tess suggests alternate solutions to Dad's plan, ranging from moving in with her for the summer to flying Aunt Jackie to Santa Cruz to recover, anything to keep me from disappearing for months. But I know there's no other solution because Dad loves me, and he knows I love home, and he wouldn't move us out to Nebraska for the summer unless he had to. And beyond that, I know I should *want* to go, I should *want* to help my family.

But knowing and wanting are two very different things.

"Maybe I can visit," Tess says. Her hand leaves mine as she sits up, jarring me more than it should. The longest we've ever been apart was when she visited her extended family in Samoa for two weeks last summer.

"Maybe," I say. "But what about work?"

Tess works at her parents' restaurant, a small café off one

of the crowded tourist strips that serves up authentic Samoan dishes, like these sweet coconut buns so obnoxiously delicious they were featured on one of those Food Network shows.

"The problem isn't getting off work so much as not being able to afford a plane ticket. As much as my parents love you, I don't think they're going to foot the bill for a trip to Nebraska."

"Why? Don't they know it's a destination hot spot?"

We both laugh, then fall silent.

"Look." Tess nudges my leg. "The others are coming. And I spy a very striking sir by the name of Eric."

Eric. I dig my fingers into the sand. I think of our bodies drawing nearer all afternoon and the way our eyes kept meeting. This summer could have changed everything for us. We could have pressed closer each day until there was no distance between us. Tomorrow, I'm not just leaving Santa Cruz—I'm leaving the possibility of us.

No Eric, no Tess, no surfing, no Surf Break—the punishments continue to pile up for a crime I didn't commit. Before I can give it more thought, Eric, Marie, and Cassie arrive, laden with surfboards, drinks, and food. Tess and I stand to greet them.

"What's happening with this Nebraska trip?" Eric asks. I imagine his eyes wide with panic. It's hard to tell in the dark.

I quickly relay the story once more. My friends look as devastated as I feel. "But dude," Marie says. "It's final summer. You can't miss final summer." Along with Cassie, Marie will be gone next year too, starting prelaw at Northeastern on the other side of the country. By the time I get back we'll only have a couple of days together.

Maybe this was a bad idea, inviting all my friends out tonight, giving myself a taste of what I'll be missing for months...and then forever. Even though I still have another full year with Tess and Eric, they're both applying out of state for college, and I'm staying here and applying to the University of Santa Cruz.

I'm not ready to know what good-bye feels like.

"Come on," Cassie says. Her dark skin is luminous in the moonlight. Between her toned muscles and confidence, she always looks so strong. The navy should put her in one of their brochures. "Let's get some driftwood and get this night started. If this is the only Anise I'm going to get all summer, I want to make it count."

We split off to hunt for whatever sticks and brush the sea has churned out for us, baked dry from a day under the blistering sun. Eric walks by my side. He seems to be nearer than usual. But the night does that to your senses, makes it feel like everything is closing in.

We walk in silence, drifting down the coastline and occasionally picking up bits of wood. I want to say something, but the words don't form. As we turn back toward the Litchfield Dunes, Eric reaches out and grabs my hand. The scraps of wood I've gathered almost fall to the ground as I turn to face him, my heart pounding in my ears, like that ten footer is staring me in the face all over again.

He catches my gaze.

This is it. He's going to kiss me.

But then he doesn't.

He takes a small object out of his pocket and hands it to me. My body tightens at the sight. I have to shift the pile of driftwood in my arms to accept it.

"I found it on the walk over here." He takes a short breath. "Anise," he says, his voice taut. "This summer won't mean anything without you."

I look down at a milky-blue sea marble in my hand.

When I glance back up, Eric is heading back to the dunes alone.

———

An hour later, more friends have arrived. A small campfire burns away, Motel/Hotel, our favorite electronica band, plays lightly from someone's iPhone speakers, and marshmallows crisp by the flames. I'm sitting nestled between Eric and Tess, my two anchors. Conversation flows over me as my eyes flit between the fire and the waves.

"Anise." Tess pokes me in the shoulder. "Anise," she repeats.

"What?" I snap back to attention.

"Truth or dare."

I laugh. "You can't be serious."

"Come on," Spinner says, pulling his hair into a tangled

ponytail. Spinner moved in across the street from me six years ago and has been using my boardwalk to access the beach ever since. "We haven't played in forever. It'll be fun."

"There's a reason for that," I say. "Remember the incident with Cassie and the sea bass and the annoyed paramedic?"

"Yeah," someone says. "Pretty sure that was their first and only distress call to help save a saltwater fish."

Everyone laughs, including Cassie.

"Yes, but now we're older and wiser," Tess says. "Come on. It'll be fun. One last hurrah and all that."

I eye her. "If you're so into the idea, you go first. Truth or dare?" I ask. I'm not really into Truth or Dare, but Tess wants to play, and as she nestles deeper into the blanket we're sharing, I realize I'm not the only one who'll be spending the summer without my best friend.

"Turning the tables, very nice," Tess says. "Okay, truth."

"What did you tell your parents you were doing out this late?"

Tess's parents are notoriously strict. Most of our parents are thoroughbred hippies and beach bums and keep us on loose leashes, but Tess's older sister was rebellious, to say the least, and it made her parents extra wary Tess would turn out the same way. "Volunteering at the women's shelter downtown," she says.

"God, you're shameless." I laugh. "You know you're going to Hell, right?"

She grins and squeezes my hand. "I'll take you with me.

Besides, I *am* volunteering there. I just confused *tonight* with *tomorrow morning*."

The game continues for another half hour, secrets slipping out from friends I didn't think had any secrets left to share. When it's Tess's turn again, she faces me. "Truth or dare?"

"Dare," I say.

"Shocker." Eric grins and nudges my shoulder. "Have you ever picked truth?"

I shake my head. I'm a strong believer in actions over words.

But as I look at Tess's face, I know I've made a big mistake. She tricked me. My pulse quickens as I realize there's a 95 percent chance she's about to dare me to kiss Eric.

Instead she says, "Go catch a wave."

"What kind of dare is that?"

"*Naked.*"

I stare at her. Then I stare at her some more. Then I stare around the circle to make sure everyone else is staring at her too. Growing up on the beach, we've all skinny-dipped more than our fair share of times, but there's a big difference between stripping down and jumping in the water and stripping down and getting on your surfboard. It's dangerous. My wet suit saves me from a lot of potentially nasty cuts and burns. Whenever I go out in just a bikini, I always come back littered with scratches.

"Come on," Tess says. "Memories and all that."

"I don't know…" I say slowly, but I'm already giving into the idea.

Because I'm not one to turn down a dare.

Because why the fuck not?

Because I need something to remember this summer by.

"Actually," Tess continues. "I'm going to modify that dare. I dare you *all* to surf naked."

Laughter erupts around the campfire, people shouting, "nice try" and "not happening."

Marie cuts in among the fray. "Umm, the rules of truth and dare do not work that way. You can only dare one person at a time. The only way more than one person can be involved is if you are daring the intended party to do something with a different party."

"How legalese of you," Cassie teases and leans over to give Marie a quick kiss.

"Which is exactly what I'm doing," Tess continues. "Daring Anise to do something, i.e., surf naked with all of you."

"I'm down," Eric says.

I whip my head in his direction. "What?"

He shrugs. "Sounds like fun." And then he stands and strips off his hoodie. The firelight ghosts off the shadows of his defined abs. I'm supposed to fly two thousand miles away from *those*?

Tess smiles and claps slowly. "And here we have discovered one brave soul. Shall others join him, or shall I subject them to horribly embarrassing truths?"

I bite my lip. I look at Eric's abs. "Okay, I'll do it."

I stand up and Eric smiles at me, wrapping an arm around

my shoulder and pulling me into his bare chest, his body giving off more heat than the warmth of the fire. I ignore the flush rising to my face and turn to everyone else. "Marie? Cassie?"

They look at each other without speaking, the way couples who have been together for half of forever can do. After a few moments of silent communication, they both nod and stand, faces bright in the curling firelight.

"We're in," Marie says.

"So in," Cassie agrees.

"Excellent," Tess says. "Anyone else?"

There's a long pause as I glance around at my circle of friends. This is an all or nothing situation. Either they join us, or the dare will fizzle to smoke.

Finally, Spinner stands, shaking out his long hair from its constraint. "Let's do this."

Everyone else echoes his words and climbs to their feet.

"Now if you don't mind," Tess continues, "I'll just get my camera out and—"

"No!" The objection comes from all of us at once, followed by laughter. The last thing I need is to wake up tomorrow to photos of my bare ass.

"Fine, fine." Tess waves her hand. "It was worth a shot."

⸺

The water isn't freezing, but it's cold enough to make me crave the wet suit lying by my feet. I try to let my skin and mind adjust, working up the nerve to strip off my bikini too. About twenty feet away on either side of me stand Eric and Cassie, with the rest of my friends spaced twenty feet from them, dappling the coast with our nude silhouettes. The moon lights everything in odd angles, so I can't see much more than their outlines. Still, my eyes hover over Eric, tracing the contours of his strong thighs and shoulders.

"Ready?" he shouts. The whipping wind distorts his voice.

I take two short breaths and one deep one, then shimmy out of my bathing suit. The air prickles my bare skin, and I rub my hands up and down my arms and jog in place for warmth. "Ready!" I shout and turn to ask Cassie the same.

She shouts back, "Hell yes! Go, go, go!"

Usually when we surf, only one of us goes out at a time, leaving plenty of space for each person to catch a perfect wave. But tonight, we all rush into the water at the same time, spray kicking up around our ankles. The most familiar action in the world feels alien, salt water rushing over each and every pore, wind catching my hair, flying it over my bare skin. And yet, my body still knows what to do.

As soon as I'm waist-deep, I climb on my board and paddle out to the crest of waves. My arms slice through the water with heavy strokes, warming my body with the exertion. Every element feels magnified. The biting sting of the salt. The sharp musk of the air. The tranquil thunder of the waves. My body hums as I paddle out into the moonlit water, and abruptly I let out a wordless shout, a euphoric call to the world and the waves. That call reverberates around me, over the crash of the water, my friends are doing the same, hollering to the moon and thanking it for its tides.

Up on the glowing horizon, I spot a wave pulsing toward me. It's smaller than my usual fare, but maybe that's good considering my state of dress, or lack thereof. I paddle fast strokes with one arm, turning my board back to the coast, spotting a glimpse of Tess on the shore. She's dancing and skipping and jumping around, and I think perhaps she too is hollering to the moon.

As the wave launches itself behind me, I jump to my feet with a perfect takeoff. I shout once more as the current surges beneath me, hurtling me down the coast, invigorating me with adrenaline akin to when I was seven and caught my first wave. For a second, I'm transported back in time, born once more into the water, everything fresh and new, yet also filled with an overwhelming sense of home.

The ride ends all too soon, and I find myself back in the shallow water. Tess is closer now, still dancing, twirling as if on an invisible string, rippling in the shadows cast by the fire. To my right, Eric dips along on his board, staring in my direction. I can't see the details of his face, but I know him, and he loves what I love, so I know he's smiling because I'm smiling. There's nothing to feel but happiness in this moment.

———

Truth or dare fizzles out after that. It's better to appreciate certain experiences than try to top them. Instead, we all sit around the fire, cracking open a few beers stolen from parents' pantries or bought with shitty fake IDs, huddling in oversized terry cloth towels and fleece blankets, eyes and ears on the crackle and pop of the fire.

We talk about the same things we always talk about. The waves from earlier today. What college will be like. The different pro tours all over the world. I sit and listen, finding it hard to speak because somehow I already feel the distance growing between us. Each minute stretches into another mile of separation. As they all talk about a plan for tomorrow, my stomach clenches because I won't be there. And then, as they graze the topic of Surf Break, I retreat even further. How much will I miss while I'm gone? What if so much changes I don't even recognize home?

Eric, perhaps noticing my silence, leans into my shoulder. "Want to take a walk?"

I hesitate, the word *yes* stilling on my lips, because I think I know what this walk will bring, and as much as I want it, want *him*, I'm scared. Pulling off a Band-Aid can't sting if you don't get cut in the first place. So as much as I want him, is it worth it only to be ripped apart the next day?

But then Eric nudges me again, the warmth of his lips near my neck, and I find myself nodding and saying, "Sure."

We stand from our spot around the fire and retreat with a mumbled, "Be back."

I love my friends because they don't chorus with *oohs* and *ahhs*. They just say, "chill" and continue with their conversations. Well, except for Tess, who winks at me from across the fire and howls softly like a coyote in the distance.

Eric and I make our way down the beach, walking along the shoreline, bare feet padding through wet sand, water lapping behind us, erasing our freshly-made footprints. Eventually, when the light of the fire is just a small glow behind us, we stop walking, and Eric turns to me. It's too dark to see his eyes clearly, but I know their exact color: blue with a hazel ring around the center. He runs his hand through his curly hair.

"I—" he starts to say.

But I don't want to hear what he has to say, because that will make this real. He'll acknowledge that I'm leaving, that tomorrow I'll be in Nebraska instead of running out to meet the tide, that the summer will be ending by the time I'm back, that everything that could have been will never be.

I don't want to hear it. Any of it. So instead of waiting for him to piece together his thoughts, I tug his hand, step forward, and kiss him.

It's so simple.

Our heights the same. Our lips level. We fit together with an ease that seems impossible.

His lips part slightly, and I shiver into their warmth, stepping closer to him so our sand-freckled bodies press together, arms wrapping, hands exploring. My toes curl into the damp ground as his lips graze over my cheek, my neck, my collarbone. As his tattered breathing skirts across my bare skin, I feel the moon above us—watching, glowing.

And as we stand there under its careful eye, I wonder: If the moon has the power to turn tides, does it also have the power to still time?

———

Dad wakes me up the next morning—after approximately two hours of sleep—and tells me we're already late for the airport, and *no*, I can't go back to sleep, and *no*, I don't have time to shower, and *no*, the airplane can't pick me up from home. I'm so exhausted I actually crawl out of bed without further complaint and follow him to the car. It's not until I'm at the airport, through security, and walking onto the plane with a duffel bag slung over my shoulder, a boarding pass in one hand and a to-go cup of green tea in the other, that it actually registers. I'm leaving Santa Cruz for more than two months, and nothing short of a natural disaster, which of course would be terrible, will get me off this plane.

Dad gives me the window and then promptly puts in headphones and falls asleep. I settle into my seat and lean my head against the cool, vibrating wall. My stomach churns with anticipation…and maybe the one and a half beers I drank sometime around three in the morning. A few hours ago, I was on the beach with my friends—surfing, talking, *kissing Eric*, and now I'm here, on a plane, taking me away from all of it.

I slip my phone out of my pocket and glance at the display, which is filled with messages, wishing me good-bye. The one from Tess reads:

If you're not back in two months, I'm sending a rescue squad.

There's a message from Eric too. Just the sight of his name heats my cheeks. But then an overhead announcement comes on, asking everyone to turn off their phones, and since I've never been on a plane before, I'm not sure if that's a rule no one pays attention to or a real rule, so I shut mine off and slip it into my ragged tote, still damp and sticky with sand from last night, and then curl further into my seat.

The plane crawls down the runway, then races down the runway, then tears down the runway, and as we shoot up into the sky like blasting off from an epic wave, the ground turning into air and Santa Cruz shrinking away beneath us, I think of the note I scribbled last night around four in the morning, head buzzed and lips swollen, the note I taped to my mom's favorite mirror in the guest bathroom: *Aunt Jackie was in a car accident and broke both her legs. We'll be at her house all summer if you want to find us there.*

THREE

"WHY IS IT hot?" I groan. "And humid?"

Six hours, one flight change, two snack-size bags of peanuts, and two cans of Coke later, I'm standing with Dad outside the Omaha airport, bags around our feet, sweat dripping down our necks, and no taxis in sight.

"This isn't fair," I say. "No ocean should equal no humidity. Isn't that like a meteorological rule or something?"

"Anise, enough," Dad says. "Now grab a bag and help me find the taxi stand."

I'm not used to this problem, the problem of finding things. For the last seventeen years, I've lived in the exact same place, which means I never had to *find* a grocery store or *find* a pharmacy or *find* a goddamn taxi stand. But this place isn't home. This place is dirty concrete instead of sand; this place is pigeons picking at overfilled garbage cans instead of seagulls scavenging under the boardwalk.

"Fine." I swing my giant duffel bag over my shoulder and grab the rolling carry-on with the half-broken wheel. "You know, we should invest in some real luggage."

"Remember a couple summers ago when I asked if you wanted to go to DC and you basically had a heart attack at the suggestion that you'd want to do anything but surf all summer?" Dad asks.

"Umm…"

"We haven't taken a trip since you were eleven, so we've never needed better luggage."

"Right," I say. "Well, maybe we should buy some. It might make these impromptu trips to Nebraska a bit easier."

Dad halts in front of me. I stop short but still half-crash into his back. He turns and gives me *the look*. You know, the one all parents have, the one that says *I brought you into this world, and I can take you right back out.*

"Anise, honey, I know this isn't fun for you, so you can complain to me as much as you want—"

"Really?" I interrupt.

The look intensifies. "But if you make so much as one ungrateful, selfish, immature comment around your aunt and cousins, I swear you'll never see the pit of a barrel wave again. Understood?"

The duffel bag strap digs into my shoulder. I readjust it and keep my eyes on the ground. Dad and I are close, so when he's upset with me, it slices deep. Plus, he's right. I shouldn't be complaining. I should be *happy* to help my family. I *am* happy to help my family. I'm just not so happy to be helping my family in *Nebraska*.

"Understood," I say.

"Good. Now come on. I think I see some taxis over there."

———

I'd always imagined Nebraska to be some giant, flat dust bowl, a place my mom would want to run away from at seventeen, but as we speed down the interstate toward Aunt Jackie's house in the Omaha suburbs, grass stretches in every direction. It's slightly yellowed from the heat of summer, but it's grass all the same. The tall stalks wave in the wind, like Nebraska's pathetic attempt at an ocean.

"You've been here before," Dad says.

"What?" I look at him. He's staring out his own window. "I've never left California."

"You were barely a year old," he says, turning to face me. "It was the first time your mom left, and I panicked. Booked a flight. We stayed with Jacks while I tried to track down your mom. Your aunt was only twenty then, in college, living alone in the house since both your grandparents had passed away. The look on her face when I showed up with you—it was like..." He trails off.

"Like what?" I ask.

"Like she'd been expecting me. Your mom lived with me for two years straight. I wasn't familiar with her…her habit."

"I didn't know," I say. I have a dozen memories of my mom's famous disappearing acts, but of course I wouldn't remember one from that long ago. I glance at Dad, wondering yet again how he raised a kid with an absentee wife. No, not an absentee wife. Worse than that. A wrecking force, flying in and out without notice, not caring what destruction she leaves in her wake.

When I was younger, I remember Gabriella, one of Dad's only serious girlfriends, left him because she found out he was still technically married. My mom never had the courtesy to sign divorce papers. I wonder if he was ever tempted to quit parenting too and what my life would have been like if I'd had two parents who didn't want me instead of just one. I run my fingers over the rough texture of the seat belt as the taxi pulls into a neighborhood. We must be close. "Did I like it?" I finally ask.

"What?" His forehead wrinkles.

"Did I like Nebraska? The first time?"

Dad pauses and then gives a short laugh and shakes his head. "You cried for three days straight."

⸻

The house is two stories of chalk-white bricks and blue shutters. A bicycle sits haphazardly in the small yard, its front wheel sticking up to the sky. Shrubs dot the borders along the neighbors' properties. I think of our beautiful, dilapidated beach home and try to keep my expression bright. I think of my mom living here as a kid. I try not to think of my mom living here as a kid.

Dad pays the taxi driver, and we grab our bags and head up the concrete driveway. As we approach, the front door slams wide open, and two compact figures rush out. "Uncle Cole! Anise!"

They crash into us with energetic, small-armed hugs. "Hey guys." I smile down at my younger cousins, hugging them back. Parker and Nash are nine-year-old twins. Technically they're fraternal, but if it weren't for Parker's jet black hair and Nash's lighter brown, it'd be impossible to tell them apart.

Emery emerges from the house, trailing behind her brothers. I falter when I see her. This is definitely not the kid I played with last summer. Emery is almost thirteen and seems to be a few inches taller than she was last year. She's wearing a flower-print romper, and her dark hair is pulled back into some fancy braid that puts my plain ponytail to shame.

After getting over my shock, I walk over and give her a hug. "Hey, you."

She hugs me back, kind of, and then quickly steps away and mumbles, "Hey, Anise." Her gaze lingers on me, maybe taking in my outfit—worn-out jean shorts and a cotton tank top.

"Come on," Dad says to everyone. "Let's get our things inside so we can go see your mom. How's she doing?"

Aunt Jackie is still at the hospital, where she'll be for her second surgery and several weeks after that for recovery. One of her friends stayed over with the kids last night, and a neighbor has been checking in all day until we could get here to take over.

The cousins lead us inside the house. Parker and Nash even help grab the bags. I hold back from saying anything as they struggle with the weight.

"She's okay," Parker answers Dad, panting.

"No, she's not!" Nash says.

"Yes, she is!" Parker repeats.

"Guys! Shut. Up." Emery bites out the words, low and sharp.

The boys quiet immediately, and Dad and I exchange worried looks. Emery has always played her big sister role but never with a sharp tone. I wonder if she's always like this now or if she's just freaked out. She was seven when her dad passed away, and her remaining parent was just in a near-fatal car accident. I tense, remembering a few years ago when Dad fell off a roof at a construction job and was one wrong angle away from breaking his neck. I was so scared of losing him, of having no one left. I want to say something to Emery, but I can't think of the right words, so instead I wrap an arm around her skinny, freckled shoulder as we head to the house. She looks up at me with a small smile. "Come on," she says. "I'll show you guys your rooms."

Parker and Nash drop our bags at the foot of the staircase and veer left into the living room where I can hear a television on. Dad and I follow Emery up the carpeted stairs.

It's weird to walk on the soft fabric when I'm so used to the familiar creaks and groans of our wooden floors. Family photographs line the beige wall. I focus on a black-and-white one of Uncle Scott with the twins as newborns. They only visited once as an entire family before he passed away. I was eleven that summer, and for a few weeks, my whole family, including my mom, was together. But the night before Aunt Jackie, Uncle Scott, and my cousins were supposed to leave, my mom disappeared again. She stayed fewer days than ever that visit, almost like with more family there, the more she wanted to leave.

I'm both disappointed and relieved there aren't any older pictures, none of my mom, no indication she grew up in this house. I'm not too surprised, though. There are so few pictures of her to begin with. Aunt Jackie once told me that even as a kid my mom rarely sat still long enough for someone to snap her photo. It must be strange to disappear so completely from your own home. I imagine my bed with the crocheted quilt Tess made me, the living room with my old, cracked surfboard on the wall, the kitchen with the pictures of Dad and me stuck to the fridge. If I disappeared, left home and traveled far away for college, would all proof of my existence eventually disappear too?

Once upstairs, Emery leads us down the hall and opens the door to the master bedroom, which must be Aunt Jackie's. The bed is made, the linens turned down neatly, like in a hotel room. A pair of running shoes sits by the door. My eyes focus on them. Aunt Jackie runs daily, religiously, like Dad. It'll be months until she can lace up those shoes again.

"Mom said to put you here," Emery tells Dad. "When she gets back home, she'll stay in the downstairs guest room because of her...her legs."

"Thanks, sweetie." Dad brushes a hand against Emery's shoulder before dropping his canvas backpack in the middle of the room.

Emery nods and then turns back down the hallway. "This way, Anise." I follow her and end up at her room. Band posters and art—most of which looks like album covers—plaster the walls. An outdated Mac sits on a desk, which is covered with pens and markers and crumpled paper. Two twin beds press against opposite walls, one with a bare mattress and one neatly made, corners tucked in and everything. Emery flops down on the made bed and gestures to the other one. "When Mom gets home you'll sleep here with me. I can help you set up the bed and stuff. Until then, you can have your own space in the guest room downstairs. Want me to show you?"

"I think I can find it. Thanks, Emery."

I smile at her and she gives another small smile back, one that doesn't really hit her eyes. Then she pulls on a pair of chunky green headphones and opens a magazine, settling more deeply into the bed.

"Aren't you coming to the hospital with us?" I ask.

She doesn't look up, just softly says, "No, I went yesterday." I decide not to push it. Even though I'm sure Aunt Jackie

43

would love to see her again, hospitals can't be on Emery's list of favorite places.

I leave her room and take a slow inventory of the rest of the house. The twins' room is also upstairs, complete with bunk beds and those glow-in-the-dark stars on the ceiling. Downstairs in a corner is the guest room. I drop off my tote bag and then head to the kitchen, an old layout with laminate countertops but, unlike ours, appliances that actually came out of this century. It'll be nice to make toast without worrying about blowing up the house. It's a running joke between Dad and me that he runs a construction company, yet our own home probably breaks every building code in the book.

I wonder which room my mom grew up in, and if I scavenged through it, would I be able to find anything she left behind? It's strange to brush my hands against the same walls she did as a child. I swore off thinking about her last time she left me, but avoiding her here feels impossible. Even without her pictures and things, I can feel her presence, a living ghost haunting its old home.

I can't believe I left a note telling her we're here. This summer is already enough of a disaster. The last thing anyone needs is for her to show up and wield her particular brand of devastation.

I step into the living room. The twins are splayed out on the carpet, playing some video game with gunfire and green alien splatter. "Wanna play?" Nash asks, his eyes glued to the screen and fingers rapidly pressing the controller buttons.

"Yeah, wanna play?" Parker asks, glancing at me for half

a second before turning back to the screen to blow off some alien's head.

"Next time," I say. I almost never play video games. Some of my friends like playing this old surfing game on Xbox, but I never really understood the point with an actual ocean steps away.

A sliding glass door opens the living room to the backyard. I walk outside. My skin immediately misses the cool blast of AC. There's a pool out here, which would be great if it had any water in it. I pad across the cracked cement, my flip-flops smacking the backs of my feet. The pool probably hasn't seen anything but rainwater for years. I guess that's what happens when you have three kids in three years and then your husband passes away before two of them are even in kindergarten. Time and money for things like fixing pools don't exist.

Sighing, I sit down at the lip of the bowl and dangle my feet into the empty space. I grab my phone from my pocket and play "No Night to Sleep," my favorite Motel/Hotel song. I start to text Tess but stop. What's there to say? *Nebraska sucks. See you in two months?*

I tell myself to be positive, to be happy that I can help my family, family I love.

But that positivity feels difficult to grasp when I look up and see rows of asphalt-shingled roofs instead of lines of lush saltwater waves, when my friends are almost two thousand miles away, when my family is hurting, when I'm stuck here all summer—trapped in the home of a woman who broke free.

I have a lot of experience with hospitals. Between dislocated shoulders, lacerations, and common yet dangerous dehydration, at least one of my friends lands in the ER every few months. It's pretty easy to get hurt out on the water, especially during tourist season when there are crowded breaks and too many distractions. So entering through the automatic double doors into the distinct, recirculated hospital air is, in an admittedly strange way, comforting.

Dad starts toward the help desk to ask for directions, but Parker tugs his arm. "I know where to go," he says. "She's in the same room as yesterday."

"Oh, okay. Great," Dad says, and then we all follow the four-and-a-half-foot boy through the labyrinth of hospital halls. Parker maneuvers through about a dozen twists and turns with confidence. I wish I'd inherited the same memory. As we walk, Nash zigzags back and forth across the hallway, knocking on every closed door until I catch him by the shoulders. He grins up at me like I should find his behavior endearing.

Eventually Parker stops in front of room 1109. The door is slightly ajar, but Dad knocks anyway. No response.

"Let's go in," Nash says, then pushes open the door and enters without further thought. Nash doesn't seem to put further thought into most of his decisions.

I hesitate before entering the room, suddenly realizing

my mom could be inside. Maybe she somehow heard her sister was injured and flew straight here instead of going to Santa Cruz. Maybe she's standing by Aunt Jackie's bedside, a flower from a *get well* bouquet tucked in her hair and a small Styrofoam cup of tea in her hand. Maybe she'll turn to me and smile, and maybe I'll—

She isn't here.

But I'm fixed in shock in the doorway anyway.

Aunt Jackie is rigged up in so many contraptions, threaded with so many tubes and wires, that she looks like an illustration out of my paperback copy of *Frankenstein*. I've seen a lot of injuries, but this is by far the worst. Her left leg is slung in a metal gurney with some kind of weird plastic wrapping around it, and cuts and bruises cover every inch of exposed skin. Tears prick at my eyes as I realize I actually could have lost my aunt, one of the most important and caring people in my life.

"Fuck," I say.

"Anise said a bad word!" Nash shouts.

"Shh," Dad whispers. "Don't wake up your mom."

"But we're here to see her," Parker says.

"I know," Dad answers, "but…"

"Cole, Anise? Is that you?" Aunt Jackie mumbles and shifts slightly in the bed, leaning her head toward us and cracking open her eyes. Her dark brown hair is pressed in tangles against the pillow, and I think of how patients on hospital TV shows always look so groomed, like they stepped right out of a beauty parlor and into the ER.

We all scoot forward. Well, Dad and I do, while Parker and Nash launch themselves onto the armchairs by the bed. "Hi, Mom!" they both say.

"Hey, Jacks. How you feeling?" Dad asks.

"Hi, boys." Her eyes open more fully, scanning the room. "Where's Emery?" she asks, her voice hoarse from medicated sleep.

I rub my arms and wait for Dad to answer because I can't think of a positive way to say *your daughter's at home because your life-threatening accident traumatized her.*

"She's just tired, Jacks," Dad says.

Aunt Jackie's eyes flicker and she swallows. "Hey boys—" she stops to clear her throat. "Why don't you run and get some sodas—*caffeine-free* sodas. Cole, do you have any change?"

Dad nods and hands Parker and Nash a few dollars, which they grab and then run from the room, their sneakered feet pounding down the hallway at a pace much too fast for an establishment of sick and dying people.

Through the stitches and bruises, Aunt Jackie manages half a smile. "They're pretty cute, aren't they?"

I nod. "Pretty fucking cute."

Her gaze lingers on the doorway. Then she blinks a few times. "Sorry," she says. "The meds they have me on are strong. I'm feeling a bit toasted."

"Toasted?" I ask.

Aunt Jackie nods. "Oh, you know—stoned, high, baked, riding the green—"

"Okay, okay, word defined," Dad cuts her off.

She rolls her eyes at him. "Please, Cole. Your daughter is seventeen and lives in California. I think she knows what marijuana is."

I *do* know what marijuana is. When I was fifteen, Cassie said I had to try it for this concert we were going to. I'd be lying if I said I didn't have a great time at that show, but I've only smoked a couple of times since because I'm not really into messing with my lung capacity and edibles are too strong. Still, Dad doesn't need to know about those rare occasions. Before I have to defend myself, Aunt Jackie speaks again, "Is she okay?"

For a second, I think she's talking about me.

"Emery will be fine," Dad assures her. "I think she's a little shocked, a little scared. She's still digesting it all."

Dad would make a great counselor if he ever got sick of construction. He's very direct and Zen. Apparently back in the day he used to be a bit of a mess. His parents were both elderly and sick when he left for college. His sophomore year, they went downhill fast, so he left school and came home to take care of them. They died within a year of each other, and he never went back to college. Instead, he spent his days drinking and smoking and surfing. My mom told me that's how she met him, with a can of Bud Light in one hand and a joint in the other. They spent an entire year enjoying the bliss of nothing until my mom found out she was pregnant. Dad knew she was a wanderer from her tales, but she said I was a sign to put down roots, that her family had found her. So my parents got married, and I was born, and everything was picture-perfect. That is, until my mom couldn't *deal*, ripped out those roots, and ran.

Dad became an adult real fast. He quit drinking, quit smoking, and worked in construction until he could open his own business. As the years went on, he found ways to decompress from all the stress in his life—running and green tea and yoga. He not only was a parent to me but also a counterbalance to my mom's instability. Saying I love him is like saying the Beatles had a decent career.

"I'm sure you're right. I hope she'll come around soon," Aunt Jackie says. Her hand plays with the edge of the comforter, smoothing it and crinkling it again and again. Her eyes drift closed, and she speaks once more, the words slurred, half-spoken in sleep. "A girl needs her mother."

―――――

I can't sleep. The guest room, with its white paint, white comforter, and white curtains, has less personality and warmth than a chain motel. I crave my room—the crocheted quilt Tess made me, the walls plastered with posters of my favorite surfers, the shelves stacked with tangled medals from surfing competitions, books and magazines, odd-looking shells and sea marbles. It's hard to think of my room without me in it, my things just sitting there, hoping I'll come back for them.

As I toss and turn at one in the morning, it occurs to me I've never experienced complete silence before. My entire life has been filled with the crash of waves, the squawk of seagulls, the humming conversations of people walking the beach. Never once have I experienced this terrible buzzing silence. Every time I close my eyes, it eats at me, and I yank them back open in mute anxiety.

Giving up, I grab my phone from the nightstand and scroll through my texts, opening the one from Eric I didn't have time to read earlier:

Wish we could repeat last night all summer. Hope everyone is okay. Call me if you have time.

His words flush my skin. I bite my lip, but it doesn't compare to the feel of his touch. I wish we could repeat last night all summer too—exhausting our limbs from surfing, exhausting our lips from each other. I can't believe I kissed him last night. But I kissed him and left. This summer could have been everything, and now—

I press Eric's number, heart thumping slow and hard as I wait. He picks up on the second ring. "Anise?" His voice sounds different over the phone, and for a second his face blanks out of my mind, as if I were talking to a complete stranger and not one of my closest friends. I can't remember ever talking to him on the phone before. Why would we when we could just text or walk to each other's houses?

"Anise?" he repeats.

"Hey!" My voice comes out squeaky. "Hey. Hi. How are you? What'd you do today?"

"I'm okay. I did the usual, you know, surfed and stuff. It's not the same without you showing me up. How's your aunt?"

I sink into my pillows and clutch the comforter to my chest. Sleep presses more heavily now, my eyes blinking from the frenzy-induced exhaustion of the last twenty-four hours. "Um, not great, but she'll be okay…"

"That's good."

There's a long pause, and that terrible buzzing silence fills the room again. "Hey Eric, can I ask you something weird?"

"Sure. What is it?"

"It's really weird."

"Try me." I can almost hear him smiling over the phone. Throughout the many years of our friendship, he usually does the weird things, while I watch and laugh and judge only a little.

"Um, will you go out on your deck and put the phone on speaker? I miss the sound. You know, of the ocean."

After a short pause, Eric says, "I'll do you one better. I'll take you right to the waves."

And he does.

And I fall asleep, not to Eric's voice, but to the crackling roar of the water.

FOUR

IT ONLY TAKES three days of helping out around the house for me to decide I never want kids. Ever. Unless I'm a millionaire and can pay other people to take care of them. But even then, I'm pretty skeptical about the whole thing. I don't know how Aunt Jackie does it. I have a lot of endurance, but after less than seventy-two hours, I'm ready to drop.

One of Aunt Jackie's friends had a lead for construction work on the new city hall, and Dad jumped at the opportunity to bring in some money while we're here, which is great and all, but that leaves me stuck alone with all the kids trying to keep the house standing.

Emery is pretty easy to handle because she spends 95 percent of her time in her room and online. Every now and then she comes out, phone in hand, and settles next to me on the couch. I wish I could offer to take her to her friends' houses or the movies, but I don't have a license, and even if I did have a license, I don't have access to a car, and even if I *did* have a license and access to a car, part of me thinks I'd pile all three kids in the backseat and head straight for Santa Cruz.

It's the boys who are out of control. I'm trying to be patient. I really am. My chest gets tight when I think about all my cousins have been through. They only have one living parent, and she's currently in the hospital. Sure, the worst is over. Aunt Jackie has a long road of recovery ahead of her, but she'll be okay. But that doesn't make *what could have happened* any less scary. I want to be sensitive, but it's hard to be sensitive—to stay sensitive—when living under the same roof as Parker and Nash.

I'm not sure if all kids have this much energy or if I just hit the familial jackpot. Sometimes I get a break when they play one of their multiplayer games on the Xbox, but most of the day, they trail me around the house with a never-ending chant of, "We're bored. We're bored. We're bored."

This was never a problem in Santa Cruz because there's an ocean, and nine-year-old boys can boogie board and fly kites and throw seashells at one another to their hearts' content.

But Nebraska doesn't have an ocean.

It has yellow grass and central AC.

Everyone is particularly on edge today because Aunt Jackie is having her second surgery. After that she'll be in recovery at the hospital for a while before she can come home. Since

Emery still seems so nervous, Dad and I decided it was best I stay home with all the kids, so he's at the hospital alone with Aunt Jackie. Emery has spent most of the morning on the living room couch with us, instead of in her room like usual. Of course, she's still silent and glued to her phone, but it's nice to all be in the same physical space.

The boys are on a sugar high (probably because their genius cousin made them waffles and ice cream for breakfast), and they won't stop begging me to take them to the park. "Please, please, please," they chorus.

I hate it when they speak in unison. It's obnoxiously twin-y of them. I put down my phone, where I'd been days deep into my friends' Instagram feeds. "You guys," I say, "I would love to take you to the park, or anywhere for that matter, but you know I don't have a car."

"But that's the thing," Nash says. He's standing in front of me, jumping from one foot to the other. I don't know *why* he's jumping from one foot to the other, but if it's using up some of that extra energy, then I'm all for it. "We don't need a car. The park is really close. We can skateboard there."

Skateboard there? Really?

None of my friends back home skateboard. There's a divide, I guess. The surfers spend all their time on the beach, while the skaters bum around in a littered skate park after school and smoke cigarettes. I wouldn't call skateboarding a sport so much as an excuse to be a burden on society. But with no ocean, surfing isn't an option.

"I don't know guys," I say. All I really want to do today is sit at home, watch the Big Wave Awards on ESPN2, and maybe text with Eric since I ended up sleeping through 99 percent of our last conversation. I don't know where things stand with us. Aside from that one text message he sent, we haven't talked about the kiss. I'm worried the distance will not only ruin what we started but also weaken our friendship. Ocean water erodes a lot back home, dissolves paint and rusts metal, but it can't chip away at relationships. Distance, however... Well, I'm worried that's a stronger force.

I push away the thought and concentrate on the kids. Parker and Nash have upped their puppy dog eyes game from JV to varsity, and even Emery is glancing up with interest. I guess I could text Eric from the park and watch the awards later...

"I should ask your mom first."

"But she's in surgery," Parker says with a quiet, yet surprisingly commanding, voice. "Our *mom* is in *surgery*."

"Don't try to manipulate me," I say.

"We're not trying to manipulate you," Nash, who for some godforsaken reason is now doing jumping jacks, says. "We're just giving you the facts."

"It could be fun," Emery chimes in. "Some of my friends are there."

If the park has caught her interest, then maybe we should go. It'd be good to put her mind on something besides Aunt Jackie, and despite my best (okay, moderate) efforts, I haven't served as a very good distraction. "You think?" I ask her.

She gives me one of those small smiles and nods.

The park isn't a terrible idea. It might even be a good one. Three days indoors is unheard of for me. The last time this happened, I had the flu, and Dad caught me sneaking out to the beach with my surfboard when I still had a hundred-degree temperature.

I bite my lip, quickly weighing the situation in my head. Nothing too catastrophic can happen, and I'll text Dad where we are. It'll be good to give them something to think about other than the whole Mom-on-an-operating-table thing, so I nod and say, "Okay. Let's go to the park."

In reality, the "close" park is a brutal two-mile journey. Parker and Nash have their skateboards to ride, and Emery has her bike. I have a choice of Emery's Rollerblades that I can barely squeeze my feet into, the boys' bicycles where my knees bump against the handlebars, or walking. I choose walking.

On the way, we pass rows of plain, two-story houses, complete with white picket fences and trimmed lawns. It's an older neighborhood, with suburban cookie cutter homes, so different from Santa Cruz, where one house is an ancient bungalow like ours and the next is a multimillion-dollar mansion. The streets are relatively empty, save for the occasional car that slows to an impossibly safe speed before passing us. As we travel, the houses become more spaced apart, and grander trees appear, their leaves dark green despite the crisp summer heat.

After a few more minutes, Parker announces, "We're here!"

Thank god. I'm dripping in sweat, even dressed in athletic shorts and a loose tank top. Sweating never bothered me in Santa Cruz since the moisture constantly mingled with ocean water, but here there's no avoiding the volume of my own perspiration.

I glance at the park, one hand shading my eyes against the bright sun. I'm not sure what I was expecting—something smaller, I guess—but a gravel lot is filled with a few dozen cars, and behind it stretches an expanse of grass and trees so great I can't begin to see the end of it. At the entrance stands a giant wooden sign with etched white lettering reading *Holly Commons.* A wide and winding concrete path cuts through the grass, allowing easy access through the park, which must be at least a few square miles.

"Okay, see you guys later," Emery says, leaning forward against her handlebars to bike off.

"Hold on there." I step forward, blocking her bike. "Where are you going?"

She looks confused before saying, "Oh, right. Sorry. I usually hang out with my friends at the courts. Is that okay?"

"The courts?"

"The basketball courts." She dismounts from her bike and walks toward a map posted behind Plexiglas under the park sign. "See?" She points. "We're here. Down this path, a left here, a left there, and a right, and there you go. Right next to the lake."

A lake?

I'm a bit nervous to let Emery go off alone, but when I was her age I spent hours at the beach without direct parental supervision. And seeing her friends will be the best distraction from her mom's surgery. "Okay," I say. "But text me when you get there, and if you don't, I will come find you, and I will embarrass you."

She smiles, a full smile this time, which crinkles the soft skin around her green eyes. "Promise," she says, then climbs back onto her bike and heads down the tree-lined path.

"Okay guys." I turn back to Parker and Nash. "To the skate park. Lead the way."

Ten minutes later, after we follow a lengthy trail that's actually kind of beautiful with the surrounding trees and flowers and Snow-Fucking-White chitter-chatter of birds, the wooded path opens up into a giant, ungainly slab of concrete. Benches, rails, and what I think are called quarter pipes and half-pipes are interspersed throughout the park, and more than a dozen skaters ride around, trying out tricks, shouting, and being altogether way too loud. Immediately I yearn for the crashing of waves that drowns out all other sound—or at least the relative quiet of the wooded area we just left.

"You wanna come watch us?" Nash asks, eagerly scanning the park.

"I'm going to watch from over there." I point at a metal

bench that looks out of the way from most of the action. "I'll come closer later. You guys have fun." I want to join them, but all the unfamiliar noises and people bombard my system. Adjusting to an unfamiliar yet quiet house was one thing. Adjusting to this cacophony is entirely different. My chest feels tight, my breathing short.

I need to sit; I need space.

"Okay!" They seem just as happy to go off without me.

I settle down onto the long, flat bench, wishing I'd brought something to read, maybe a Detective Dana novel, this old, cheesy series circa the 1970s about a female police officer who quits the corrupt force to start her own private agency. The books are absurdly plotted, and I can only find the tatt paperbacks on eBay and in old bookstores, but for whatever reason, I love reading them. I never get sick of tagging along as Detective Dana solves each ludicrous case.

Back home, I never get the urge to read outside. Tess is the one who does that, racing through novels while tanning. It feels wrong to have the sun burning my neck and wind cutting through my hair without a surfboard beneath my feet.

Without my friends by my side.

I pull out my phone and send off a few texts, including one to Eric, but they're all probably too busy surfing to respond. I guess I can't blame them. What's better: a friend thousands of miles away or a barrel wave?

I scroll through my Instagram feed, soaking up pictures of sand, surf, and my friends. I notice a new haircut, a new bathing suit, a new tourist they're hanging out with. Each picture makes my pulse race and my stomach clench. I've been in Nebraska less than a week, but already my friends' lives are moving on without me. How long will it take for me to disappear from their feeds and then their thoughts entirely?

I put my phone down and close my eyes. The sun continues to beat steadily, lulling me into a warm haze. In my half-asleep state, I find myself focusing on the sounds around me. The scrape of wheels against concrete. Shouts and jeers. The hard crack of landing a jump. Every time I start to drift off, these sounds yank me awake, because they remind me this is not home.

––––

"Hey."

The voice is smooth and deep. Definitely not one of my cousins.

I pry open my eyes and then immediately close them when assaulted by the piercing midday light. Why didn't I bring sunglasses with me? Did I think Nebraska wouldn't have a sun? I raise my hand to shield my eyes, cracking them just enough to see a black guy about my age standing in front of me.

"Hey," he says again, smiling. Why is he smiling?

"Hi…" I respond, still groggy from dozing off. Did one of my cousins break something? Do I owe someone money for ruined property? I rub my eyes and focus on the person speaking to me.

He's tall and wearing jean shorts and a sleeveless flannel shirt. And he only has one arm. His right arm is dark and muscled, and his left—just isn't there. It ends about six inches below his shoulder in a smooth, rounded nub.

"I'm Lincoln," he says and offers me his right hand, because he doesn't have a left one, or because people shake with their right hands. One or the other, or both I guess.

I train my eyes away from what isn't there and lean forward to shake his hand. "Anise," I say.

"My parents aren't weird or anything."

"What?" My gaze keeps flicking back to his missing arm. I wish someone would squirt me with a fucking spray bottle or something.

"You know, naming me Lincoln and living in Nebraska. We aren't *from* Nebraska."

I give him a blank look. I have no idea what he's talking about; maybe it's impossible to think in this apocalyptic summer heat. "Huh?"

"You know, Lincoln, Nebraska? The capital?"

Now that he says it, the name sounds familiar. I think Detective Dana solved a murder there. "Right," I say. "Sorry. I'm not from around here. I'm visiting from Santa Cruz."

"Ah, Cali life. I'm going to hike the Pacific Crest Trail next year." When he smiles again, I notice a particularly dimply dimple on his right cheek. I have a weird urge to reach out and touch it. But that's probably just the heat again. "What brings you to this fine state?" he asks.

"Umm, family stuff," I say. And right then I realize I've been asleep for who knows how long, and there are three little people I'm supposed to be keeping an eye on. "Shit." I rise to my feet and step around Lincoln to scan the skate park. I find relief before my heart launches into full-on racing mode. Parker and Nash are at a set of low rails, trying to jump and skid on them. Thank God I made them wear helmets. I slip my phone out of my pocket and find a message from Emery:

> Btw tell me when you want to leave and I'll meet you at the entrance :)

No messages from Dad. My stomach tightens. What if Aunt Jackie's surgery isn't going well? He would text, right? Would he have the time? I quickly send off a message, and within seconds he texts back: so far so good, still in surgery.

"Everything okay?" Lincoln asks.

I whip back around to find that I'm *very* close to Lincoln and Lincoln's dimple. I have to look up to meet his dark eyes behind his chunky, black-framed glasses. Since I'm five ten, it's rare for me to ever have to look up at anyone. For a second, I think of Eric and our perfectly level eyes and our perfectly level lips. "Fine." My face flushes, and I take a step back. "I'm fine. Everything's fine."

He smiles. *Again.* "Don't worry," he says. "You were only sleeping for like ten minutes tops."

This statement sets off all kinds of alarms. "Were you watching me sleep?"

"No!" He looks away for a second, clearing his throat. "I was just aware that you...aware of you...and your eyes were closed." He stops again, takes a breath, and seems to regain his confidence. "I wasn't watching you sleep. I've only seen Parker and Nash here with their mom, so I noticed you were new. I *noticed* you. I didn't *watch* you. Very big difference."

"Very," I agree.

Two guys skate past us. "Yo, Lincoln!"

Lincoln turns and salutes them. He calls out, "Jason, remember to *look* where you're skating. We don't want another Wildcat incident!"

"Roger that!" one of the guys calls back.

"Anyway." Lincoln turns to face me again. "What was I saying?"

"Something about not being a creepy stalker who watches people sleep."

"Right. Definitely *not* a stalker." He runs a hand over his close-cropped hair. "You have cool eyes by the way. Very green. Like seaweed."

"Really not helping your not-a-creepy-stalker campaign," I say. And yet, I'm flattered. I think.

"Right," he says. "Fair point."

Another voice calls out from behind us. "Hey! Lincoln! Come show me that varial again!"

Lincoln doesn't turn around this time. Instead he cocks his head back and yells. "One sec!" Then he steps toward me and turns so we're standing next to each other and facing the action of the skate park. His right arm brushes against mine, and even though he's a stranger, the touch feels oddly comfortable. "That's my younger brother," he says, pointing at the guy who just called out; he's dressed in head-to-toe black with chunky silver chains looped through his pants.

And he's white.

Like white, white. Like whiter than me at the end of winter when my wet suit hasn't come off in months.

"Um, cool," I say.

Lincoln must sense what I'm thinking because he says, "We're both adopted. And our dad's Vietnamese. Makes for very interesting Christmas cards." Before I have a chance to comment, he jumps on the skateboard resting by his feet and kicks off toward his brother, calling out, "I'll see you later, Anise," as he rides away.

"Right. See you, Lincoln."

I lie down on the bench, intent on falling back asleep, but as I close my eyes a warm buzzing in my mind keeps me wide awake.

The twins are skateboarding zombies as we wait for Emery at the entrance to the park. They trail back and forth across the concrete path, their heads dipping in exhaustion. Honestly I'm surprised they're still standing. After resting on the sidelines for another half hour, I went and joined them at the rails, cheering them on as they attempted to ride the full length without falling. The task looked markedly less impressive than surfing, but it was still fun to watch my cousins slowly accomplish their goal as the hot sun pressed overhead. Obsessive athleticism must run in the family.

At one point Lincoln joined us, standing next to me in comfortable silence, watching the twins grind halfway down the rail before falling off. After observing for a bit, he called them over, crouched down to their level, and started talking and gesturing at the rail. He even got on the rail himself once, the twins watching with steadfast attention as he smoothly slid across the metal, flipping his board at the end before landing with a solid *thwack* on the ground.

During this maneuver, he also managed to, I shit you not, *wink* at me, dimple flashing as he smiled. I wanted to say something along the lines of *nice wink, stalker*, but by the time the thought formed and I stopped blushing, he was already waving good-bye and skating back to his brother.

I look back toward the park path, and Emery comes around the curve of the trail, walking her bike next to two other girls about her age. They look like they should be on the cover of some preteen magazine, all in bright summer dresses and

wearing complicated hairstyles designed to look uncompli-
cated. I feel a pang for my girlfriends back home. Tess, Cassie,
Marie, and I could be walking down the beach right now,
gossiping about all the wonderfully meaningless shit that happened today. Maybe Spinner, the biggest gossip of them all,
would even join in. My fingers itch to text them, but to say
what? Besides, I'm supposed to FaceTime with Cassie tonight.
We'll catch up then.

I almost tell Emery to hurry up because I know Dad will be
waiting with news of Aunt Jackie's surgery. He texted me a little
bit ago saying all good at hospital, low battery, be home soon. I'm
sure the rest of the surgery went fine yet worry sticks to the back
of my mind. Still, I let Emery take her time walking over to us.
I don't want to embarrass her by insisting she hurry up. Dad and
I have always had a pretty tight relationship, but I remember
being a mortified twelve-year-old when he would talk to my
friends like he was *their pal*. No way am I going to do the same
thing to Emery.

But then Nash shouts, "Emery!" and zooms over to her
with all the energy of someone who hasn't been skating for
hours and proceeds to forget how to stop with all the coordination of someone who has *never* skated, crashing into Emery's
friends with enough momentum to hurtle all of them to the
ground in a jumble, and I realize my speaking to her friends is
low on the list of potential humiliations.

I run over to mediate the situation, Parker trailing at my
heels, but by the time I get there, Emery's friends are already

on their feet and walking back into the park. One turns and gives a halfhearted wave, but the other doesn't even glance back. My friends would never react like that. They'd laugh it off and probably even give Nash a high five. But I've been friends with the same people my entire life. Maybe Emery's friendships are new—tender.

As soon as the girls round the corner, Emery turns on Nash and the screaming begins.

"You're so annoying! Why would you do that? God, you're embarrassing! Why can't you be more like Parker?"

Her words are quick and harsh. Nash sits on the pavement, staring at the ground, his face red and his eyes welling with tears. I don't know *what* to do, but I have to do something. I try to channel Dad's Zen-ittude.

"Um, Emery." I place a hand on her shoulder, which she shoves away. I don't blame her. Who wants a hand on the shoulder when your mom is in the hospital, and on top of that, your brother just embarrassed the fuck out of you? "Look," I continue, "I'm sure Nash is very sorry for what happened. It was an accident. Right, Nash?"

"Yeah," Nash says with a quiet sniffle. Oh god. Did he really just sniffle? I do not know how to take care of sniffling kids. What on earth gave Aunt Jackie and Dad the idea that I'm responsible enough to deal with sniffling kids? "I'm sorry."

I'm preparing for the worst—another outburst from Emery, perhaps even some physical altercation in retribution for her friends—but instead she pauses, takes a slow breath, then leans down and rubs Nash's shaggy hair. "It's fine. Never mind. I'm sorry for yelling. Come on. Let's go home."

Nash hesitates then grabs her offered hand. She tugs him to his feet, and all three kids start toward home, leaving me openmouthed behind them. Did we really just avert World War Three in all of five seconds? Is this normal sibling behavior? I guess I should embrace it, rather than standing around second-guessing my good fortune.

"Right," I say, even though no one is close enough to hear it. "Let's go home."

―――

As we round the corner to our street—I mean, *their* street because *my* street is back in Santa Cruz and has an ocean attached to it—I notice Dad sitting on the front stoop, dressed in his running gear, an electronic cigarette perched between two fingers. He gave up smoking years ago, but he still pulls out one of these when he gets stressed. I tense at the sight. What if the surgery...

I try to read his facial expression, but he's kind of far away and also I'm shit at reading facial expressions.

"Hey." I turn to my cousins. "Why don't you guys go inside and get showered, and I'll get dinner ready?"

"But we want to know how Mom is," Nash says.

"Yeah, how's Mom?" Parker asks.

My shoulder muscles tighten. I also want to know how she

is. But bad news can wait, and good news will still be good news a few minutes from now.

When I don't answer, Nash asks again, loud enough that the words carry over the quiet street. "How. Is. Mom?"

"She's great!" Dad calls out. "Everything went great." The tension immediately eases from my shoulders. "I'll tell you guys more over dinner. Go shower like Anise said."

They don't protest further. They drop their gear in the garage and then head into the house. Emery gives me a lingering glance, as if she wants to ask something else, before rolling her bicycle into the garage and leaving me alone with Dad.

"Hey," I say, walking up to him. He looks exhausted. He was up early this morning to meet Aunt Jackie at the hospital before her procedure. Suddenly I feel guilty for how annoyed I was earlier when my Google alert informed me to expect six foot waves in Santa Cruz all afternoon. I'm not the only one sacrificing this summer. I'm sure Dad would much rather be doing yoga on the beach than dealing with his sister-in-law's surgery schedule. "Is she really great?" I ask. "And how are you?"

"She's good," Dad says. "Recovering, but the surgery went as well as it could. She'll be up to seeing the kids tomorrow, and the doctor said she's still on schedule to come home in a few weeks. And I'm good too. Just tired and…"

"And what?"

"It's just…being in this house, *her* house—" He isn't talking about Aunt Jackie. Dad shakes his head, then smiles.

"It's nothing." He pats the stoop. "C'mon. Hang with me for a bit. I've barely seen you since we got here."

I settle down next to him. These aren't the wooden chairs on our back deck, but it feels good to sit out here next to Dad.

"Thank you again for taking care of your cousins," Dad says. "I know three kids can be a handful. God, I know *one* kid can be a handful."

"Hey." I nudge him in the shoulder. "Don't insult your legacy to this world. And it's okay. The park was actually kind of cool." I think of Lincoln, or more precisely Lincoln's dimple and self-assured smile. "And it seemed to wear out the boys."

"Anything that wears out those guys is cool in my book." Dad takes another drag of his cigarette and then blows out the artificial smoke in one quick burst. "This thing is shit," he says.

I fake gasp. "Cursing? Aren't you supposed to be setting a good example?"

"Eh, your cousins are inside, and I already fucked that one up with you." He grins at me, and I laugh.

We relax into comfortable silence for a few minutes until the front door opens behind us. Parker and Nash stand there, hair wet, towels wrapped around their waists. "We're hungry," they say together.

I groan and stand up from the stoop, surprised to find my muscles protesting, like they've already begun to atrophy from three days without exercise. Maybe I should lift weights or run to maintain some strength this summer. "Come on," I say. "I'll cook you guys dinner. Uncle Cole's going to hang out here a bit longer."

And by cook I mean PB&Js or maybe mac and cheese, if there's any left. Too bad Dad didn't pass on his culinary skills to me. Maybe he would have if I ever stayed inside the kitchen long enough to learn.

"Oh, no cooking," Dad says. "Tonight's pizza night. Your mom told me if I feed you guys anything else for dinner she'll ground me."

Instead of laughing, Parker and Nash stare at Dad. "That doesn't make sense," Parker says. "Mom can't ground you. You're an adult."

"Yeah, Uncle Cole. Grown-ups can't be grounded."

I snicker and join in. "Yeah, Dad. Grown-ups can't be grounded."

"You're right." Dad stands. "But grown-ups can pick the pizza toppings."

"*Wait!*" my cousins wail, shadowing Dad as we all follow him into the house.

⸻

Later that night, I'm in my room and about to FaceTime Cassie. She texted earlier that she got her info packet for boot camp, and I told her I want to hear all about it. But as I'm about to call her, someone knocks on my door. "Come in!"

Emery opens the door and takes a hesitant step into the

room. "What's up?" I ask. She shrugs her shoulders. I pat the open space next to me. "Come join me."

"What are you doing?" she asks as she settles on the bed, grabbing one of the extra pillows and holding it in her lap.

"Well, I was going to talk with my friend, but—"

"Oh, I can leave."

"No!" I control my voice and close my laptop. "I mean, stay. Let's hang out. It'll be nice to have some alone time without those brothers of yours." I'm dying to talk to Cassie, or any of my friends for that matter. Every time I see a picture of them laughing at the Shak or they tag me in a post about legendary swells, my heart sinks a little more. Today, they're still tagging me, but what about a week from now? A month?

I push the fear away because I know Emery needs someone right now, and since Aunt Jackie's at the hospital, I guess I'm that someone. And besides, as much as I want to talk to Cassie, I'm also worried catching up on everything will only make me miss home more. I send Cassie a quick text saying I have to reschedule and then turn my full attention to Emery.

I want to ask about the incident with her friends and how she's doing with Aunt Jackie in the hospital, but I'm sure she doesn't want to talk about either subject. So instead I go with the one topic, besides surfing, I never get sick of.

I look over at her and raise my eyebrows. "So, have a crush on anyone?"

"No!" She blushes and looks down at the comforter. "I mean, not really. There are a few guys I kind of like."

"Do any of them like you?"

She shrugs. "How would I know?"

"You could ask one," I suggest, though I'm not sure why. It's not like I'm a wealth of dating advice. I've only dated a few guys. The longest was for a full six weeks before I realized his favorite thing about the beach was watching all of the girls in bikinis. So most of my romantic knowledge comes not from my experiences but from hearing Tess talk about hers. I wonder if she's already targeted her first summer fling of the season. She loves tourists because she doesn't have to break up with them. The end of summer does that for her.

"I don't know," Emery says. She hugs the pillow tighter. "It's too scary, you know? When someone is really cute and funny? Your whole body feels weird. It's hard to get the right words out."

I expect an image of Eric to flash in my mind, but it isn't him—it's someone taller with dark skin and glasses. "Yeah, I know what you mean." I push the thought away and clear my throat. "Hey, you want to watch a movie or something?"

She nods, so I open my laptop and pull up Netflix. We scroll through the movies, and I let Emery pick one she wants. I don't mention I've already seen it twice.

"Hey, Anise?" she asks as the opening credits play.

"Yeah?"

"Mom is going to be okay, right?"

Mom. I think of the postcard my mom sent and the note I left behind and how at any minute she could breeze through the front door like she left two days not two years ago. I hate that a small part of me wants to see her. I don't need anything from her. Maybe when I was younger I thought I did, but I don't now. If anything, I need her to stay out of my life. I wish she never sent that fucking postcard because once again I'm wasting time thinking about her, why she always leaves, and if she'll ever come back.

I wrap an arm around Emery and lean into her. "Yeah," I say. "Your mom's going to be okay."

Her shampoo smells like ocean water. I breathe her in.

FIVE

THE HOSPITAL IS packed. Sunday afternoon must be prime visiting time. It reminds me of those perfect summer days in Santa Cruz when *everyone* is outside. The nurses and doctors are like the locals, filling out charts, taking care of patients. They're completely comfortable in this frenzied environment. The families are like the tourists, eyes flicking back and forth over the chaos, trying to find their place in the throng.

We file down the hallway. Every few steps someone rolls by in a wheelchair, or a doctor rushes past. Emery's joined us today, but she's lagging so far behind it's like she'd be perfectly fine with never making it to her mom's room.

As we approach the door, Dad turns toward all of us—and by all of us, I mean Parker and Nash—and says, "Okay, guys.

Now remember, your mom just had surgery, so be sure to be quiet and—"

Before he can finish speaking, both boys scoot around him, burst into the room, and start singing Destiny's Child's "Survivor" on maximum volume.

Dad and I rush in behind them to find them dancing with lots of arm pumping. I'm about to shush them before we get kicked out of the hospital when I notice that Aunt Jackie is laughing and clapping along to the beat. Bruises and scratches still cover her pale face, and her legs are still strung up in the *Frankenstein* contraption, but she's smiling, and I'm not going to be the one to ruin her good mood by muzzling her kids.

It turns out I *don't* have to be the one to ruin her fun because just as Parker and Nash are reaching the climax of the song and climbing on top of the armchairs, a nurse appears in the doorway. I'm sure the last thing she wants to deal with are two nine-year-old boys belting out Destiny's Child. "What's going on in here? Boys, please lower your voices!" she commands in one of those whisper yells that seem exclusive to hospitals and libraries.

"Sorry." Dad turns on his charming smile, which is alarming to see on my own parent, and leans in to speak quietly with her.

Her expression turns from annoyed to flattered. "All right," she says. "Just keep it down. This *is* a hospital."

"Absolutely," Dad says. "Thank you for being so understanding."

Thankfully Parker and Nash are finishing the song and moving on to giant bows.

We all clap, even the nurse. Well, hers is one of those unenthusiastic golfer claps. She gives the boys another warning look and Dad a smile before leaving.

"My favorite song! That was wonderful, guys," Aunt Jackie says, still smiling. "You sing beautifully out of tune like your father. He couldn't even sing 'Happy Birthday' without the neighborhood cats howling. Now come give me a kiss."

The boys go to her bed and kiss her cheek with more gentleness than I knew they possessed. Then they settle down into the armchairs. Parker grabs the remote and flips through the TV channels, and Nash pulls out his Nintendo 3DS. Performance over, I guess.

"Hey, sweetie," Aunt Jackie says.

It takes me half a second to realize she's not talking to me. I turn to find that Emery has yet to enter the room. She's still standing in the doorway, her hip pressed against the frame.

"Hi." Her voice is quiet. She fiddles with her phone, flipping it around and around in her hand. "I'll be back in a bit."

And then she's gone.

I wonder if this was the hospital where her dad passed away, if she sat here scared and confused while doctors failed to keep him alive. I want to go after her, console her, see if she needs anything, but maybe all she really needs is to be alone. And I'm not going to take that away from her.

Aunt Jackie tries to smile. "It's not her fault," she says. "You know, bad memories and all."

I nod and move further into the room, perching on the windowsill by her bed. "How are you feeling?" I ask.

"Okay," she says. "Tired. Loopy. A little queasy from the drugs. The doctors still have me pretty…what was the word again? Ah, toasted."

"What's that mean?" Nash asks, looking up from his game.

"Warm," Dad says, coming over to stand next to me. "Toasty. See? Lots of blankets."

Nash gives one of those I-know-you're-lying looks but goes back to his game, muttering, "Grown-ups are weird."

Parker, eyes still on the TV, nods his head. "Very, very weird."

I decide *not* to point out that they were the nine-year-olds just singing Destiny's Child at the top of their lungs in a hospital.

━━━

About half an hour later, Emery sidles into the room with a magazine in one hand and a giant bag of McDonald's in the other. Why there's a McDonald's in a hospital is beyond my comprehension. The scent reminds me of the fryers in Tess's family's restaurant. Maybe she's there right now, serving coconut chicken curry and *panikeke*. Parker and Nash launch themselves off their chairs and at the bag, but Emery yanks it into the air and out of their reach. I'm half-expecting them to pull some kind of circus act and climb on each other's shoulders to get to the food.

"Want some fries, Mom?" Emery asks.

"Well, I had surgery on my legs, not my heart, so I think that's probably okay." Aunt Jackie smiles. "Bring 'em over."

I wonder if, when you have children, your DNA mutates so that you'll do anything to make your kids happy. Because I *know* Aunt Jackie is nauseous, and I *know* scarfing down McDonald's french fries won't ease that discomfort. And yet, Aunt Jackie isn't going to say no to Emery's proffered fries because rejecting the fries would basically be like rejecting her daughter.

I wonder if my mom's DNA forgot to mutate.

"Come on," Aunt Jackie repeats, patting the bed. "There's room."

All three kids climb on cautiously. The boys sit at the foot, and Emery sits at the head, scooting in right next to Aunt Jackie. Then Emery opens the bag, and the golden fried scent fills the room. For a few minutes the only sounds are munching and licking of salt off fingers. Dad and I move to the periphery of the room, giving them space for what seems like a McDonald's-fry-eating family ritual.

Emery seems more comfortable now, less scared. Her mom is still here, still the same person she was before the accident. She was in trouble, but now she's okay. I want to tell Emery how lucky she is that her mom loves her and will do everything in her power to stick around as long as possible. Aunt

Jackie would sacrifice anything and everything for her. But the thing is, I think Emery already knows that. And that's probably why she's so scared of losing her.

"What's this?" Aunt Jackie asks Emery, tapping the magazine with a fry.

"Just a magazine. *Seventeen*," Emery says.

"Ah, but you're only twelve."

"*Almost* thirteen," Emery protests.

"Which, correct me if I'm wrong, is still four years away from seventeen." Aunt Jackie smiles and nudges Emery in the shoulder. "Read some to me."

Emery hesitates. "Really?"

"Really."

Emery glances around the room, as if expecting one of us to protest, but no one does. So she flips open the magazine to a random page and starts reading about "Seven Summer Fruits Guaranteed to Give You a Healthy Boost." As she reads in a smooth voice, calm envelops the room. Aunt Jackie slowly leans into Emery, and the boys slowly lean into each other, and across the room I slowly lean into Dad.

Maybe hospitals have McDonald's for one simple reason: fries stitch families back together.

———

The next few days pass in molasses torture as the reality of my summer sinks in. With Aunt Jackie in the hospital and Dad working full days on the new city hall, my cousins continue to be my sole responsibility during the mornings and afternoons, a responsibility I'm struggling to get used to. Besides the odd summer job helping out at Tess's family's restaurant or teaching the rare surfing lesson, I've never had any obligations but homework and keeping myself occupied. Now I have three trailing shadows.

We go to the park almost every day, but the sweltering heat usually sends us back home dripping with sweat within a couple of hours. Every time we go, I keep my eyes alert for Lincoln, but I haven't seen him since that first day when he said my eyes were seaweed-green.

This morning I'm sitting in the kitchen, staring at wave forecasts on my phone because I like torturing myself, contemplating whether to throw together lunch or pray that Dad gets off early and makes us something edible with actual nutrients and vitamins and whatever, when my phone rings—a FaceTime from Tess.

I answer and am greeted with a sun-glared smile.

"Hey, stranger!" she says. She must be lying on her stomach, because behind her tanned face I can just make out the edge of the beach and the lapping water. I turn the volume all the way up to catch the sounds of the crashing waves and seagulls. The sight of her face and the sounds of the ocean make the wooden chair I'm sitting on suddenly very uncomfortable. I should be pressed against the warm sand or floating in the cool water. I should be with my friends. I can't believe how many days have passed since my feet have been firmly planted on a surfboard, since I've spent hours unwinding next to Tess, sharing headphones as she sketches seagulls and swells.

"Hey, stranger," I say back. "How are you?"

"Good!" she says. "Parents let me off work early yesterday, and we set off some fireworks that Spinner not-so-legally acquired. We missed you."

Back home, I never would've missed out on a night like that. I have flashes of memories I don't possess—fireworks lighting up the sky over the dunes, smoke ghosting over the water, shadows flickering over my friends' laughing faces.

"How goes life in Nebraska?" Tess asks. "How's your aunt?"

"Okay…" I say. "Everything is okay…"

I'm trying to think of something interesting to tell her, something she can share with the rest of our friends, make sure they're all still thinking of me, like the boys singing *Survivor* at the hospital or—Tess cuts off my train of thought. "Oh, I have some very exciting news!"

"What?" I ask.

"Okay, so you know how they never finalize the band lineup for Surf Break until last minute?"

"Yeah…"

"Well, guess who they just added?" Tess doesn't give me a chance to guess. "Fucking Motel/Hotel! Can you believe it? Right here in Santa Cruz!"

My stomach drops. I *can't* believe it. Motel/Hotel. Our

favorite electronica band. Possibly our favorite band flat-out. They're really small and almost never tour too far from their hometown of Athens, Georgia. This will definitely be their first time in Santa Cruz. And I'm going to miss it. One more thing my friends will experience without me. One more thing that separates their lives from mine.

So instead of smiling, instead of squealing and cheering and flipping the fuck out, all I can do is gnaw on a hangnail that's been bugging me for the past few days. Because I won't get to see Motel/Hotel. Because my friends will talk about the show for months to come, and every time they do, what has always been an *us* thing will suddenly be a *them* thing.

Tess, either sensing my lack of excitement or a bad connection, leans closer to the screen. "Earth to Anise Sawyer! You there? Did you hear me?"

"Yep," I say. "And maybe *you* can figure out why *I'm* not excited." I don't mean to snark at her. Tess is my best friend. We don't snark at each other. We snark at other people together. But I can't help it. This is one more nail in the coffin of my shit summer. More proof of what I always knew because of my mom but never experienced personally: when you lose a place you lose its people too.

"Dude, but wait. If you tell your dad what a big deal it is, he'll probably let you come home early. I mean seriously, your flight is, like, a week later, right? Would he really mind?"

"Tess, I told you this before. He's planned everything out. We're flying home the day after Aunt Jackie is supposed to be out of her wheelchair. Trust me. He knows how much I love Surf Break. If he could have booked us earlier, he would have."

"I know, but what if you—"

"Look, can we talk about something else? I love you, and when I see your face I want to be in a happy mood, not in a life-is-the-worst mood. So let's change the subject, okay?"

Tess looks like she's going to protest, but then she nods. "Okay. Right, you're right. Sorry, Anise. Oh, Eric says hi by the way! He's out in the water, but I'm sure he'd *looovve* to talk to you."

Eric. We've barely communicated since I got here. We were texting while watching the same YouTube surfing tutorial yesterday, but then Nash decided to see what happens if you put bubble bath in the washing machine, and I completely forgot to message him back. And even that conversation was stilted. Our relationship has always been immediate, tangible. This distance has made everything difficult; plus, we haven't brought up the kiss again. I *want* to want him, but I can't wrap my mind around wanting someone who isn't here, and he probably feels the same way about me. Maybe that first kiss would have led to many more. But now I'm gone all summer, so maybe that first kiss was our last.

"He hasn't hooked up with anyone else yet, by the way," Tess continues. Relief comes, but only a little. The word *yet* lingers in my ears. "I think he's hung up on you. God knows why. I mean you have absolutely zero attractive qualities."

"Thanks, jerk," I say. "Love you too."

I think of Eric—his blond curls, blue eyes, sculpted shoulders—but the image that comes to mind is out of focus, like when you have a bad connection and a picture won't load properly. I know I like him, like how he encourages my competitiveness instead of being turned off by it, like how without saying a word, he's always there with extra support when my mom skips town. I know our kiss made my heart race and skin tingle. And yet, part of me wishes the kiss never happened. Because now when I think of us, I only see a giant question mark.

I'm gathering the nerve to ask Tess to grab him when Parker and Nash bounce into the kitchen. "Let's go to the park!" Nash shouts.

"Yeah, please," Parker says.

"Please, please, please."

Their pleas make it almost impossible to hear Tess. "I think that's my cue to go," she says, laughing. "Have fun at the park. Love you!"

"Thanks, love you too," I say. "Talk soon, okay?"

"Definitely," Tess agrees before signing off.

The screen goes blank. No more Tess. No more ocean. I'm sad yet grateful. I really do need to clarify things with Eric, but there's no harm in putting it off a little longer. Right? My throat feels tight as I ask the boys, "Do we really want to go to the park again? Don't you want to, like, rot your brains on video games or something? I don't know if you've noticed, but it's very hot outside."

"Pleeeasssseee," Parker says. "I want to learn this new trick, the crooked grind, and Austin, you know Lincoln's brother, said he'd help me with it today."

Lincoln's brother. That means Lincoln will also be at the park. Probably. Not that I'd go to the park just because Lincoln is going to be there. I'd go because Parker wants to learn this grind trick. Parker and Nash both cheer while I go change in a room that isn't mine. Dad never said no when I wanted to learn something new. Once he even worked twelve-hour days all week and still came out with me at the crack of dawn on a Saturday because I wouldn't shut up about learning a frontside bottom turn. I have no desire to deny my cousins the same opportunity. If I can't enjoy my summer, I'm damn sure going to help them enjoy theirs.

The park paths are emptier than usual today, undoubtedly because the temperature is already breaching the ninety-degree mark. Most kids are probably down at the public pool, splashing around in lukewarm water, their parents hunting for shade in the handful of umbrellas. Apparently it's rare for the temperature to climb this high in Nebraska; apparently the scorching sun showed up special for me.

Emery waves good-bye and heads for the basketball courts again. She seems happier since Aunt Jackie's successful surgery. Part of me wants to follow her to get a closer look at these friends of hers. But I remind myself that although I'm not her parent, I am her quasi–guardian–cousin, and my presence might embarrass the hell out of her.

Instead I follow Parker and Nash to the skate park. They rush off toward the same cluster of short rails, where they high five and bump fists with a few kids. I hope Parker learns his new trick today. I hope he learns it, and then another trick, and then another. I hope the thought of skateboarding wakes him up each day with clawing excitement. I hope when he closes his eyes at night he only sees the grit of asphalt and hears spinning wheels. The thrill of learning something new out in the water has never left me, and through Parker, maybe I can snatch a shred of that adrenaline rush.

After watching them for a few moments, I scan the rest of the park and spot Lincoln and his brother by the edge of the giant bowl. The pair couldn't look more different, and not because of their physical differences. Lincoln looks like some kind of redneck–meets–hipster with his jean shorts and sleeveless flannel shirt and chunky black-framed glasses and his brother looks like he Googled punk-goth and bought the first clothes he saw.

Lincoln looks up and catches my gaze. I hate getting caught staring. The whole appeal of watching someone is ruined if they watch you back. He leans over, says something to Austin, then jumps on his skateboard and glides over to me. The move is so fluid that for half a second, skateboarding impresses me. It's not as beautiful as slicing down the coastline as water trundles beneath you, but for solid ground, I guess it's not as pathetic of a sport as I've always thought.

"Hey," he says and slides to an easy stop in front of me. He remains on his skateboard, popping it back and forth, lifting each side a couple inches off the ground and then dropping it back with a sharp rattle. It's like the action is more natural to him than standing still.

"Hey," I say back. He's even more attractive than I remembered—tall with broad shoulders, dark eyes, and smooth skin completely unmarred by scruff or acne.

He gestures to his skateboard. "You ever try one of these?"

I shake my head. "Not my sport. I'm a surfer actually." I'm not sure why I divulge this information. Something about Lincoln makes me feel comfortable despite the unfamiliar terrain.

He adjusts his glasses, tilts his head, and appraises me. "A surfer. You must hate it here."

"Unless there's an ocean hiding under these great plains, I'm pretty much destined for a summer of torture."

"All summer?" Lincoln asks. Instead of popping up his skateboard, he starts riding back and forth in a semicircle around me. His hand jingles by his side. He might have more excess energy than the twins. "Why all summer?"

"Well, you know Parker and Nash, right?" Lincoln nods, and I continue. "Their mom, my aunt, got into a pretty bad car accident, so my dad and I flew here for the summer to help while she recovers."

"Ah, that's why the disastrous duo disappeared for a few

days. Poor guys." Lincoln glances at the twins and then back to me. "Hope your aunt's doing okay."

"She is, thanks." I pause. "Disastrous duo?"

Lincoln nods. "Oh, yeah, that's what everyone calls them. A few weeks ago, there was an ice cream truck situation involving some neighborhood dogs, a clown from a kid's birthday party, and—actually, it's kind of a long story. I won't get into it. But let's just say they've been the source of many fiascoes."

I make a mental note to be on guard around ice cream trucks and clowns for the rest of summer. "Do you, like…hang out with them?" I ask.

Isn't it weird to hang out with younger kids? I don't ask.

"Yeah, you know, we all do. Kind of a skate park thing, I guess. If you hang out here enough, you get to know everyone. Our own little four-wheeled family."

I think of my surfing family back home—Cassie with her infallible energy, Marie with a work ethic even more intense than mine, Spinner with his ability to laugh off even his most outrageous fuckups.

"So you want to try?" Lincoln asks, snapping my attention back to him.

"Try what?"

He kicks up the skateboard with one quick stomp of his foot and offers it to me. "Skating."

"No thanks," I say.

"Why not?" The board hangs there between us. "Look, I know I'm pretty great looking and everything, but there's no need to impress me. I promise I won't judge when you fall on your ass."

"Um, who said anything about you being good-looking?"

"*Great* looking," Lincoln corrects. "And it's kind of a known fact. Lincoln is great looking. Lincoln has one arm. And Lincoln is better at skating than Anise."

"You remembered my name," I say.

"Memory of steel, another one of my many amazing talents."

"Your modesty is overwhelming."

"So is my smile." He grins and his dimple pops out once more. "Come on, give it a try."

I'm about to refuse again when I notice Parker and Nash skating toward us, like two puppies hunting down a whiff of leftovers.

"What's up?" they ask in unison after skidding to stops at the exact same time.

"You guys plan that, right?" I ask.

"Plan what?" they respond.

I stare them down. "That twin timing."

"Nope." They both grin.

"Hey, guys," Lincoln interrupts. "Don't you want to see Anise try to ride a skateboard for the first time?"

"*Try?*" I ask.

"Yes!" Parker and Nash shout.

"Me too," Lincoln says. "Come on then." He offers me the skateboard again, and I look at it with distrust. There has to be a catch. I can't comprehend what could possibly be entertaining about watching me roll around on a slab of wood for a couple of minutes.

But also I can't think of a legitimate reason for saying no besides the obvious *I don't want to*. "Fine. One ride and then I'm done."

"Excellent." Lincoln smiles. I eye his dimple with suspicion, wondering if it has powers to persuade people into doing things they most definitely don't want to do. "Follow me, please."

I follow him over to an empty part of the skate park. Parker and Nash trail behind us, giggling and poking each other in the sides like this is the most entertaining thing that's ever happened to them.

"All right," Lincoln says. "First you step up with your—"

"I don't need how-to instructions," I say. This already feels absurd enough. I don't need Lincoln guiding my movements with his hand like we're in some cheesy made-for-TV movie. Okay, maybe I am a *little* curious what his hand would feel like, pressed into my back, adjusting my stance, but I'm sure that's just the dimple talking. "I've been surfing since I was seven. I think I've pretty much mastered the whole plant-feet-on-board-stay-standing-thing."

"Right," Lincoln says. "And they're the same sport, so—"

"No, they're not; surfing is much more difficult."

Lincoln grins. "Okay, sure. You've got this. Totally."

"Totally," the twins echo, laughing even more.

"All right, all right." Lincoln raises his hand, and the boys quiet. "Sorry to offend, surfer girl. I'm sure you'll wow us all. Please, go ahead."

After giving Lincoln a healthy dose of my evil stare, which seems to have zero effect on him, I grab the board. It feels foreign in my grip. The top surface is rough, grittier than my surfboard. I could probably grate a block of cheese on it if it weren't for all the dirt. It's also about a third of the length and less than half the weight, making me wonder how stable it is. How can this plank of wood carry Lincoln's bulk or even mine?

I waver. Maybe this'll be a *bit* more difficult than anticipated. But I can't back down now—not after rejecting help, not with my cousins and Lincoln watching me.

Taking a short breath, I drop the skateboard onto the ground. I go to take a surfing stance, feet perpendicular to the board, knees locked slightly inward, but realize that might be wrong for skating. I glance around the park, taking in the postures and feet placements of everyone around me. Front foot parallel to the board and back foot perpendicular. Right. Can't be too difficult. I cautiously step onto the board. It wobbles back and forth, and I know my *mask of confidence* must slip for a second because Lincoln says, "Easy there, surfer girl. Sure you don't want some help?"

I lift my hands into the air, as if to showcase my incredible athletic dexterity. "I'm fine. It's fine." My ankles feel locked. The board wobbles again, but I refuse to show my hesitation a second time. "See? Everything's fine."

"Sure. Great," Lincoln says. "Now why don't you try the actual skating part?"

"I was getting there."

"Want a push?" Nash asks, rushing forward with arms outstretched.

"No!" I shout—just in time to keep his hands from launching me forward and most likely to the ground. "Absolutely not. No pushing." And then I mutter, "I should probably be wearing a helmet…"

"Excellent idea!" Lincoln calls. Apparently supersonic hearing is also one of his many talents. He pops off his own helmet and throws it to me. I reach forward, stumbling off the skateboard, and grab it with clumsy hands. I do not stumble. I do not have clumsy hands. Nebraska is obviously poisoning my coordination skills with its oppressive heat.

The helmet is too big for me, but not wearing it would set a bad example for those kids I'm supposed to be keeping alive. "Right." I reposition myself on the board once more and gather a breath. "How hard can this be?"

Slowly, I remove my right foot from the skateboard, plant it on the ground, and then kick off. I almost lose my balance, but somehow manage to bring my right foot back onto the board and ride for all of two seconds across the pavement. My heart is racing. I don't know why it's racing. I'm three inches off the ground and moving at a speed of approximately half a mile an hour, but it's racing all the same.

I grab the board, walk over to my audience, and drop the board on the ground. "See? Not that bad. Am I done now?"

"No, no, no," Lincoln says. "That was not skating. That was inching. At a maximum it was scooting. But definitely not skating."

At this point, all I really want to do is shove the board in Lincoln's face and say *I don't give a damn about skating or inching or fucking scooting*. But I don't aspire to spend my summer with taunting cousins, which will inevitably happen if I give up now. Plus, I've never exactly been one to back down from a challenge, even a challenge as pointless as this.

"Fine," I say. "What would you consider a respectable amount of movement to prove this *sport* is mind-numbingly easy?"

"Hmm." Lincoln rubs his chin in mock thought. He turns to my cousins and bends slightly so he can look them in the eyes. "I don't know. What do you guys think?"

All three of them debate back and forth while I stand there, hands on my hips and sweat dripping down my neck. Finally, they deign to speak directly to me, telling me I need to skate the length of the back fence of the skate park. The distance is short enough, about a hundred feet, but it looks like a marathon compared to my last tiny stunt.

"No problem," I say, because if I say *no problem* it will be *no problem*, right? "But after this, no more challenges. My skating career will be over. Understood?" I direct this question at my cousins, and they nod in agreement.

I grab the skateboard once more, wishing that it were about four feet longer and in the ocean, and walk over to the far corner of the skate park. Two sides of a chain-link fence corner me in. Setting the board down on the ground, I once again balance myself and then kick off, a little less cautiously this time.

Okay, a lot less cautiously. I kick off so hard that I only manage to keep my "balance" for about three terrifying seconds until I crash to the ground, my arms bracing my fall and chafing hard against the rough cement.

"Shit!" I curse, clutching both arms to my chest to quell the stinging. I sit in a huddle on the ground, trying to breathe out the pain. "Shit, shit, shit," I repeat.

I hear the twins laughing, which is very inappropriate considering their cousin is on the ground bleeding. At least, I think I'm bleeding. There's no way I can feel this level of pain without some quantity of blood. Unless I'm mistaking pain for unadulterated embarrassment. Lincoln walks toward me, looming over me, his form blocking the sun so he looks like an absurdly tall version of one of those Victorian silhouettes.

"You okay down there?" he asks.

"Excellent," I mutter.

He offers me his hand, but I ignore it, proudly lifting myself off the ground despite the protests of my throbbing arms. I inspect them and find only a few drops of blood. It's mostly rubbed-raw skin. I pick out a couple grains of gravel and flick them to the ground, knowing I'll need to pour rubbing alcohol on later. Years of surfing injuries have taught me it's better to be safe than sorry when it comes to infections.

"You know," Lincoln says. "I hate to insult an injured party, but I *did* try to warn you it's harder than it looks."

"Warn me? You goaded me into doing this, which is like the opposite of warning me."

"I thought you'd enjoy it. You know, once you get past the bleeding and bruising. Well, you never get past the bleeding and bruising, but you get really good at ignoring it."

"I have no idea why you'd think I'd enjoy skating," I say. "Surfing is ten times more interesting and difficult. Not many people can literally ride on water. Anyone can slap some wheels to a piece of wood and ride it."

"Umm, actually though, you couldn't," Lincoln says.

"It was my first time! You can't—I can't—" Frustration rips through me. I've been forced away from my friends, my ocean, my board, and dropped in the middle of the country with no warning. I've been torn from comfort and stability, thrown out to sea without a buoy. I hate feeling powerless. I hate it, and I'm over it.

"I'll tell you what," Lincoln says right as I'm ready to boil over. He clasps a hand onto my shoulder and leans toward me. "How about a chance at redemption?"

"Redemption?" I ask.

Lincoln steps back onto his own board and rides in those tidy half circles in front of me. "Sure, redemption. If you think skateboarding is so easy, I'll give you a week to prove it."

I eye him with suspicion. "And how exactly do I prove it?"

"One week from now, we meet back here for a little competition. If I win, you admit skateboarding is just as difficult as surfing. And if you win—"

"You give me a hundred bucks."

Lincoln smiles. "That's a pretty uneven bet."

"How long have you been skating?"

"Seven years."

"Seven years. One week." I narrow my eyes. "Sounds pretty even to me."

His eyes flicker with *something*, and I flush with warmth. "Fine," he says. "Deal."

Still smiling, he holds out his hand. We shake on the bet.

SIX

DINNER IS QUIET tonight. We sit around the table, pick-ing over reheated shepherd's pie, the least impressive dish in Dad's culinary repertoire, and all the less appetizing in its days-old form.

The embarrassment I feel from earlier today is unprec-edented and unsettling. The memory of my cousins and Lincoln laughing at me hurts worse than the scrapes on my arms. Because the only thing worse than failing is failing while someone watches. I've always been a natural at sports, and not only surfing. I've played beach volleyball with friends, rowed crew for a year, and I even do yoga with Dad sometimes. Why should skateboarding be any different?

After we finish eating, Dad and the kids head to their rooms for the night. Instead of doing the same, I go outside for some fresh air. The temperature drops fast here, and the shorts and tank I sweltered in this afternoon now leave me with prickled skin. Parker and Nash's skateboards sit in the yard, stationary yet somehow more menacing than approaching ten-foot swells. I can't believe I agreed to that bet. Why on earth would I do something so senseless? I guess I could get out of it by avoiding the skate park for the rest of summer, but the park is the only form of entertainment that doesn't require a car and makes all three of my cousins happy.

And there's no *way* I'm going back there to face the mortification of defeat. So—

I have to learn to skate.

And I can't do that without practicing.

I grab one of the boards from the grass and throw it onto the concrete driveway. It clatters to the ground, a raw echo in the still night. The quiet of the suburbs makes my skin crawl. Every rustle and whistle can be heard without the crashing of the waves to smooth the world out. I still haven't adjusted to life without the privacy of white noise, still haven't slept well in this thunderous silence.

I sigh and step cautiously onto the board, willing my body to adjust to this new equilibrium. But my body refuses. Everything about this feels unnatural, from the wheels threatening to roll without my permission to wearing shoes instead of standing barefoot, naked toes digging against waxed grit.

I should go inside, curl up on the old corduroy recliner, and message with Eric while watching ESPN2. If I can't be in Santa

Cruz, I might as well live vicariously through surfing marathons and incessant communication with my friends. But I haven't talked to Eric for days. On my phone, I find more online pictures *of* him than texts *from* him. He messaged me daily at first, asking about my day, but with nothing really new to tell him, my answers back have become shorter and more sporadic.

I should focus on the now. What I can do in Nebraska. I've never backed down from a challenge, and I'm not making an exception for Lincoln's.

So I lock my jaw, place one foot down on the concrete, and push off. Slowly. I don't want a repeat incident of earlier. The board scoots down the driveway about a foot, then wobbles, then stills. How can *this* possibly compare to the thrill of a solid frontside floater or the overwhelming ecstasy of my first aerial?

It can't.

But if I want to beat Lincoln, I'm going to have to do a lot better. I step off the board, pull out my phone, and YouTube binge basics. If I can get good enough, maybe I'll knock that ever-present smile from his smug, attractive face.

⸺

"Yes, yes, *fuck!*" I stumble off the board and almost twist my ankle. Again.

Two hours of practice. My thighs burn. Sweat drips down the nape of my neck. But I like it, the feel of exertion. Plus, I can now ride the entire length of the driveway without stumbling. But I can't ollie, which according to YouTubers, is the simplest trick in a skater's repertoire. If I can't master the simplest trick, I definitely can't beat Lincoln. I pick up the skateboard and slam it back onto the ground for no other reason than the satisfaction of that piercing clatter.

I step up and position both my feet perpendicularly to the board, left foot resting above the raised edge at the end. I go over the three simple steps:

1. Jump with the board by slamming my back foot down on the back lip.
2. Slide my front foot up.
3. Land.

Now if only my feet would agree with my thoughts.

"You can do this, Anise. You can do this," I mutter. "No hesitation."

I take a quick breath and then jump. My left foot comes down hard against the board, and it pops up into the air with me, then miraculously, we land as one. The adrenaline I've been missing since I left California rushes through me. I did it. I ollied. A shitty ollie, but still—if a tree falls in the forest, and it was a shitty tree, the tree still fell, right?

I'm about to try it again when I hear the front door open behind me. Dad, in striped pajama pants and a gray T-shirt, walks outside. "You should really be wearing a helmet," he says, settling down on the lawn in one of his yoga poses.

"I know," I say. "But the kids' helmets are too small, and it's not like I wear one when I'm surfing."

"Yes, well, when you're surfing I don't have to worry about you cracking your head on concrete."

I grab the skateboard and sit down next to him. "Okay, point made. But I'm pretty sure forcing my head into a child-sized helmet would be just as harmful. Lots of skull squishing."

"True." Dad readjusts his pose, stretching his legs out in front of him and arching his feet back so his toes point toward the moon. I copy him, relishing how the stretch unwinds my sore muscles. "I guess we'll have to risk it then. There are worse things in the world than finding my daughter's pretty brains splattered all over the driveway."

"You've always been such a sweet talker, Dad."

We continue to stretch in silence, the night air cooling my overheated body. I think of home, of the evenings spent on the beach with Dad, performing this exact routine, except tonight dry grass tickles my skin instead of damp sand. We've always been in sync like this, always shared so much with each other. For a second I'm tempted to tell him about my mom's postcard and the note I left behind, warn him that at any moment our human hurricane could disrupt this relative peace. But I quell the idea.

I hate hiding things from Dad, but I don't want to talk about her. Besides, even though he tries to hide it from me, I know he gets upset when he thinks about her. How could he not? The first decade or so he was as forgiving as humanly possible. Sometimes they'd even "get back together" when she'd come into town. But he hit his breaking point around the sixth time she ditched us, so he now welcomes her with all the consideration and distance of a hotel concierge.

After a few minutes, Dad speaks again. "If you're serious about skating, we'll get you a helmet. Maybe a board of your own too."

I turn to him. "I'm *not* serious about skating."

"Okay, but you *did* just skate for two hours straight."

"It's not... I just..."

"You miss surfing?" Dad asks.

"That's probably the understatement of the century—of the millennium, actually."

It's not only surfing. I miss everything. My friends. My home. My ocean. But I don't tell Dad that. He already knows it. No point in making him feel worse.

"I'm sorry," Dad says. "I didn't mean to uproot you. Being here's—"

"—the right thing to do. I get it, Dad. I do. Family helps family, and I'm happy to be here. Well, not *happy*, but you know. It's the last summer before Marie leaves for college, before Cassie leaves for boot camp, and I just really wanted to spend it with them."

"I know," he says, then brings up his knees and hugs them to his chest. "*You* could apply to colleges all over the country. You don't have to stay in Santa Cruz when you graduate."

"Trying to get rid of me?" I smile, but the corners of my mouth feel rigid. I hate when Dad brings up college. I hate when he tries to nudge me out of the nest. There's nothing wrong with wanting to stay in Santa Cruz. In fact, wanting to leave is absurd. Why would I want to abandon everything and everyone I love? Being here less than a month has already made the details of home slip away. Is it the bottom or top kitchen drawer that gets stuck when you open it? Five or six steps up to our boardwalk? If I leave for college, vanish for so many months, these details will continue to fade until my memory of home disappears entirely.

Dad sighs. He leans into me, bumping my shoulder. "You know I'm not trying to get rid of you, Anise. I love you. But I want you to consider your options. There's a lot of world out there."

"But why leave when I'm already living in the best part of it?"

Dad glances at me, like he wants to push this further, push *me* further. But before he gets the chance, I stand and head toward the house. "Taking a shower and going to bed," I call out. "Night, Dad."

He probably says *night* back, but I'm inside before I have a chance to hear it.

———

Two days later I'm sitting at the kitchen counter and chowing down on a giant bowl of Cap'n Lucky Puffs. I've been spending almost every free moment under the oppressive sun, trying to learn how to ride a damn skateboard, so my appetite is back to its usual ferocity. I'm midbite when Dad walks into the room. My shoulders tense. We haven't talked much since he brought up college, and I'm hoping time has erased the issue from his mind. Most parents would be *thrilled* their kids don't want to move away for school. Why does my parent want me gone?

"Morning," he says.

I nod and swallow a bite of my cavity-certified cereal. "Morning."

He pulls a carton of eggs and shredded cheese from the fridge. Even though it's already nine, he's still wearing pajama pants. "Want an omelet?" he asks.

I stare at my giant bowl of cereal. Then I think about the frosted brown sugar cinnamon Pop-Tarts I ate before it. Then I shrug my shoulders. "Sure."

He starts heating a pan. "Don't you have work?" I ask. Most days he leaves for his job before I'm even awake.

"Not today. There was a delay in supplies because of delay in payment because of delay in someone signing off on paperwork. Gotta love working for bureaucrats."

"Wait a second," I say. "You *don't* have work today."

"Correct."

"Which means you're free."

"Correct."

"Which means *you* can watch the kids."

Extraordinarily long pause. Like a *Rocky Horror* antici…pation pause. Dad looks at me. "Well, I was thinking we could all go visit Jacks."

"As in all five of us?"

"Yes…"

I sigh. It's not that I don't love my cousins. I do. I really do. Especially Emery, who I've established a nightly routine of popcorn and Netflix with. I *still* can't believe she's never watched *The Office*. I'm just not used to being responsible for three kids almost twenty-four hours a day. When my cousins visit us in Santa Cruz, Aunt Jackie is around to take care of them, and I pitch in. I'm not the sole caretaker. Keeping the boys from destroying the house on a sugar rampage all by myself takes up more energy than a full day's surf in hostile waves.

Since Dad doesn't have work today, I want to take advantage and grasp a little responsibility relief. "How about this," I say. "I go to the hospital to hang with Aunt Jackie, and *you* take the kids to the pool or whatever."

I glance at the omelets. Dad is sprinkling on the cheese. "More cheddar, please. No, like more, more. Like personal cow more. Thank you. Now does that sound like a deal? Me, aunt. You, kids. Me, hospital. You, pool."

"I don't know…" Dad says, drawing out the words like it'll help him make a decision. "Jacks probably wants to see them…"

"So come after. After they've exhausted themselves swimming, they won't have energy to wreak havoc on innocent hospital patients. We'll avoid a Destiny's Child repeat. Come on. Please, please, please?"

"Getting in some swimming *does* sound nice…"

"Yes!" I hop off the stool, rush forward, and give Dad a hug from behind. "Thank you! Love you!"

"Careful! Melting cheese here! And love you too."

———

When Dad drops me off at the hospital, I feel like a little kid getting dropped off for a playdate or camp. For years now, I've walked everywhere or gotten rides from friends, so being dropped off in a minivan by Dad feels like I've taken a time machine and am seven years old all over again.

And yet, as the van pulls away, I'm relieved. This is the first time in a week that I've been completely alone. Sure, I've had a room to myself every night, but is privacy really privacy when at any moment Parker and Nash can bang on the door, wanting to know if it's bad they accidentally cracked the box that makes the Internet be the Internet? This is the first time in days I don't have to be responsible for anyone. I'm here to spend time with Aunt Jackie, but she has doctors and nurses to look after her. I'm just visiting. I'm not *responsible* for Aunt Jackie.

I take a deep breath. The air is warm as always, but clouds cover the sun, and a light breeze whips through my hair. I sit down on a wooden bench near the hospital entrance, close my eyes, and try to replace the sounds of the hospital with the sounds of the beach. Not a car rushing to the emergency entrance but a Jet Ski slicing through the spray. Not sneakers thumping down the concrete but flip-flops smacking along the sand. Not pigeons cooing but seagulls crying.

"Excuse me, miss?"

I crack open my eyes. No ocean, just an elderly man wearing a fleece jacket, despite the heat. "Yes?"

"Do you know what time it is?"

I glance at my phone and tell him, "Just past eleven."

"Thank you, sweetheart." The man smiles at me before leaving.

I nod and smile back, but now my oceanside illusion is ruined. I stand and head toward the hospital entrance. As I walk, I watch the old man in front of me, dragging a rolling oxygen tank along with him.

Ocean air is good for the lungs, I want to tell him. *May I suggest moving to the beach?*

Aunt Jackie is sitting up and reading when I enter the room. Her black-framed glasses remind me of Lincoln's glasses, which make me think of his face...and his lips.

Aunt Jackie looks up. "Anise!"

"Hi! Book any good?"

She grins. "Terrible, but I love it." Her voice is smooth today. Perhaps they lowered her painkiller dosage. She slips off her glasses and cocks her head to the side. "Are you trying to copy me?"

"What?" I ask.

"That collection of bruises you've got could rival mine."

"Oh, right." I've gotten pretty banged up from a few days of learning to skateboard.

"Just don't let my kids start thinking injuries are cool, okay?" Aunt Jackie says.

"Promise," I say. I've told the boys if they skate without helmets I'll *personally* give them brain injuries, but I should probably also lead by example.

I settle into one of the armchairs. "Huh," Aunt Jackie says, staring at me in a way that makes me think they didn't lower her painkiller dosage after all.

"What?"

"Nothing, you just look a lot like your mom when she was your age."

"Oh." The *mom* topic startles me. It's an unspoken rule in the family only to bring her up if she demands to be brought up—basically whenever she appears in town or leaves again. We discuss the logistics of my mom, not my mom herself.

"I think it's the sunburn and the scratches," Aunt Jackie continues. "And the messy hair. You know, the whole bedraggled look."

"The what look?"

"Bedraggled, disheveled. You know, the 'I've been out all night and don't have time to shower before class' look. She was a true wild child. And after our mom passed away, she stopped even pretending to act like a good kid."

Aunt Jackie shifts under the crisp hospital sheets, tilting toward me. Her eyes are animated but trained past me, like she's watching a movie projected on the far wall. "She'd leave the house one day looking all put together and return the next at the crack of dawn with bruises from going dumpster diving for *found art* or racing motorcycles she wasn't licensed to drive. Oh gosh, and one time—when your grandfather was out of town—she jumped off the roof into the pool. It was filled then, of course, but still, it was about the most reckless thing she could do."

Aunt Jackie reaches for the water on her nightstand and sips from the plastic straw before glancing back at me with that nostalgic-drugged look again. "She was your age, you know."

The question pops out of my mouth before I can stop it. "My age when?"

"When she ran off. Two years after your grandmother passed away. Your grandmother was born and raised here, and she always talked about finally seeing the world after we graduated from high school, but then she got cancer, and…

"Your mom was terrified to end up like her, to live and die in the same place without seeing the world. That fear and grief just built up. So she left. I was Emery's age at the time and devastated. And when she didn't come back, I got angry. One night, a couple months after she left, while your grandfather was sleeping, I ripped up papers and pictures, threw her books in the pool, destroyed all of her stuff. When she finally came back to visit, two years later with a GED and a boyfriend from

Mississippi, there wasn't even a T-shirt of hers left for her to sleep in."

"Oh." I shift uncomfortably in the chair. Dad always tells me it's not my fault my mom leaves, but he's never gone into detail about her childhood. I never knew Aunt Jackie's anger is why there's no evidence of her at the house. I always assumed that, like in our home, she's a ghost, leaving nothing behind but an unsettled atmosphere.

I try to imagine what my mom's room would've looked like when she was seventeen, but I draw a blank. I can't conjure her favorite band, let alone her favorite color. One of the strongest memories I have of her is a faint musky scent because she prefers men's deodorant.

I don't know how to respond. Talking about my mom, spending time thinking about her, makes me uncomfortable. Why should I spend time on someone who never spends any time on me?

I scramble for diversion. "Do you want a snack? I can grab us something from the cafeteria."

Aunt Jackie doesn't respond, and for a moment I'm scared she won't leave the topic alone. Then she smiles, one of those smiles that make you feel sad not happy. "That sounds good, Anise. Chocolate pudding if they have it."

"Will do."

As I leave for the cafeteria, I can't help but think of my mom as a teenager, wild hair framing her pale face, visiting the grandmother I never met, perhaps already beginning to plan her escape. I glance back at Aunt Jackie's room, and my heart squeezes as I realize something: I wasn't the only twelve-year-old girl abandoned by someone I love.

———

Aunt Jackie and I spend the rest of the afternoon together. We eat chocolate pudding. She reads me excerpts from her paperback romance that put even the cheesiest bits of my Detective Dana novels to shame. I go back to the cafeteria to get us more chocolate pudding. She tells me all of the hospital staff gossip, both of us breaking into hysterical giggles as the nurse we were just talking about comes in to take her vitals. By the time Dad and the kids arrive, Aunt Jackie is nodding off to sleep, and I'm picking through her romance novel, texting Tess the best excerpts, including my personal favorite, *Rafael's scepter pierced her guarded honeycomb*. Messaging back and forth constantly almost makes it feel like I'm back home. But then a blast of recirculated air hits me instead of the ocean breeze.

"Hey," Dad whispers from the doorway with Emery. Parker and Nash slip into the room. "She sleeping?"

I nod, then turn to Parker and Nash and put a finger to my lips. It looks like the pool really did exhaust them because they collapse quietly into the extra armchairs by the bed. I stand and gesture for Emery to take my chair. She smiles at me and joins her brothers. I walk over to Dad at the doorway. "You guys have fun?" I ask him, keeping my voice soft.

He runs a hand through his graying hair. "You know what's more exhausting than building a city hall?"

"What?"

"Toting three kids to the pool and the mall."

I gasp. "The *mall?* You hate the mall. You must have made Emery happy."

"Emery? More like Parker and Nash. Those boys spent two hours in the Discovery store. Emery and I had to pry them away with the promise of cinnamon sugar pretzels."

Oh god. Cinnamon sugar pretzels. The bakery next to Tess's family restaurant makes the most delicious ones but only during the holidays. I swear I eat three a day all through December. "Did you…"

Dad pulls a crumpled wax paper bag from one of the shopping bags at his feet and grins. "I did. Because I am—"

"—The best father ever. Thank you, thank you." Despite eating chocolate pudding all afternoon and a ton of sugar this morning, I open the bag and tear off the still-warm dough, popping the piece into my mouth. "And thank you for taking them today," I mumble while chewing.

"Happy to do it," Dad responds. "How was hanging with Jacks?"

"Pretty good. I forgot how much I missed her, you know?" When they visit us in Santa Cruz, the trips are always so relaxed. Aunt Jackie and I have spent countless hours sitting by the surf, sipping Arnold Palmers, and inventing increasingly absurd backstories for all the tourists walking by. When

I was younger, I used to beg Dad to let them come live with us. I wanted my aunt and cousins to be around all the time, a big, loud family like the ones on TV. He had to explain that they had their own home. And soon enough, Eric and Tess and my other friends and their parents became that big, loud family anyway. It was only late at night, when it was just Dad and me that I still felt a little alone. Sometimes I'd slip one of my mom's postcards out of my nightstand and run my fingers along it like a magic lamp, wishing, "Come home, come home, come home."

I imagine her finding the note I left in Santa Cruz. I wonder if she'll care that her sister is hurt, if it will even register for her to care. I can't believe she up and left her sister and dad for two years without a word, yet of course I can believe it because she does the exact same thing to me. No wonder Aunt Jackie ruined all of her stuff. It's probably healthier than stashing keepsakes in a nightstand.

"I do know," Dad says. "I've missed Jacks and the kids too. It'd be nice if we lived closer and could see them more often."

"You mean if *they* lived closer," I correct.

"Yes, of course." Dad shifts on his feet. "Oh, I almost forgot. I got you something else."

"A cinnamon sugar pretzel *and* something else? Watch out or I might turn into one of those spoiled Willy Wonka kids."

"Think of it as a thank you for being there for your cousins," he says and then reaches for the largest of the shopping bags by his feet.

Parker and Nash nudge each other, and Emery half glances over from the screen of her phone. I hesitate, then open the bag and find two things inside: a skateboard and a helmet. The presents are unlike Dad's usual gifts—Mr. Zog's Wax, a new wet suit, a gift card to the Shak. People identify who you are and buy you presents accordingly. What do these presents say about me, about how much I've changed since leaving home?

"You like them?" Dads asks.

"Yeah, do you like them?" Nash asks loudly. Parker shushes him. Nash swats him. Emery shushes them both. Aunt Jackie stays sleeping.

I nod a couple times but don't say anything because the skateboard and helmet are white and teal, which are the colors of my surfboard. My throat gets all tight.

"You like the colors?" Dad asks. "They're your favorites, right?"

This is sweet. This is thoughtful. This is Dad saying, I'm sorry your summer isn't turning out like you planned, but I hope this makes it better. So I cough, trying to loosen my throat, and say, "Awesome. Thank you. Really, thanks."

Dad has always been one to take words at face value, so he hugs me and smiles. "Glad you like them."

And I do like them. Well, part of me likes them.

But a different part of me feels like I'm looking at gifts that belong to a different girl.

"I don't need help packing," Emery says. I'm sitting on her bed as she pulls out a duffel bag and stares into her closet.

"I know," I say. "Just thought I'd keep you company since I won't see you over the weekend."

Emery's friend has a lake house, and as we were leaving the hospital this evening, she texted Emery to invite her up for a few days. Emery jumped at the chance, even as Dad was muttering something about it being rather last minute. "Okay, thanks I guess. But you know, you are here *all* summer." She looks up from inspecting a pair of shorts and smiles. "You'll survive a few days without me."

Thanks for the reminder. I still have fifty-seven days left in Nebraska. Not that I'm counting. "So who else is going?" I ask as Emery places the shorts on the extra bed and pulls out two blue summer dresses that look exactly the same and holds each one up to the mirror, switching them back and forth.

It's amazing how Emery and I can spend hours talking and watching TV and laughing yet basically have no shared interests. She's all music and clothes. And I'm all surfing and…surfing. But maybe that's part of what family is—loving people you have nothing in common with.

"You don't know them. People I hang out with at the park. From school and stuff."

"All girls?"

"Yes, *Mom.*" She says it teasingly with a grin, but the word unsettles me. Maybe because of my conversation with Aunt Jackie. I knew my mom left home young, but I never got many details. Looking around Emery's room now, crowded with her own things, I wonder if...

"Hey, Emery?" I ask.

"What?"

"Do you know...um, was this your mom's room when she was a kid?"

She doesn't seem to notice the tension in my voice as she keeps sorting clothes. "Nope, oldest kid gets the biggest room. It was your mom's. Do you like this top?"

"Yeah, it's great," I say, but I'm not looking at the top. I'm looking at the closet's door frame and wondering if the notches in it were made to mark my mom's height, wondering what color the room was painted when she lived here, wondering how her furniture was arranged.

Emery continues, "Yeah, so the trip is all girls because Charlie's dad doesn't want any boys there. He's, like, super uptight. Are you allowed to have boys sleep over?"

Boys? Sleeping over? Emery now has my full attention. "Um, not really," I say, having a flash of this one night Eric stayed over until four in the morning watching movies while Dad was fast asleep. Eric was dating someone then, so he was just my best friend Eric. But now, looking back, I remember my flushed skin as we wrestled for the remote on the couch, my racing heart when we decided to share a blanket because both of us were too wiped from the wrestling to get up and grab a second one. I guess I liked him before I knew I liked him. And now because of almost two thousand miles of separation, I'm losing my chance to explore those feelings.

Eric has had a few girlfriends over the years. Has he met a long-stay tourist to hang out and hook up with? Is that why our texting has gotten awkward? It's not like I expect him to wait around for me, and I'm not sure I even want him to, but the thought leaves me unsettled. Eric is one of my best friends. When I get home I still want my best friend.

As I lean back, I notice a CD case on Emery's desk. "What's this?" I ask, grateful for a distraction. The label says it's a Beatles' *Abbey Road* CD, but the cover art is from a different point of view. All four Beatles are in black and white and sitting on top of a building, looking down at the famous Abbey Road instead of walking across it.

"Nothing." With flushed cheeks, Emery crosses the room and plucks the CD from my hands.

"Did you make it?" I ask. Her walls are plastered with pictures and posters and album designs. "Did you make all of these? They're awesome." They really are. I don't have an artistic bone in my body. I'd kill to be able to make stuff like this. Sometimes Tess sketches the ocean and portraits of us out in the surf. Her hand flies across the page like it's controlled by magic. The most I've ever been able to draw is inside the lines of a coloring book.

Emery sits down in her desk chair and toys with the CD case. Finally, she mumbles, "It's kind of silly. I know."

"Silly?" I ask. "It's awesome. How'd you make them?"

She shrugs her shoulders. "I mess around with Photoshop and stuff. For fun. But it'd be cool if I could do it for a job one day or something." She gets up and returns to her packing. "I have a blog where I post them. People like them, I guess. They request their favorite albums and everything."

"I'd love to see it," I say.

She turns to me, eyeing me as if trying to see if I'm kidding. Maybe someone made fun of her at some point. People can be assholes for no reason. Or without realizing it. I know I've had my moments.

"Okay, maybe." She continues to fold clothing. "I can make one for you, if you want."

"I would be honored. They're great. Seriously."

She doesn't respond again, but when she turns to put the stack of clothing in her duffel bag, I spot the most natural smile on her face I've seen all summer.

SEVEN

THERE HAS TO be a limit to how many times one can fall on one's ass in the same day. And I have to be really close to reaching that limit. "Try again!" Parker insists as I get up from the ground, rubbing my tender backside.

"Why?" I groan.

"Because you have to beat Lincoln."

I laugh, loud and short. I'm supposed to meet Lincoln at the park today for our challenge, and the stark truth is that I have a zero percent chance of skating better than him. I've looked into the average skills a skater acquires after seven years of skateboarding, and I've barely learned the tip of that iceberg. And yet, I'm still trying. Who knows? Maybe some skateboarding deity will come down to Earth and bestow me with killer talent.

"Come on," Nash says. "Try it one more time. You almost had it, I swear. Here, I'll show you again."

I don't get embarrassed easily, but watching my nine-year-old cousin breeze through a trick that has me on my ass every ten seconds isn't easy on the ego. I watch for the millionth time as Nash skates down the driveway, kicks his board into the air so that it spins in a full circle, and then lands on it. The trick is called a kickflip. Apparently it's easy. Apparently anyone who skates can do it. Apparently I'm a double-right-footed failure.

"See?" Nash asks, skating back toward me, his floppy brown hair sticking out of his helmet. "Easy as pie."

"Apple pie," Parker agrees.

"Is apple pie easier than other types of pies?" I ask.

The boys don't laugh. They just look confused and skate back down the driveway. Guess I left my coordination *and* my sense of humor in Santa Cruz. "All right," I say. "I'll try again, but we're heading to the park as soon as your sister gets back."

Or never go back to the park again.

But I don't want to be the worst cousin ever. I've already deprived them of the park for a week so I could practice in private, and they've gone along with it since I've let them help me practice. I'd be the ultimate asshole if I kept them away all summer.

As I'm about to step back onto my board, a minivan stops in front of our driveway. A side door opens, and Emery pops out with her duffel bag. Before I can ask how the lake was, she rushes past us into the house, eyes welling with tears, and then slams the door behind her.

"Umm…" I say.

The oblivious dad driving the van waves and then pulls away.

"Umm…" I say again.

"I think Emery's in a bad mood," Nash says.

"I think so too," Parker agrees.

I nod. "I think so three."

———

Okay, so here's the thing—I'm supposed to be at the park to meet Lincoln for this challenge. If I don't go, he will inevitably mock me the next time he sees me. Or worse, give me some sad, sympathetic look, like a puppy that's about to be put down. But I also need to comfort and talk with Emery who just ran into the house with tears in her eyes.

The *problem* is that Emery is currently in her room, door locked, music blaring.

I knock for the tenth time. "Emery, are you okay? Please let me in. I need to know you're okay. Emery? Come on. Answer me, please."

No response.

I sigh and slide down the door. Hopefully it's nothing serious. I remember overreacting at Emery's age when Dad said I couldn't go to the Beyoncé concert without a parent.

I remember giving him the silent treatment for a week when he said I couldn't surf on my sprained ankle. It's probably just preteen hormonal drama, like when Marie was pissed at us because we almost missed Cassie's dance recital. But then after a few uncomfortable junior high lunch periods, Marie realized she'd given us the wrong date for the recital in the first place.

Crap. That reminds me I need to text Cassie good luck. Her summer dance recital is tonight. Her last recital before boot camp. I've attended every one since middle school, but this year I'll only be able to watch whatever shaky video someone posts online. That is, if I even go online to look. I've been avoiding my news feed the past few days.

"*She's fine*," Nash says. He tugs my hand. "We're gonna be late!"

Parker and Nash don't look too concerned. Still, worry gnaws at me each second she doesn't respond. "Has this happened before?" I ask.

"Only like every month," Parker says.

"Good." I shake my head. "I mean, not good, but you know—if this happens monthly, it's probably not anything serious, right?"

"Mom always waits until she calms down or gets hungry," Nash says.

"How long does that usually take?" I ask.

Nash shrugs his shoulders. "Long enough for us to be late to the park."

"If you don't want to wait…" Parker runs off down the hall.

"What?" I ask, but he's already disappeared into his room. A few moments later he returns with a paper clip and starts jimmying the lock.

"Parker, stop it!" Emery yells from inside her room.

I'm surprised that Parker, not Nash, is the one who picks locks. But then Parker is quiet and patient and logical, which would make him an excellent burglar—not that burglary is a career path he should consider. He'd just be good at it.

A few seconds later, the lock clicks. "I'm coming in," I tell Emery, then open the door.

Emery sits on the bed, her eyes red-rimmed, a magazine in her lap. "Get out!" she shouts. Her voice is more choked than loud, kind of like when a dog is scared and can't get out a full bark.

"Guys, downstairs," I tell Parker and Nash. The boys hesitate, glancing at their sister, but listen and leave. Once they've thumped down the carpeted stairs, I hover by the door in a way I hope says I'm-only-invading-your-privacy-as-much-as-necessary. "You okay?"

"Fine."

"Right." I play with the hem of my tank top. "But, here's the thing. Obviously something happened, and I need to know what it was, so I can figure out if I need to tell your mom."

Okay, not as smooth as Dad's communication skills but not the worst either. Crap, who am I kidding? I'm total shit at this. I should be comforting her, not threatening to tell her mom.

"Don't," Emery says, a sharp cut in her voice. She looks up

at me from her magazine. "It's not—it's not a big deal. Don't bug her with it."

"If it's not a big deal, then maybe tell me?"

"Look, it's nothing." She shoves off her covers and stands. "I'm okay, really. Let's just go to the park so you can do your skate thing."

Except of course it's *not* nothing. Something shut her down, caused her to come home practically in tears. I want to hug her, tell her she can confide in me, reassure her, but she's standing in this tensed, arms-crossed, fuck off position, and at least for now, I want to respect her desire for space. She doesn't look physically hurt, and the tears have stopped, and the boys want to go to the park, and I have to do this absurd challenge, so for now, maybe I should listen to her.

"All right," I relent. "But…when…or if you decide you're not fine, let me know, because you know, it's okay to be not okay."

Emery rolls her eyes, then brushes past me and out the door.

———

The sun presses higher into the air, turning a hot day into a blistering one. It feels like a sin to step out of the bliss of air conditioning. By the time we get to the park, my clothes are dripping off me like the clocks in those Salvador Dali paintings. Definitely not attractive. Not that there's a reason for me to look attractive. I would just prefer if my perspiration levels weren't reaching new highs today. At least I managed to skate all the way here without incident. Twisting an ankle before arrival wouldn't have been good for my already depreciating self-confidence.

We enter the park, and for the first time, Emery doesn't bike toward the basketball courts. "Umm, Emery?"

"What?" she responds, continuing to ride alongside us to the skate park.

"Aren't you going to the courts?"

She doesn't respond. Oh, I'm actually that dense. Of course she's not going to the courts. Whatever happened this weekend had to do with her friends, so she doesn't want to see them right now. I'm a total asshole for even asking. My mind races. "Oh, great. You want to watch me get my ass kicked too, right?"

"Right." She even grins. Or not-frowns. Which is a giant leap forward from an hour ago. "Totally right. Gotta take pictures for posterity and all."

I not-frown back at her. "So sweet of you. Thanks, Emery."

As we enter the skate park, the boys follow close behind me, like they're bailiffs keeping me from running without posting bail. My goal today is to be collected. I might not skate better than Lincoln, but at least I can lose with grace. I can be the bigger person. I can suck up my battered pride for my cousins and their love of this sport.

But then I see Lincoln. He's wearing his jean-shorts-flannel-combo that is either style or a complete absence of style. My pulse thuds, and I almost stumble off my skateboard. My nerves of steel aren't looking so steely.

The twins holler for Lincoln from across the park, attracting the attention of almost everyone here. Lincoln glances up, and even from this far away, I can see him smiling. He doesn't look the least bit nervous. And why would he be? This is his sport. His skate park.

Lincoln and Austin skate over and slide to easy stops a few feet away.

"Hey there," Lincoln says to Emery. "You must be the third Sutter sibling." He holds out his hand for her to shake. "I'm Lincoln."

She hesitates a moment, then shakes his hand. "Hey, I'm Emery."

"Hey Emery," Austin says, his voice peppier than I expected from someone who wears only black. His genuine smile mirrors Lincoln's. Emery nods back. I wonder if they know each other from school. Then he turns to me. "Austin," he says. "Nice to meet ya!"

"Yeah, hey, hi," I say and try to smile back, but I'm too busy worrying about Emery and my kickflip to give it any real effort.

Then, without a word, Emery goes to sit on one of the benches.

Parker and Nash have already turned to Austin and are gushing over some trick he pulled off the other week, asking if he would teach them how to do it. As the boys and Austin enthuse over each other, Lincoln turns to me and smiles. Like we're friends. Like this is normal. Like it's totally perfectly normal to challenge a relative stranger to a skating competition. Maybe it is. Maybe, with a lack of better options, competitions with strangers are normal forms of entertainment in Nebraska.

Or maybe it's only a normal activity for this particular guy who makes my skin flush deeper than sunburn.

"So," he says, gesturing to my new board and helmet. "I see you've taken a liking to this fine sport."

"Not exactly," I say. "My dad just didn't want to see, and I quote, 'my pretty brains splattered all over the driveway.'"

"Makes sense," Lincoln says. "You do have pretty brains."

Lincoln has a talent for doling out the world's strangest compliments.

"Anyway," he continues, "I figured we'd both hop on the quarter pipe for a few minutes each, scoring points for the most 360s, hardflips, noseslides, the usual, with points factored in for speed and style. Sound good?"

I stare at him, mouth open. He can't be serious. Is he trying to kill me? I've barely figured out riding without falling off and ollying, and I still haven't mastered the kickflip. I'm not even sure what most of those other moves are, much less have the ability to perform them.

Lincoln bursts out laughing. He pats me on the shoulder. "Sorry, sorry. I was joking. Apparently I need to take my poker face on tour. Don't worry, I didn't expect you to turn into Cara-Beth in a week."

"Who?" I ask.

"Cara-Beth Burnside?" He stares at me as if I'm from another planet. "A pioneer of women's skateboarding and snowboarding? Anise, my new friend, I demand you go home tonight and watch her Villa Villa Cola footage."

Her Villa Villa what? "I'm sure she's not *that* famous. I mean, have you ever heard of Conner Coffin or Malia Manuel?" I rattle off the names of a couple of my favorite surfers.

"Actually, I have. Not all of us obsess over a single sport. I spread my ESPN time around. Perhaps you should try the same."

See, that doesn't make any sense to me. Why spend small chunks of time on a dozen sports when you can spend all your time on the best sport of all? I'm not saying all sports besides surfing are terrible—they're just terrible in *comparison* to surfing.

"So." I shift my balance and place one foot on my skate-board, rolling it back and forth a few inches. "How are we actually competing?"

"I was thinking we each make three laps around the perim-eter of the skate park, finagle in as many tricks as we can, and we let the boys judge who's better."

"Did you really just say finagle?" I ask.

"Finagle is a great word," he says.

"It's a weird word."

"Weird and great aren't antonyms."

I narrow my eyes but don't respond. "Don't two cousins against one brother make the judging a little biased in my favor?"

Lincoln smiles. "Ah yes, but I'm betting on the fact that I'm still better than you."

His smugness is infuriating, particularly because it reminds me of my own smugness and its quickly evaporating quantity. Back home I'm nothing but confident. Here, I'm stuck on concrete ground, but it doesn't feel very solid.

"Ladies first?" Lincoln asks.

"Isn't that a bit sexist?"

"I was going for polite, but we can go with 'losers first' if you'd prefer that."

I roll my eyes. "So much better, thank you."

"Guys!" Lincoln snaps his fingers and cuts off the boys' chatter midsentence. "We're about to start." Then he turns to the benches and waves at Emery. "Come join the judging!"

"Come on, three against one," I say. "Now that's really biased."

It turns out not to matter. Instead of coming over, Emery pulls her giant headphones out of her backpack and shoves them over her ears. I hope I'm doing the right thing by giving her space. One glance at the ever-eager Parker and Nash tells me I'm at least doing something right for two of my cousins.

"Okay, let's get this over with."

"Good luck!" Parker and Nash chorus.

Lincoln and Austin wish me luck too, which is nice of them but also a little useless.

Despite skating all the way to the park, I hesitate before getting back onto my board. I'm nervous my unease will show in front of everyone, or worse, my body will betray me in some spectacularly embarrassing way. But walking over to the wall would be embarrassing too, so I take two short breaths and one long one and then jump on the board.

My ride to the far side of the park is seamless. So far so good.

"Ready?" I call to everyone. Parker and Nash are standing on top of a table to best view my humiliation, and Lincoln and Austin stand on the ground in front of them.

"Ready!" they all scream.

"Okay!" I call back. Then a few seconds pass, and I say, "Okay," again because I still haven't started moving. A few seconds later I say, "Okay," again, and then I realize I should probably be skating and not talking since this is a skating competition and not a how-many-times-can-you-say-okay-in-one-minute competition.

"Come on, Anise!" Emery shouts. I smile at her voice.

I kick the ground hard and rocket down the first leg of the course. As I rush across the park, I thank the gods for whatever athletic aptitude they've bestowed upon me because I don't fall or waver. Some stiffness eases from my muscles. Maybe I'm not going to make a *complete* fool of myself.

I finish the first lap quickly, wind rushing through my hair, ears and eyes pricked and stinging like riding a wave in Santa Cruz. And then, as I'm starting to feel comfortable, I remember that I'm supposed to be doing tricks too and that a dog (literally a dog—I watched the YouTube video) can ride a skateboard. My feet act before my brain and I pop an ollie. The trick is faultless. My board smacks back on the pavement, and I kick off again, barely losing any momentum. So I pop another and another, hearing a whoop of applause and cheering from the table, before gearing down and gaining more speed and confidence with it.

The exhilaration takes over. As I complete my second lap, the concrete under my board feels almost as natural as churning ocean water. And for the first time here, I'm at ease. Near the end of my third lap, it's time to show how comfortable I truly am. I kick the board into the air. It spins perfectly and effortlessly. Then the board and I both fall to the ground, a cocky grin spreading across my face as I steady my balance with my arms and secure my footing and—*WHAM*.

I'm on the ground. My bruise-battered ass is defeated and embarrassed because I missed my goddamn footing. My skateboard is half the length of my surfboard, and where I expected board, I only found air. The fall is no worse than the dozens I've had all week, yet I'm mortified.

The next thing I know, Lincoln is in front of me, reaching over to help me up. I hesitate, then take his hand, which is calloused, yet soft. I'm waiting for the taunts, the mocking, but he says, "Very nice. Like, scary nice actually."

"Are you kidding?" I ask. "Or really bad at sarcasm?"

"Not at all," Lincoln says. "That was pretty dang…hmm… What's the surfer term for it? Rad?"

"Sure. Rad. In an outdated, eighties kind of way."

"Okay, sure, you fell on your ass," Lincoln continues, "but you fell after pulling off an almost perfect kickflip. Do you know how long it takes the average person to learn one of those?"

"Uh, no…" I wonder what kind of signal it would send if I massage my sore ass in front of Lincoln.

"Three months," Lincoln says and holds up three fingers to emphasize his point. "I mean, it only took me one, but I am a bit of a skateboarding genius. And, you know, an all-around genius. I *did* just graduate top of my class—that is, if you don't count the valedictorian, the salutatorian, and whatever the third-torian is. So nailing an almost perfect kickflip in a week . is, as I said, rad."

I shift from one foot to the other, still trying to process exactly how bruised my ass is and how to respond. "So does that mean I won?"

He laughs. "Absolutely not. I'm still going to kick your ass." He throws his board onto the ground and hops on. "Feel free to join the judging panel and watch the magic happen."

Lincoln is…perplexing. I'm not used to being complimented and mocked within the same relative breath. I guess some might call it honesty, but I call it damn unnerving.

I watch him. He's incredibly balanced. I wonder if having one arm throws off your natural equilibrium; though, maybe he was born with one arm, so it *is* his natural equilibrium. He's taller than a lot of my friends, making quite an impressive figure. Not that I think he's impressive or anything. He jumps and lands two perfect kickflips in a row. The sound of wheels hitting pavement carries across the park.

Okay, he is kind of impressive.

I make my way back to the table, where the boys are cheering for Lincoln as he speeds around. Austin watches Lincoln with intent and awe. I wonder what it'd be like to have a sibling to cheer me on. Would it feel different than support from my friends? When I was seven, my mom stuck around for a couple of months straight. Even Dad got up his hopes that we could be a family for the long haul. One morning, I got up the nerve to ask her if she could give me a brother or a sister. She smiled and said, "Sure, why not?"

Two days later she was gone again.

"Your kickflip was awesome!" Parker says, jolting me back.

"Very awesome!" Nash agrees.

I don't understand how my falling down translates to awesome, but instead of arguing, I just say, "Thanks guys," and sit down, resisting the embarrassing urge to stand on top of the table with them for an optimal view. I can see Lincoln clearly enough, looping around the park, successfully performing ollies and kickflips and a trick that I think is called a bigflip. He executes each move without a break in stride, always hitting the pavement with speed. Jealousy seethes through me, in part because he's better than me, but mostly because he's at home here. This is his turf. I miss that feeling.

As he's making his third lap, Lincoln suddenly veers off

course, shooting diagonally across the skate park for the giant bowl. "Dropping in!" he calls out to the few people around it.

"Oh, come on!" I shout. "That wasn't part of the deal!"

But I can't begrudge him too much. Who doesn't want to show off doing something they love? Parker and Nash jump off the table in excitement and run off toward the bowl, while Austin follows at a slower pace. I hesitate. I shouldn't care—I know I shouldn't care—and yet curiosity tugs at me. After watching what Lincoln can do on a flat surface, I want to see more, so I grab my board and ride over to the edge of the bowl.

The bowl is a free-form shape, like someone took an oval and pulled and pushed it like taffy. Lincoln glides along the sides, skimming down the walls and then back up, riding the whole length in one fluid motion that almost reminds me of surfing. All around the edges of the bowl, other skaters watch, some even clapping and cheering Lincoln on, basking in his success like it's their own. As Lincoln loops up again, he jumps out of the bowl across from me and lands with a firm crack against the concrete. He kicks up the board, holds it under his nub, then looks my way and grins.

He bumps fists and high fives some other skaters before making his way over to us. A young girl drops into the bowl, and she zooms around without an ounce of hesitation. I'm mesmerized, the tension tightening then easing in my shoulders every time she skates up and skims over the lip of the bowl.

"Not bad, huh?" Lincoln asks. He stands next to me now, his face lightly sheened with sweat. He runs his hand over his cropped hair.

My competitive nature goes to point out a flaw in his performance—any flaw—but the thing is, I'm not sure there were any. And even if there were, I'm not experienced enough to have caught them.

"It was okay," I say. "I mean, ignoring the part where you blatantly broke the rules of the competition." My words are quick and stiff. I can't help it. I came here today knowing I would lose, but that's not making the loss any easier. I've been the best for too many years to take defeat lightly, even if this defeat is in a brand new sport.

Lincoln grins, then asks, "Judges, do you have a decision?"

"The judges need to confer before delivering final results," Austin says in mock seriousness. He turns to my cousins and motions them into a huddle. "Anise, Lincoln, please give us some space."

We let them deliberate even though there's nothing to deliberate. The twins are enjoying themselves, and that's what's important. Lincoln's hand presses against my bare shoulder and guides me away from our judges. The touch is easy, reminding me of Eric. How can a familiarity that's been cultivated over almost two decades with one guy be achieved in just a few encounters with another?

Lincoln nods at my cousins. "They're pretty cute," he says, then drops his hand, yet stands close to me, close enough that

I notice a small scar on his right eyebrow, slanting diagonally through the fine hairs. Before he can catch me staring, I clear my throat and step a bit to the side.

"Yeah, they're not bad," I say. "Until you're trapped in a house with them for an entire summer. Did you know nine-year-old boys require feeding? Like multiple times a day?"

"Huh," Lincoln says. "I did not know that. I thought you just threw some kibble in the bowl and let them have at it for a week."

I laugh, and my smile lingers. "So, what about you?"

"What about me?"

"What are you doing this summer?"

"Besides converting surfers into skaters?" He scratches his head again. "You know, now that I think about it, I'm basically a skateboarding evangelist."

"Yeah, besides that."

"Well, I just graduated, but I think I mentioned, I'm going to hike the PCT—the Pacific Crest Trail. So I'm going to take a year off before college to train and work to save money."

"What's the job?" I ask.

"Skateboarding evangelist." Lincoln somehow manages to keep a straight face.

"That come with benefits?"

"Excellent benefits. I actually work at a nature store—you know, hiking gear, trail food, that sort of stuff."

"Sounds appropriate."

"Yeah, it's—"

Before Lincoln has a chance to continue, Nash cuts him off. "We're ready!"

All three boys walk toward us. Parker and Nash try to maintain serious faces, but they keep breaking into giggles.

"So?" Lincoln asks. "What's it going to be?"

Austin says, "After careful deliberation, we've come to the unanimous decision of naming—"

"Lincoln wins!" Parker and Nash scream.

"—Lincoln our victor," Austin finishes. He rolls his eyes and smiles at the boys.

I take a deep breath, sucking in all my pride along with it, and say, "Nice job."

"The bet," he prods.

"Fine." I sigh and then quickly mutter, "I admit skateboarding is just as difficult as surfing."

"Ah, thank you, gracious loser," he responds. "But seriously, you should feel pretty good about yourself right now. I've been around a lot of different skate parks over the years, and I've never seen someone learn so quickly."

"Skate *parks?*" I ask.

"Remember, I wasn't born here either. You're not the only Nebraska transplant. Austin and I have only been in this fine state for two years."

Only two years? I already knew he wasn't born here, but Lincoln glides around this place like he's the goddamn mayor—like he appeared first, and then the world grew up around him. I just assumed he'd lived here for most of his life. I'm about to ask more, but then Austin steps forward. "Lincoln, we've got to go. Dad wants us home early today, remember?"

"Damn. Right." Lincoln turns to me and hesitates, his eyes sweeping over me, lingering longer than normal. "I'll see you later, Anise."

My cheeks flush. Don't ask me why. My cheeks just seem to do that around him. "Right," I say. "See you later."

He skates away, then flips his board and comes back toward me. "Hey." He slides to a stop. "You should come to the park again tomorrow."

"I should?" I ask.

He nods with an easy smile, a smile that warms my body slowly, like when the sun first peeks out, promising a day of pure heat. "Definitely you should. Earlier the better, okay?"

"Umm, okay," I say.

And then he skates away a second time. Parker and Nash come up behind me. "That was fun," Parker says.

"Yeah," Nash agrees. "He's, like, way cooler than you."

"Awesome, you guys," I say. "Thanks so much."

"Come on, let's go skate," Nash says.

For a second, I'm actually tempted. I was so close to nailing that kickflip, I'm convinced that one more crack at it will be a success. Though I'd never admit it to Lincoln, it's invigorating to learn a totally new sport, getting my body to move in a completely new way. But then I glance over, and Emery's rooted on the same spot of the bench, and I decide my presence is more needed there.

"You guys go on," I tell the boys. After they skate off, I walk over and sit down next to Emery, and even though she has on her headphones, I say, "Hey."

She turns to me, eyes hard again. "What?"

"I just said 'hey.'"

She sighs and lifts off the headphones. "Dude, I can't hear you. What?"

I wonder if she's fucking with me. I know she's upset, but this shift in temperament feels extreme. "I just said 'hey,'" I repeat.

"Is that all?"

"Look, Emery," I pause, trying to formulate my thoughts. "Here's the thing, you said everything is okay, but you aren't hanging out with your friends, and you're being, you know," *a pain in my ass*, "short-tempered with me, and I know I'm not the brightest person in the world, but I've got to take that as a hint that everything is actually *not* okay."

Her stone face wavers, eyes blinking a bit faster than usual. But then she crosses her arms and sets her jaw. "It's not a big deal. I'm just taking a break from them, okay?"

"And I want to believe that. But if you could tell me a little about why you're taking a break from them, I'd be more comfortable keeping this from your mom."

Dammit. I did it again.

"You're not keeping anything from her because there isn't

anything to keep. Nothing happened, okay?" Her voice rises. "Don't you get it? Nothing. Happened."

But the problem is—the more she says nothing happened, the more I'm convinced something did.

EIGHT

"FUCK!" I GASP as the knife slips and slices through the thin skin of my index finger. "Fuck, fuck, fuck." I bring the finger to my mouth and suck the few droplets of metallic-tasting blood.

"You okay in here?" Dad pops into the kitchen.

His skin is damp from his morning run. I wave him away. "Fine, fine. Just accidentally cut myself instead of the PB&J."

"Let me see that." Dad gestures for my finger. I open my hand and let him inspect the small wound. He brings it close and takes his time.

Once, I think I was nine, Dad was at work and my mom was taking care of me. We were out somewhere I'd never been before, riding bicycles on this empty road, going faster and faster and faster, when I lost my balance and fell, scraping both my knees. The skin was shredded and bleeding enough to drip down my legs. I began to cry and expected my mom to baby me like Dad always did, to hush me and hold me and tell me it'd be okay. But she didn't. She ran over, her mess of curls golden-brown in the sun, and said, "Look!"

Ahead of us was a giant downhill slope, much steeper than I'd ever biked before, injured or not. I looked back at my mom, and she was smiling and laughing, and she said, "Let's go, come on!"

Her enthusiasm ensnared me, and the pain went away. I remember getting back on my bike and riding next to her, too excited to care about my scraped knee dripping blood all the way down the hill.

"Doesn't look too bad," Dad says, letting go of my hand. "Just make sure you clean it out whenever you touch that dirty skateboard, okay?"

"Okay," I say. "Shouldn't you be at work already?" I rinse my hands in the kitchen sink so I don't accidently make PB&J blood sandwiches. It's just past nine in the morning, and since the weather forecast promised a rare cool day, I'm packing lunches for the kids so we can spend all day at the park. There's also maybe a part of me that wants to go early because Lincoln asked me to. But it's tiny. Miniscule. Not even a real factor.

"Going in late today. Want some help with those?"

I nod, and for the next twenty minutes, Dad and I stand side by side and make pasta salad, sliced fruit, and of course, PB&Js. We work in comfortable silence. I consider telling

Dad what happened with Emery yesterday, but last night she seemed to have calmed down once more. If I tell Dad I'm worried about her, he'll tell Aunt Jackie because parents have that universal rule about never keeping information about their children from other parents. I'm concerned about Emery. Remembering the tears in her eyes still cuts at me, but I want her to trust me, and I should do the same and trust her. So I will. For now.

"You guys want a ride to the park?" Dad asks as we finish up. Parker and Nash have come to hang out in the kitchen, and I have to keep swatting away their hands as they grab bits of the lunch.

"That's okay. Thanks though." A week ago I would have said yes, but I'm actually itching to get back on my skateboard, muscles burning, wind whipping my hair, relishing the exhilaration my body craves.

—————

The park is almost empty, which is not surprising since it's not even ten in the morning. Emery once again heads to the skate park with us instead of going off to find her friends. When I ask why, she says none of them are here. It is early, but I still don't believe her, yet it's only been a day since whatever happened. It's probably fine to give her more time to figure it out.

When we get to the skate park, she plants herself on the same bench as yesterday. I go to keep her company, but then Parker and Nash spot Lincoln and Austin by the quarter pipe and drag me in their direction. Lincoln waves at me and I get the same feeling as when a perfect overhead wave is approaching.

"Hey guys!" Austin gives Parker and Nash high fives. His cheerful attitude once again surprises me given his black T-shirt threaded with safety pins. Parker and Nash beg Austin to help them with yet another trick, and Austin agrees. All three head off toward the rails, while Lincoln stays by my side.

"Hey there." He stands next to me, shoulder to shoulder, so that we can watch Austin and the twins from a distance. Though the air is cool today, my skin flushes with warmth when I glance up at Lincoln.

"Hi." My right foot rests on my skateboard, pushing it back and forth across the pavement, an idle movement, like how I sometimes play with the zipper on my wet suit, sliding it down a few inches and then back up.

"You're here early," Lincoln says.

I nod. "I am."

"Is it because I asked you to come?"

I clear my throat, ignoring the heat flushing my cheeks. "It's a nice day," I say.

He leans in close, a teasing flicker in his eyes. "It's not that you couldn't wait to see my adorable dimple?"

Of course he's aware of his dimple and its effect on those attracted to males. How could he not be? That dimple is like a goddamn superpower. And yet I don't want to fuel his already fired-up ego, so I tease, "Dimple or deformity?"

As soon as the word leaves my lips, the blood drains from my face.

Holy fuck.

I just said *deformity* to a guy with one arm. I am officially the most awful—no, most cruel—human being on the planet. "Oh—fuck…I mean, shit…I mean, *sorry*…" I stumble for an apology, but before I can form a string of coherent words, Lincoln smiles at me, like really smiles, like he's entertained by my repulsive comment.

"You should see your face right now," he says. "Very adorable. Possibly even more adorable than my dimple."

"Lincoln—" In my moment of embarrassment, I realize this is the first time I've ever said his name and how much I like the feel of those two syllables passing through my lips, "I am so sorry. Seriously. That was awful and—"

He places his hand on my shoulder. The touch drains some of my panic, redirecting my focus toward the feeling of those smooth calluses on my bare skin. "Dude, seriously, it's okay. The only uncomfortable thing you're doing right now is making it a thing. I know that's not what you meant, but yeah, you know, next time maybe—"

"Speak before I think?" I smack my head. "Oh god, I mean, think before I speak."

He grins. "Exactly." His hand lingers for a second longer, then drops away. I watch as his long fingers curl by his side, relaxed yet controlled. "And you know, if you're really torn up about it, you can make it up to me."

I narrow my eyes. "Make it up to you how?"

"Go on an adventure with me."

"An adventure? Here?" I ask. "Is that even possible?" Besides the skate park, all I've seen of Nebraska are mini-malls, fields of dry grass, and suburb after suburb. And of course, the hospital. Not exactly a hot spot for a good time.

"Oh, most definitely," Lincoln says. "As someone who has lived in his fair share of these United States, I can attest adventure can be found anywhere."

Lincoln is only a year older than me. How many places has he lived? "As promising as that sounds," I respond, "I can't exactly leave my cousins alone at the park."

"Ah, but that's where my true genius comes in. You have a twelve-year-old cousin, and I have a twelve-year-old brother. Put them together, and I think we're looking at a fine set of babysitters."

Part of me knows he's right. But the other part of me doesn't want to leave Emery alone when, even if she's not saying it, she might need me around. So I say, "I don't doubt Emery and Austin's abilities, but I can see the headlines now: beautiful park destroyed by twin boys due to ridiculously irresponsible older cousin. *You* were the one who called them the disastrous duo."

"Come on, Anise. Think about it. Also, Austin is first aid certified."

"He is?" I bite my lip.

"And he babysits all the time—"

"He does?" An image of goth-punk Austin playing Monopoly Junior with two J. Crew toddlers pops into my head.

"You deserve a little fun," Lincoln continues. "Especially after getting your ass kicked yesterday."

"Your powers of persuasion are miraculous."

"I'd like to think so." Lincoln smiles that cocky-ass smile. The thing is, he really is persuasive. All my days are starting to meld into cousins, park, park, cousins, and mix in a little hospital time for seasoning. I could use a break from the routine, do something for *me*. And the thought of doing something with Lincoln isn't exactly unappealing. "Come on," Lincoln continues. "At least ask Emery and see if she minds. I know Austin will mostly handle the boys. He sometimes likes when I'm not here so *he* can be the older, cool kid."

I stall, pushing my skateboard back and forth with one foot and contemplating my options: I can stay here all morning tiptoeing around Emery in the slight chance she wants to open up to me and making sure the twins don't destroy property or I can go on an adventure with Lincoln.

And Lincoln's dimple.

"Okay. If Emery agrees to it, then okay."

———

Emery agrees, which more worries than relieves me. She'd rather take care of her brothers than hang out with her friends? Two more days. I'll give her two days to tell me what happened until I give her the ultimatum: tell me or I'm telling your mom.

After I make her promise to send pictures of the boys every hour on the hour or text if she wants me to come back and then also get approval from Dad that it's fine to leave them at the park for a bit, I feel slightly more comfortable about the whole "abandoning my cousins to hang out with a hot guy" thing. I leave them the majority of the food stash, keeping a few sandwiches and water bottles in my backpack for Lincoln and myself. I have no idea if this adventure will include food, and I want to be on the safe side.

"Ready to go?" Lincoln asks after we go over the stay-safe instructions one more time.

"I guess so…" I feel anxious about leaving my cousins. I mean, they're nine and twelve. Nine- and twelve-year-olds stay by themselves all the time. But these aren't any nine- and twelve-year-olds—these are *my* nine- and twelve-year-olds.

I turn toward Emery. I must have the most expressive face on the planet because she says, "Anise. Seriously. We're fine. Go."

And she looks fine, content with her phone. And the boys look fine too, already ignoring me and trailing Austin around the park like he's a world famous skater.

"Are *you* fine?" Lincoln asks, his hand brushing against my shoulder again. It feels natural, and I wish it lasted more than a half second.

"Yeah. I'm good. Okay, let's adventure. Where are we adventuring to?"

"That's a surprise of course." Lincoln shoots me a scheming grin. "Part of the adventure."

―――――

"Downhill coming up!" Lincoln shouts.

I brace down, knees locked, blood pulsing, eyes fastened on the giant decline in front of me. Lincoln took me through some practice runs on a smaller hill before we started our journey, but it didn't fully prepare me for these steep gradients. On the first hill, I backed out halfway through, grinding my board to a clumsy halt. On the second hill, I made it to the bottom, but my stomach wouldn't stop churning at the thought of my imminent death. This time, I'm going to treat it like any towering wave and conquer it with confidence instead of submitting with fear. This time I'm going to enjoy it.

Lincoln flies down the road, body angled, board swerving back and forth in calculated cuts, as if looping around invisible traffic cones. The hill is monstrous, the grade as deep, if not deeper, than the hundreds of overhead waves I've ridden over the years. The wind rushes past me as my board picks up speed, gaining enough momentum that the wheels shake beneath me, rattling over every pebble and crack in the road.

And yet—despite the rattling, despite the knowledge that one wrong move and I could crash, a thousand tiny laccrations shredding my skin—I feel no fear. Because this unfiltered adrenaline, this surrender to the wind and the ride, this is my comfort, and this is my love.

As the hill tapers off into flat ground, the tension eases from my shoulders and knees, leaving me a bit disappointed. I'd rather feel scared than bored. Lincoln breaks in front of me, almost coming to a full stop before hopping onto the sidewalk in one fluid motion. I follow his move, managing to do so without falling or even stumbling.

"How was that?" Lincoln asks.

We're both breathing heavily. My body already aches, and we're not even to our destination yet, which according to Lincoln is six miles from the skate park. But I'm grinning. "Not bad." I pause. "Okay, kind of awesome."

"Thought you'd like it—a little more exciting than flat turf."

I bend down to relace my sneakers, and as I do, the hot sun bites at my neck. "Crap," I mutter, rubbing the exposed skin, already feeling the telltale signs of sunburn. "I really should've brought some sunscreen."

"Here, use mine." Lincoln digs through the pockets of his jean shorts and pulls out a tiny bottle. He tosses it to me, and I catch it—and then I stare at the bottle, and then at Lincoln, and then back at the bottle. He sighs and shakes his head. "Quick black people lesson: we get skin cancer too."

"Oh," I say. "Right. Of course. I knew that." But actually I didn't, probably because Cassie is my only black friend, and she spends her days slathering on tanning oil for optimum color.

Before I can embarrass myself further, I pop open the cap and coat my arms, legs, and face as quickly as possible.

"Hey, leave some for me," Lincoln says.

I look up when he speaks, because that's what normal people do, look up when someone is talking to them. But the thing is, at that exact moment, Lincoln is unbuttoning his sleeveless plaid shirt and stuffing it in his bag, his defined abs on display. I am doing very little to keep from staring at said abs; as in, I'm literally staring, and there might be the tiniest bit of drool dripping from the corner of my mouth.

Then my vision shifts, and I follow his chest up to his left shoulder. Even though Lincoln wears sleeveless shirts, I've never had a full view of his left arm. The sight unsettles me for a moment, kind of like taking a sip of water to find it's ginger ale. It's not bad, just different. I force my gaze away from his nub, which means back to his abs.

Lincoln smirks. "I'd think you'd be used to shirtless guys, living on the beach and all."

I blush (blame it on the sunburn) and toss him the sunscreen. I'm tempted to ask about his arm—his lack of arm—but I struggle to form words in my mind that don't sound rude, so instead I say, "Hurry up with that sunscreen. If I have to burn out here much longer, I'm going to give up on our adventure."

He catches my eye, and my stomach does that twisty, fluttering thing it likes doing around him. "Trust me, surfer girl, you don't want to give up on this."

About fifteen minutes later, I follow Lincoln as he turns right onto a beaten concrete road, down a hill, and into a gravel parking lot. There are a few cars, mostly Jeep Wranglers and Ford trucks. My skateboard struggles against the textured terrain, and giving up, I grind to a halt.

"Umm, where are we?" Woods surround the gravel lot. The only breaks in the trees are the access road we just came in on and a small opening to a trail. The woods emit an earthy scent of damp soil and foliage. It's not the salted air I'm used to, and yet as I take a deep breath, it's just as fresh and soothing.

"Dodge Park," Lincoln answers, taking off his glasses to quickly wipe them clean. "Well, part of it. The whole thing is about fifty acres."

"A park." I pause. "You realize we were just at a park, right? You had us skate six miles to go from one park to another park?"

Lincoln smiles. "Ah, but this is a special park."

"Uh-huh. What makes it so special?"

"Follow me to find out. Unfortunately, we'll have to go on foot from here. I know you're disappointed about that."

"Unimaginably so."

But the truth is, I will miss the board beneath my feet. There's something satisfying about going faster than you can on the legs you were born with.

We both pick up our boards, and I follow Lincoln on the

small path. I trust Lincoln, but going into a secluded spot with someone I barely know goes against just about every stranger danger warning I've ever heard, so I slip my phone out of my pocket to make sure I still have service. I do. I also have a text message from Emery showing me a picture of the boys sitting on their skateboards and chowing down on the fruit. Parker's flipped one of the orange peels inside out and stuffed it between his lips to create a giant cartoon smile. She even sent some emojis with the picture. Emojis are a good sign. I send three laughing-tears smiles back, then put my phone away and relax.

The woods are dense, filled with moss-covered trails, ivy crawling over trunks of towering trees, and scattered logs and branches we carefully maneuver around. Sunlight filters through the canopy, spreading an early day golden light over everything, glinting off the dew-dropped grass and illuminating our path in dappled shadows. The land is startling in its beauty. I had no idea that Nebraska was hiding all of this, lush nature.

As we walk, Lincoln points out different plants. He seems to know the name for every bush, tree, and flower. "This is one of my favorites." He bends down in front of a nettle of green stalks peppered with magenta flowers. "The purple poppy mallow."

I bend down next to him, watching as his fingers skim over the fragile petals. "Why is it a favorite?" I ask.

He glances at me, grinning. "Are you kidding? Purple

poppy mallow? Can't beat that name." He repeats it like it's a tongue twister as we stand and continue down the trail.

A minute later, he stops short again, and I almost bump into him. Again. "Hey, careful—" I start to say, but stop when he spins around and places a finger to his lips.

He has really nice lips.

He whispers, "Look over here. Walk gently."

He grabs my hand and pulls me forward and then down so that we're both crouching in front of a cluster of lavender and white flowers sprouting from a knot of spiky green stalks. The flowers have long, skinny petals. Two yellow and black butterflies flit around them, the patterned shapes in their wings reminding me of stained-glass windows.

"Wild bergamot," Lincoln informs me. "Butterflies love it, and—" he drops my hand and reaches forward to carefully pluck off a couple of the green leaves "—these brew some pretty mean mint tea."

"Um, Lincoln?" I ask, still crouched by the bergamot, watching the butterflies flutter back and forth and deciding on a scale of one to very how much I like holding Lincoln's hand. "How do you know all this stuff?"

He shrugs. "You know how I want to hike the PCT?"

I nod.

"I've had a thing for nature since I was little. We moved around a lot for my mom's job, so there was always somewhere new to explore, and I guess my thing for nature turned into a rather sturdy obsession with nature." He plucks off a few more bergamot leaves and tucks them into his pocket. "Hopefully I'll get into a college with a good biology or sustainability program and then maybe work for the national parks or some job that lets me travel all over the country, see all the wild bergamot and purple poppy mallow I want."

"That sounds awesome." And it does—even if his plan is so different than mine. He wants to travel the world, and I basically never want to leave home again.

"It definitely would be." He nudges my shoulder. "Come on, time for your adventure."

"So this Lincoln-guided nature walk wasn't my adventure?"

He grins. "Just an added bonus of my lovely company. The real adventure still awaits."

I hear voices first, cheerful shouts and laughs. But then—the splash of water. My skin tingles. My pulse accelerates. "Is that…"

We walk through another cluster of trees, and the world opens up. I find myself standing on top of a cliff over a large, streaming river. The river flows into a small gulf where people are splashing in the water and sunning on the muddy banks. "Welcome to our little slice of the Missouri River," Lincoln says. "It's no Pacific Ocean, but I figured it'd do the trick for today."

I don't know whether to laugh or cry or just strip down

and jump in the water. For all my complaining, I don't think I fully comprehended how much I missed home until this moment, until this sight of breathtaking water rushing beneath me. And the fact that Lincoln brought me here? He couldn't have taken me anywhere better.

And I have a feeling he knows it.

Another splash catches my attention. Down in the swimming hole people are cheering and laughing and craning their necks upward. I follow their gazes to an opening, bunkered by more trees, a short distance away from Lincoln and me.

"What are they doing?" I ask.

"Just watch," Lincoln says.

A few seconds later, someone on the cliff runs forward, grabs a rope hanging from one of the trees, and flings themselves out into the air, releasing the rope, dropping about fifteen feet into the water, and landing with a giant splash. "Oh my god," I say. "I have to do that. I have to do that now. Let's go."

Lincoln laughs at me, and I laugh back. I'm sure there's a little wild in my eyes right now. "I had a feeling you'd enjoy this," he says and grabs my hand again, tugging me back into the woods toward the rope swing. I'm going to be in water, even if it's only freshwater.

We get to the clearing, and there are a few people standing by the long rope. They wave at us and say hey, then continue to jump off one by one. We get in line behind them, and I shift from foot to foot. "Crap, what do we do with our stuff?" I ask Lincoln.

"You go first. I'll watch everything."

At this point, a nice person would say, *oh no, you go, and I'll wait*. But the thing is, I'm not always a nice person, and I want to be in that water. Like now. "Okay, sounds good to me."

I'm wearing a sports bra, so I strip off my tank and slide off my shoes and throw both in a pile along with my backpack. I feel Lincoln's gaze on me. I duck my head and fiddle with the zipper on my bag to hide my flushed cheeks. Growing up on the beach, I've had to deal with a lot of unwanted stares, but Lincoln's stare isn't exactly unwanted. Also, I've been not-so-subtly gawking at his chest since he took off his shirt, and honestly I don't mind him doing the same.

I finish fiddling with my bag and stand, watching the person in front of me jump off the cliff and into the open air, hearing them crash into the water beneath us. I step forward and grab the rough rope as it comes swinging back to the cliff. I turn to Lincoln. "So I just take this and jump, right? I'm not missing some safety precaution that will lead to my imminent death?"

"That's it," Lincoln says. "Trust me. I've jumped from here a lot, and I can assure you that death has occurred exactly zero times."

"Okay." I inch toward the ledge, letting my bare feet dig into the pebbled dirt. The drop seems a lot higher when I'm glancing straight down. Like a lot higher. Like maybe-this-is-a-really-fucking-unwise-idea higher. But the water is beautiful and clear and looks deliciously cold. "Fuck it," I say. Then I back up, run, and jump.

As soon as my feet leave the ground and I'm swinging into the air, I release the rope and scream with sheer joy. Wind rushes past my ears, and once again I experience that unfiltered adrenaline that only comes with doing something a little bit reckless. I slam into the water with a giant splash, and instead of coming up for air immediately, I stay under, relishing what it feels like to be cut off from everything else. I crack open my eyes to swirling blue and imagine that when I break the surface, the Santa Cruz coast will welcome me home.

But then my lungs say enough, and I rise to the surface, breathing in the fresh but Nebraskan air. I crane my neck to locate Lincoln at the top of the cliff. It's hard to see his face clearly, but I have a feeling he's smiling right along with me. For a moment, I think of Eric and my last night at home, surfing in the nude and smiling at each other in sheer joy. Only two weeks buffer that moment from this one, yet this feels so real and the other like a dream.

"Nice job!" Lincoln shouts. "You good?"

I give him two giant thumbs-ups. "Definitely good!" I yell. I lean back and float in the water for a few peaceful seconds before I run back up the cliff to jump in again.

———

Two hours later, I'm soaked and exhausted and happy.

Lincoln and I took so many turns running up the cliff and

jumping that I lost count, and the exertion has left us both hungry.

Ravenous.

Starving, actually.

The kind of hungry where your stomach wants to eat itself.

"Come on." Lincoln gathers his things. "I know a perfect spot."

"What's wrong with this one?" I ask, already digging into my backpack for one of the sandwiches.

"Nothing. I just know a better one."

Resisting the urge to chow down right here, I follow him once more through the woods, traveling down a gradual decline. My sneakers, tied around my bag, knock into the backs of my blissfully sore legs as we walk. The twigs and pebbles on the path remind me of the shell-sprinkled sand. Instinctually, I glance at the path for a sea marble but of course find none. A cool wind whips through the trees, drying my drenched sports bra and shorts. Eventually we come to a second clearing by the river, but this one is much smaller, secluded. I can no longer hear people shouting and splashing into the water.

We settle down onto the muddy riverbank. I flip over my skateboard to use as an unsanitary serving platter, then set out the sandwiches and water bottles. As I reach into my bag to dig out a final sandwich, I check my phone. There are messages from two people—Emery and Eric. Emery sent another picture of the boys. I hesitate before deciding not to open Eric's message. I can read it later. It's not like responding instantly will close the many miles between us.

"Ah, man. I wish these were bánh mì Spams," Lincoln says as I unwrap one of the PBJs and bite into it.

"You wish they were *what*?"

"Don't get me wrong," Lincoln says, midbite, somehow talking while chewing without making it seem disgusting. "Peanut butter and jelly is great, but I'm just really craving some bánh mì Spam." I give him another questioning look, so he sets down his sandwich and says, "Okay, I told you my dad is Vietnamese, right? So one of his favorite things to eat are bánh mì. Think of a baguette but better and filled with cilantro, cucumber, jalapeño, pickled carrots, and whatever kind of meat you want. And my mom is like deep Midwesterner American, and she loves Spam. Put the two together and you've got bánh mì Spam sandwiches. We used to eat them on road trips all the time because Spam doesn't need refrigeration."

"Sounds…interesting?" I say.

"Interesting? Try amazing. I'll make you one someday. You'll see."

I chew over Lincoln's words: *I'll make you one someday.* Lincoln plans on hanging out with me again. My cheeks heat. Eric's message is in my bag, but I'm in an entirely different reality. And for all I know, at this exact moment, Eric might be sharing fried cod sandwiches at the Shak with another girl, like our kiss never happened. And maybe it shouldn't have happened because now a constant in my life has turned into a variable.

Life would be easier with less variables.

I look back at my sandwich, then to Lincoln. "Do you come here a lot?"

"I try to, but Austin prefers the skate park, and younger siblings have this habit of always getting their way."

I think of dinner last night when Emery, despite her bad mood, relented and let the boys have the last two slices of pizza. I'm only here for the summer—Emery has been sacrificing pizza slices for nine years now. "I like it here." I lean back, propping myself up with one hand, while keeping the other clean to eat my sandwich. "It's nice, peaceful."

"Yeah, I love the skate park, but nothing really beats pure Mother Nature."

"Agreed—surfing is always better early morning or late at night. Empty beaches, empty breaks." I take another bite of my sandwich. "Thanks for today," I tell Lincoln. "It was…well, it was perfect. I really needed it."

He glances at me, squinting in the sun. "I'm glad you had fun. You weren't half-bad on that rope swing either."

"Not half-bad? I was better than you."

"You were so not better than me!"

"Oh, yes I was."

"Anise, sweet Anise, I'm working with the one-armed handicap, and I was still leagues better than you. Just accept the facts."

My gaze flickers to his missing arm, and this time ingrained manners can't keep me from asking, "How did you... I mean, why do you only... Well..." I have a sneaking suspicion he always knows how I'm going to embarrass myself before I do it.

"Just ask, Anise. I don't mind. I'd rather people ask than awkwardly avoid the topic. I was friends with this one guy for a solid two months—we hung out almost every day—and he never said a thing until one afternoon we were playing bas-ketball outside his house and he just blurted out, *Dude, did you know you only have one arm?*"

I grin, but I'm still uncomfortable. I pick at the remains of my sandwich, flicking the crumbs to the ground, avoiding his gaze. "Okay, hopefully I'm not as bad as that." I pause. "Lincoln, why do you only have one arm?"

"Zombie attack."

"Come on, really."

"Secret Service op."

"*Lincoln.*"

He repositions himself, pulling one leg to his body and tucking his head on top of his knee. "Ever heard of ABS?" he asks. I shake my head. "Amniotic Band Syndrome. When I was a fetus, amniotic bands wrapped around my upper arm and cut off the blood supply. Most of the arm was necrotic, you know, dead, at birth, so they amputated it." He takes a swig of water and looks out toward the river. "Sometimes doctors can fix ABS in utero, but that would require the mother see a doctor during the pregnancy."

The way he says *the mother* makes my skin feel tight. He plays with the leftover plastic wrap from his sandwich, his ever-present grin disappearing. I have so many questions for him, but I'm scared if I ask him, he'll have questions for me too. And if he shares the story of his mother, I'll have to share the story of mine.

So instead I simply say, "I'm sorry."

"It's okay."

We pick at the pebbles around us, haphazardly skipping them into the river. The gentle water sounds remind me of calm ocean days, lounging in the shallows of the water, soaking my feet with my friends by my side. It's the longest period of silence I've ever spent with Lincoln, yet it's as comfortable as the constant chatter.

My phone beeps. I slip it out of my bag. Another text from Emery of Nash sleeping on one of the park benches. Hopefully he didn't do anything too ridiculous to wear himself out. "Crap," I tell Lincoln. "It's almost four. We should probably get going."

"Sounds good," he says. "Think you've got enough energy in you to skate back?"

"Do I have any other choice?" I ask.

"Nope." He grins.

"Then I guess I do." I smile. "In fact, I think I have enough energy to race you there."

By the time we get to the skate park, we're sticky with sweat. The park is almost empty, since most kids have gone home for dinner. I focus on a somewhat surprising sight—Emery and Austin sitting next to each other on a bench, sharing a pair of earbuds.

They look peculiar yet perfect together—Emery in her bright summer dress and sandals and Austin in his black and chains and Vans. Their heads are bent toward each other as they laugh and talk without pause.

"Huh," I say.

Lincoln also watches them. "Being a ladies' man is in the Puk genetic code."

"You're both adopted."

He shrugs his shoulders. "Nature. Nurture. Po-tay-toe. Po-tah-toe."

Before we can continue to stare at Emery and Austin, Parker and Nash rush over in an excited fury. Nash jumps off his board and flings himself at me, almost toppling me to the ground with a colossal hug.

"Whoa there!" I catch him and hug him back. "Is everything okay? What's this affection for?"

"Nothing." He wipes his hands on his shorts. "You're sticky."

"Guess what?" Parker asks.

"What?"

"Austin taught us how to noseslide!" He looks down at his skateboard. "Do you want to see?"

"I definitely want to see. Go on and show me before we head home."

Parker and Nash high five each other, and then Nash waves at Austin. "Come watch!" With the whole earbud/Emery situation, Austin must not hear him, so Nash starts to call again.

"Hey, how about you just show me and Lincoln? Private viewing, okay?"

Nash shrugs his shoulders. "Okay."

"What's a noseslide?" I whisper to Lincoln as we join the boys by a long, empty bench.

"I'll teach you if you want."

I roll my eyes. "Maybe next time."

We stand next to each other, watching as the boys prepare for their trick by doing a few calisthenics that look straight out of an '80s workout video. Lincoln's right shoulder brushes against mine. We watch the boys grind across the bench with just the nose of their boards, the rattling wood against metal, and I pretend not to notice—but a million percent notice—as the tips of Lincoln's fingers graze against mine.

NINE

IT RAINS FOR the first three days of July. Fat droplets hail down, beating the house without reprieve, the sun hidden beneath thick, gray clouds. My mom once showed up in a storm like this, breezing through the front door, past our shocked faces, oblivious as she dripped water onto the wooden floors. Sometimes, during a particularly loud clap of thunder, I think I hear the doorbell, and my stomach clenches as I picture her on the stoop, soaking wet and with a smile I'll be too angry to return. Or even worse, sometimes I imagine the same thing, but I return the smile.

I wonder if she really meant it when she said she'd visit this summer, or if the thought flitted through her mind, as temporary as the water dripping down the living room windows. I try to imagine her here as a teenager, grieving the death of her mom, watching rain pour down through this exact view. Why was she so determined to leave this house, her family?

Back home, rainy days equal TV marathons with my best friends. We splay out on couches and binge watch the latest season of our favorite show. Here, rainy days equal being stuck inside with three kids, my foot constantly jiggling up and down from excess energy.

"Want to play?" Parker asks. I look away from the window to where he's on the floor playing a video game. I'm lying on the couch, intermittently watching the rain and thumbing through my favorite parts of a Detective Dana novel, trying to find the section where she breaks her own suspect out of jail to solve a murder.

Emery is in her room, where she's spent the past few days. I check on her every few hours and am usually greeted with a blank face and an "I'm fine" or a "No, I'm not hungry" or a "No, I don't know where Nash hid all the batteries from the remotes and smoke detectors."

She *says* she's fine. But she still won't talk about what happened with her friends. I told myself I'd tell Aunt Jackie about the situation if Emery hadn't cracked by now, but the problem is there technically *isn't* a situation. She's not crying. She's not trying to harm herself. There aren't any bullying threats in the mail (or on any of her social media accounts, at least not publicly, and yes, I stalked her online to check). I want to protect her, but I also don't want to blow the situation out of proportion or betray her trust if it's unnecessary. So I'll give it a couple more days. A couple more days can't hurt, right?

I shake my head at Parker. "No video games for me. What about Nash?" As I ask the question, I look around the room and discover why it's been so quiet. Nash isn't here. "Parker, where is your—"

A piercing scream comes from the backyard.

I throw my book to the side and jump to my feet. "Stay here," I tell Parker. I'm not sure why. Instinct kicks in, and it just seems like the right thing to say.

I yank open the sliding glass door and rush outside into the beating rain. Heart pounding, throat thick, I scan the backyard for Nash but don't see him in the downpour. Then another noise follows, this time more of a whimper. "Shit, shit, shit," I mumble, my stomach knotting because the whimper comes from the empty pool. I run to the edge, push away my dread, and look inside. Nash is crouched in the middle of the concrete pit, helmet askew, holding his leg.

"Crap, fuck, crap, crap," I curse, sitting down on the ledge of the pool and dropping in, my bare feet almost slipping on the rain-slicked surface. "Nash, are you okay?" I rush over and squat beside him in the stagnant half inch of sludgy water. "Let me see your leg."

"I'm sorry," he whimpers. His tears mix with the rain. "I wasn't skating in the pool! I swear! I was bored, so I came out to skate, and it was wet, and I slipped and fell in—"

"It's okay," I say. "You'll be all right. I'm not mad, I promise. Let me see your leg."

Some relief sweeps through me as he removes his hands. There's blood but not much. It's all coming from a single laceration that doesn't look very deep. And what's even better, as I run my fingers over his leg, pressing lightly, he barely winces. Nothing seems to be broken. His scream was probably fear more than anything else.

"I'm sorry, Anise," he says again.

"Don't be sorry. It was an accident. Accidents happen."

"I know, but they're scary…like Mom's."

I've never seen Nash like this, so vulnerable, so somber. I guess Emery isn't the only kid in this house who realizes Aunt Jackie's car accident could have been much worse. "Your mom is okay now, and so are you. The accidents are over, and you're both okay." I hug him tightly.

"But bad things are infinite, right?" he asks.

"What do you mean?"

"Well, just because Mom got into an accident it doesn't mean she can't get into another one, right? One bad thing doesn't stop more from happening."

My heart clenches, as my mind whirs for some kind of comfort to share. He's right. Bad things are infinite. But I kiss his head and hug him tighter and say, "That's true, but you know what else is true?"

"What?"

"Good things are infinite too."

After further inspection inside and out of the rain, I'm relieved to find Nash's injury is nothing worse than fright and a small cut, so after pouring on a ridiculous amount of rubbing alcohol to prevent infection, I bandage him up and expect everything to go back to normal.

But here's the thing: Nash doesn't want everything to go back to normal because apparently even the smallest wound for a nine-year-old equates to at least twenty-four hours of indulgence. "More ice cream!" he hollers, jumping up from the couch and hopping on one leg to the kitchen, even though both of his legs are totally fine.

"Me too!" Parker shouts. He climbs out of the armchair and follows Nash into the kitchen with his own bowl. Emery goes after them so Hurricane Ice Cream doesn't destroy the kitchen again. She emerged from her room when Nash screamed and has stayed downstairs to help dote on him.

A few minutes later they're back in the living room with an extra bowl for me. We bum around watching an old episode of *Full House*, the one where Stephanie accidentally drives a car through the kitchen, which feels a little too close to something Nash might do if he ever gets his hands on car keys, especially with the amount of sugar flooding his system right now.

"What are we doing tomorrow?" Emery suddenly asks.

I turn to her. "For what?"

She gives me a weird look. "For the Fourth of July."

The Fourth of July. Normally on the fourth, we throw a giant party on our back porch and a bonfire on the beach. Dad and I invite all of our friends, and we spend the day grilling and surfing and blasting music, and we spend the night roasting marshmallows and watching fireworks illuminate the sky and paint the ocean. Aunt Jackie and the cousins usually plan their trip around the celebration so they can join in on the fun.

Who will throw the party this year? Will Cassie find someone else to compete in the how-many-marshmallows-can-I-stuff-in-my-mouth-and-still-breathe competition? Will Spinner find someone else to late-night surf with despite being weighed down by burgers and hot dogs and guacamole? Will Eric—*Eric*... I never read his message from when I was at the river with Lincoln. I forgot about it, about him.

A little more than two weeks from home, and already my life and friends are slipping away. The thought churns my stomach. I put my ice cream on the side table. I *have* to FaceTime them tonight, or better yet, tomorrow to wish them all a happy holiday. I imagine all their tanned faces gathering around the screen so they can say hello and tell me they miss me and they love me and *of course* summer is boring without me, and they promise to not do a single exciting thing until I get back.

But what if no one picks up?

What if they're too busy enjoying marshmallows and fireworks without me?

"Yeah, what are we going to do?" Parker asks, jerking me back to here.

I know Dad's original idea was to visit Aunt Jackie, then take the kids to the park for grilling and marshmallows and firecrackers, but the forecast promises at least another day of torrential rain, which means no grilling, no firecrackers, no celebration.

But I don't have the heart to tell them that, especially without a backup plan in mind, so instead I shift on the couch and say, "It's a surprise. I'll let you guys know tomorrow," because it's a better answer than, "Absolutely nothing."

As predicted, it rained all day on the fourth. We spent the whole afternoon inside with Aunt Jackie at the hospital. We played cards and ate apple pie, but being at the hospital on a holiday was still kind of depressing.

Later that night, alone in my room, I scrolled through my phone. There were a handful of texts from my friends, but I was drawn to the photos of the fireworks and ocean and crackling fires, and picture after picture of my friends smiling without me. It was our last Fourth of July all together, but we weren't all together. I wanted to text my friends back but couldn't bring myself to ask how their celebration was when mine was so bleak in comparison. Anyway, with the time difference, they were probably still celebrating and too busy to check their phones.

At least today, on the fifth, I wake up to a sky sunny and blue enough to belong on a cruise brochure. The kids and I get dressed in record time and trek to the park, the air deliciously temperate after all of that rain. As we journey, we toss the uneaten bag of marshmallows back and forth, picking one out and popping it into our mouths before passing the bag onto the next person. When we get to the park, I'm surprised to find Austin at the front entrance, skating back and forth, silver chains glinting in the sun. His gaze locks in on Emery as we approach.

I glance at Emery. She gives me the *go away* look. Austin seems like a good kid, and I'm happy she's willing to talk with anyone, even if it's not me, so I tell Parker and Nash, "Race you to the skate park!"

The boys need zero motivation for competition *and* they're extra energized with marshmallow sugar, so they burst off down the path. I follow behind at a slower pace, passing Austin and giving him a nod and a smile. When I make it to the first bend in the trail, I turn to see Austin pass what looks like a CD case to Emery. As I keep watching, Emery glances up at me, and I expect a glare and maybe even a *fuck off*, but instead she smiles at me. A real smile. An Emery smile.

It's like I just nailed a perfect ride.

I smile back, then jump on my board, intent on showing my cousins who really skates best in this family.

⎯⎯

The boys beat me to the park, but I don't mind their mocking because Lincoln is here. My stomach does its twisting and fluttering act, especially when I think about the muscles hiding under his flannel shirt. But then I stiffen—because Lincoln isn't alone.

Three other people surround him, all of whom look vaguely familiar, like maybe I saw them here another day but wasn't quite paying attention. My stomach continues to twist, but this time with anxiety. I'm used to meeting new people. On the beach, there are always tourists to give directions to, annuals to party with, and visiting surfers to meet. But the thing is, I was always meeting new people on *my* turf. Now, for the first time in my life, *I'm* the intruder. It was easy making friends with Lincoln because he basically did all the work for me, but the idea of meeting three new people at once is intimidating. And I don't like to think of myself as being easily intimidated.

My pulse races as I take in the three strangers, especially the girl in a magenta romper, popping small ollies while talking to Lincoln. It's obvious this is her environment, not mine.

My mom would know exactly what to do in this situation; she always knows how to make herself comfortable somewhere new. A few weeks after my thirteenth birthday, she swept into town after being gone for more than a year and a half, at the time her longest absence ever, and my emotions were at a full boil. I was cold, angry, harsh. And yet, she was impossible to resist, wearing me down, tempting me with giddiness and promises of adventure.

One Saturday morning she coaxed me into an old convertible and drove us down miles and miles of coastal roads, roof down, wind whipping through our hair. We stopped to grab greasy fries from one of the unhealthy fast food places Dad hates, picked wildflowers off the highway median, ran through the dunes, not caring as we tracked sand back into the car.

Later that evening we ended up wandering some unfamiliar beach, our hair twisted into dozens of tiny braids from one of the overpriced tourist booths, and we came across this small wedding party. The ceremony was long over, music pumping, bonfires crackling, and food and alcohol flowing. She insisted we go, and I insisted we didn't. She insisted until I gave in, and by the end of the night, we were taking pictures with the happy couple and playing bocce ball with some of the bridal party.

If my mom were here, she would know what to do.

But she isn't here. She's never here when I need her, which is why I've learned not to need her. I'll avoid the situation and hang out with Parker and Nash. But before I can nudge them toward a different part of the park, Lincoln waves me over. "Yo, Anise! Come here!"

Fuck.

Okay. I can do this. I'm a confident, capable person, and these are Lincoln's friends, not bullies from a cliché movie. Maybe we'll all become best friends. Maybe I'll post photos with high saturation to show I'm having a good summer too.

"You guys okay?" I ask Parker and Nash. They nod, Parker already tugging Nash toward his favorite set of low rails.

I want to pull some kind of trick as I head over—grind on one of the benches, pop an ollie or two, or even a kickflip, anything so I don't look like I'm a complete encroacher. I don't want Lincoln's friends to look at me like I look at all the tourists in Santa Cruz, the ones who fall off their surfboards before ever properly standing up. However, as strong as my desire is to look like I belong, my desire to not make a complete fool of myself is even stronger, so I skip the tricks and skate straight over.

"Anise, meet Tom, Clayton, and Sofia." Lincoln points to his three friends. "Guys, meet Anise. She comes to us from the fine city of Santa Cruz, where she spends her days surfing and surfing with a small side of surfing."

"Oh, and don't forget surfing," I say.

We grin at each other. The pleasant stomach fluttering returns.

"Very cool." Sofia smiles at me. She's pretty—undeniably so—and by the look of her toned calf muscles, she can probably skate circles around me for hours. She continues to perform little tricks on her board as she talks to me, like Lincoln does, like she doesn't have to think about what her feet are doing, like it's as natural as running her hand through her hair. "I went surfing at the Wedge last summer. I totally sucked, but it was awesome."

Great. She's talented, pretty, and humble.

"So Anise," Clayton says. He has alarmingly blue eyes and a short and stocky build. "Have you ever skated in the bowl before?"

"Not yet," I say.

Lincoln clasps me on the back for a second, his fingers on the skin exposed from my tank top. "Anise here is a bit of a skating prodigy. I'm sure she'll pick it up quickly."

I glance down into the bowl, which looks to be about eight feet deep, much steeper than my average wave. Before I have a chance to consider further, Lincoln leans over to murmur into my ear. "I'm not saying I bet these guys twenty bucks that you'd make it on your first go, but I'm also not *not* saying I bet these guys twenty bucks that you'd make it on your first go."

I look at him. "Seriously?"

He grins and raises his eyebrows. "Seriously."

My thoughts churn for a second. "Fine. But we split the winnings."

"Fine."

"Sixty-forty."

"Fine."

"I'm the sixty."

His grin widens. "I figured."

———

The first time I got on a surfboard, it was in the middle of an afternoon on a weekday in the dead of winter. The beach was as empty as the beach ever gets. Dad stood by my side, taking me step by step through all of the maneuvers like he'd been doing for weeks, assuring that I had each move memorized on the packed sand before ever wading into the water. So on that day, the day I finally surfed, I knew exactly what I was doing, and only Dad was there to watch.

Now as I stand at the edge of the bowl, one foot planted on the tail end of my skateboard, the other hovering above it, an audience of not one but six people stands behind me— Lincoln, his friends, and of course Parker and Nash. Emery and Austin still haven't shown up, and part of me wants to use that as an excuse to put this act of foolishness on hold and go check on them.

"Okay," I mutter, then rehash the quick tutorial I was provided. "Plant foot on board, drop in, turn board, keep momentum, don't lean back…definitely don't fall…"

I'm not sure why I'm doing this. It's not like I need, what— twelve whole dollars? I mean, I wouldn't say no to twelve dollars, but it's a pretty small sum of money considering I could break an arm, or worse, my pride. No, it's not the money.

This summer took away my surfboard. I'm not going to let it take away my confidence too.

So with two short breaths and one deep one, and my new mantra of "Fuck it," I stomp down on the front of the board and plummet into the bowl. The plunge is quick and steep, and common sense says it should lead to a very painful fall on my ass, but then the adrenaline floods, and reflexes take over, and I turn the board to the right and then the left at the last second, just balanced enough to stay vertical while sustaining momentum, and then I'm racing across the flat expanse of the bottom of the bowl, bringing my left foot down to the ground to kick for more speed, trying to accumulate enough to ride up the other side of the bowl.

As I get closer, I imagine that I'm not coming up on a wall of concrete, but a wall of water, a beautiful barrel wave, and I either have to face the wall or give up. I don't give up. So I kick hard three more times, lock my knees, and burst back up the other side of the bowl, the tip of my board inching past the edge of the wall, and—"Fuck!"

I lose grip of my board and fall backward into the bowl. My feet trip as I attempt to run instead of fall down the steep side. But I'm too unsteady. I fall on my ass, my board clattering down beside me.

I sit there and try to ignore the very prominent pain in my posterior. Why the fuck did I decide to try this in front of a bunch of relative strangers? Then someone starts clapping, one of those slow, sharp claps.

Someone whistles, and someone says, "Hell yeah," and someone else says, "I really didn't think I'd lose that bet."

I crane my head back to find Lincoln smoothly sliding down the side of the bowl with his full-dimpled smile. He reaches down and offers his hand, which I take. After pulling me to my feet, he picks up my board and gives it to me. "Pretty rad, surfer girl," he says.

"I'm not sure how falling on my ass equates to rad, but if you say so…"

"Dropping in without falling flat on your ass is basically impossible the first time around. So trust me, what you managed was pretty rad."

We both crawl out of the bowl, and by crawl, I mean run, climb, and then jump out of the sharp vertical slope. Lincoln's friends all clap me on the back and congratulate me, including Sofia who grabs my forehead and presses it to hers. "Girl, you are my new hero."

The thing is, even though technically I just failed, their encouragement is empowering. And the fact that I almost *didn't* fail is even more empowering. So when they ask if I want to try again, I don't think about the rather large bruise forming on my ass; instead, I think about how exhilarating it would feel to burst over that wall with a perfect landing. And so I smile and say absolutely.

⎯⎯

When I climb out of the bowl for what must be the hundredth time, I find Austin in front of me, safety pins glittering in the sun. "Nice ride," he says.

"Thanks." I wipe the sweat from my forehead and grab the water bottle that I think is mine but also might be Parker's and take a giant swig. Once my breathing slows to normal, I glance around. "Where's Emery?"

Austin looks down at the ground and scuffs his shoe against the concrete. "I don't know... She didn't want to come with me."

"You don't know where she is or you don't know why she didn't want to come with you?"

"Uhhh..." Austin scratches his forehead under the swished front of his hair. "Both. I don't know. She was in a weird mood."

My heart beats fast with the wrong kind of adrenaline. Emery is twelve. She's perfectly capable of hanging out in the park in the middle of the day alone, but still. I'd rather know exactly where she is. I pull out my phone and call her, but it rings and rings and rings.

Emery always has her phone with her.

I dial again.

And again.

Austin stares at me, his expression turning from bummed out to concerned. "Do you want me to go get her?" he asks.

The third call goes to voice mail. I shake my head. "No. I'll get her. She's fine. I mean, of course she's fine. I'm just going to go... Will you watch the boys? Wait, no. Actually..."

I spin. Lincoln's standing on the other side of the bowl, cheering on one of his friends. I speed walk over to him, my throat tight, my legs shaking from something other than exertion. "Watch Parker and Nash for me, okay? Don't let them out of your sight. I'll be back."

His brow creases. "Wait, what—"

But I don't respond.

I grab my skateboard and race toward the park entrance and, I hope, Emery.

———

Emery isn't where I left her. Not in the parking lot, not by the entry sign, not by the wooden benches along the main path. I call her again and again, but she doesn't pick up. I pace back and forth in front of my skateboard, cursing Austin for leaving her alone and cursing myself for leaving her alone with Austin.

He fooled me with his smile, with his generosity toward Parker and Nash, when the truth is I should have never trusted someone who uses safety pins as buttons. Why would he just leave her here alone? Okay, well, maybe because she asked him to, and he was respecting her wishes. This is *my* fault. I'm responsible for her, and—

"Come on, pick up," I mutter. This isn't good. This really isn't good. Emery always has her phone with her. If she's not picking up, that means... No. I'm not going to think about that.

Do I call the police? Dad? Do I go back to the skate park and ask Austin more questions? Do I—

Wait. The basketball courts. Maybe she made up with her friends.

Before the thought fully forms, I jump back onto my skateboard, following the occasional sign that points me in the right direction. I don't even have to think about my balance as I skate anymore. The movement comes naturally as I speed down the paths, curving with sharp, pinpointed turns to avoid crashing into pedestrians, ignoring my sore muscles, not pausing to take in anything around me but the same two words on each sign—*basketball courts, basketball courts, basketball courts.*

Eventually the path opens to a chain-link fence, like the one surrounding the skate park, except this fence surrounds two basketball courts. Old men, probably retirees, are midgame on the first one. But as I near the second court, I find exactly who I'm looking for—a group of preteens.

I spot Emery standing on the outskirts of a tight-knit group of kids. The flood of relief is so strong that I rush up to her and pull her into a tight hug. I do this before I remember there was drama with her friends and this is the first time she's hanging out with them since the lake.

"What are you doing?" she screeches—actually screeches—voice high and tight, face red.

I stumble away, feeling a new type of panic. Emery was making up with her friends, and now I've embarrassed her. "Umm…" I try to think quickly, but my mind spins. Her friends give me judgmental glares I swear only twelve-year-old girls are capable of. "Sorry—nothing. We need to go. And you wouldn't pick up your phone."

She rolls her eyes. "Jesus, I left it at home on accident. Fine. Let's go."

Without another word, she turns on her heel and stomps off toward the side of the courts, where she locked up her bike. I glance at her friends one more time. None of them say bye to Emery or seem upset that she has to leave. They've turned back to one another, chatting quietly. I wondered what happened. It must feel terrible to be ignored by your friends.

Emery refuses to speak to me as we head back to the skate park, except for a blunt "fine, whatever," after I ask as nicely as possible that she not go anywhere without telling me first. I can't tell if I'm mad at her or her friends or myself. Maybe I'm just mad at everyone and everything. The weight of making sure these exhausting, wonderful kids are safe is overwhelming.

No wonder my shit excuse for a mom couldn't handle it.

The second we walk through the skate park entrance, Lincoln ambushes me in almost an identical fashion to how I just ambushed Emery. He grabs my shoulder and locks eyes, melting and welding me to the ground. When he speaks, his voice is rough. "Shit, Anise, you can't fucking do that."

Emery has already slipped away from my side, so in a skate park surrounded by dozens of people, it feels as if Lincoln and I are the only ones here. "Do *what*?" I ask.

"Go off like that! Run off all freaked out without telling me what's going on."

"I—Look, I'm sorry. I didn't have time. I was worried about Emery."

"You were worried about Emery. I get it, okay?" His face changes. "But don't you understand that maybe... *Fuck,*

Anise." I've never seen him flustered like this, and it makes me feel unsteady. "Don't you get that *I* was worried about *you*?"

The pause is long as I digest what he's saying. Lincoln was worried about me. And we've only known each other for a few weeks. It's hard for me to process, so I ask, "Why? Why were you worried about me?"

He laughs, which is a relief because it's such a Lincoln thing to do. He takes me by the shoulder again, this time guiding me toward our friends and family, and as we walk, he answers, "Why wouldn't I be?"

TEN

AUNT JACKIE COMES home tomorrow, which means tonight I'm moving into Emery's room, which would be great if she'd spoken a word to me in the last five days. Okay, she's said, "Parker, please tell Anise she managed to *undercook* mac and cheese," and she's also said, "Nash, please tell Anise she managed to *overcook* mac and cheese." But that's been the extent of our communication. I feel like I fucked everything up. She hasn't been back to the courts since that day. If I hadn't chased her down, maybe she would've made up with her friends, been happy again, and therefore be talking to me. But it's not like I could've shrugged my shoulders and said *oh well, my cousin is missing.*

Dad, even with working overtime all week, has noticed something is off between us. But now more than ever, I'm driven to defend Emery, like if I bolster her silence, she'll confide in me instead of continuing to stare at me like the scum on the bottom of her flip-flops. So two days ago when Dad asked me if everything was okay between us, I told him we were both on our periods at the same time. And even though Dad has zero embarrassment about menstruation—I mean, *he* was the one who bought me my first pads—he also has no actual understanding of it, so that was a good enough reason for him.

"*Don't* make a mess," Emery says, her first direct words to me in days, as I load my few items of clothing into the small extra dresser. She's on her bed, watching me, ready to pounce if I make a wrong move.

I want to explode at her, call her a brat.

I want to hug her, tell her I'm sorry that her friends are mean and that I embarrassed her.

And beyond that, tell her I'm sorry her mom is in the hospital, tell her I'm frustrated my summer wasn't the one I anticipated, so I can't imagine how much worse hers must feel.

Instead I just say, "Okay," and fold my clothing and place it into the drawers as neatly as possible because tomorrow Aunt Jackie will be home, and everything will be okay. Her presence will restore Emery to the Emery I've always known, the Emery who spends hours picking out the most perfect seashells and gluing them onto wooden frames, the Emery who laughs when Dad tells a joke, no matter how terrible the joke is, the Emery who snuggles with me in bed as we binge watch episodes of *The Office*.

Tomorrow Aunt Jackie will be home, and everything will go back to normal, and everyone will be okay.

⸺

"Oops, sorry!"

"Behind you!"

"Watch out!"

"Ouch!"

"Sorry!"

Question: how many people does it take to get one woman in a wheelchair into her home?

Answer: too many.

Even with the help of the nurse aid who's here to set everything up and make sure Aunt Jackie is okay on home care, it still takes us about twenty awkward and uncomfortable minutes to get Aunt Jackie inside of the house. Dad constructed a temporary wheelchair ramp to the garage door, but that was before we realized the garage entrance was too narrow for the wheelchair. So then we had to move back to the front door and manually lift the chair and Aunt Jackie into the house. At one point, Dad offered to just pick up Aunt Jackie and bring her inside, but she was too worried he'd accidentally bang her legs on the door frame.

Finally, everyone is in the living room, where Parker, Nash, and Emery have created a giant banner over the fireplace that reads WELCOME HOME, MOM. Okay, it actually reads

WLCOME HOME MOM with a tiny E crunched in belatedly because Nash can't watch TV and spell at the same time. We also have plates of homemade cookies and brownies to celebrate, including a cookie concoction from Parker and Nash that has chocolate chips, Reese's Pieces, marshmallows, *and* sprinkles.

Aunt Jackie looks around, her face pale from being indoors, her frame small and hunched. "I'm sorry guys," she says, though she's not really looking at any of us. "I'm really beat. Do you mind—" She turns to the nurse aid. "Would you help me to my room?"

The nurse, an older man with thick shoulders and thin legs, nods and wheels Aunt Jackie into the guest room, where, this morning, we set up a special bed that lowers and rises so Aunt Jackie can get from the wheelchair into the bed despite the long, straight cast still on her right leg. Her left leg is only wrapped in a compression cuff.

Parker and Nash start to trail into the room, but I place a hand on each of their shoulders. "Let's let your mom rest," I whisper. "How about you help me eat some of those cookies?"

I turn to invite Emery to join us, my heart hurting that Aunt Jackie's homecoming wasn't as joyous as we'd all hoped, but she's already disappeared upstairs.

"What should we do about Aunt Jackie?" I ask Dad the next day. I thought she would be thrilled to be home, but she hasn't said more than a few words at a time. I want to help her, but I don't know how.

Dad and I are sitting in the kitchen early in the morning, sipping green tea and picking over cinnamon French toast and fresh-cut fruit. The house is quiet with all the kids and Aunt Jackie still sleeping. Last night I tried to talk to Emery. I wanted to reassure her that Aunt Jackie was tired and would be better in the morning, but by the time I went upstairs, she was already in bed with her lights off and headphones on. If I can get Aunt Jackie to cheer up, I know it will help Emery too.

Dad runs a hand through his hair. It's been growing out all summer and now curls at the ends. "Well," he says. "What makes us feel better?"

"What makes us feel better when we've been on bed rest for almost a month with another month to look forward to?" I ask.

Dad gives me a hard look. I sigh and tear off a piece of the French toast, squishing it with my fingers before popping it into my mouth. What makes me happy? Surfing, of course, then Tess and all my friends who I haven't seen for weeks. I don't think anything would make me happier than being surrounded by all of them. And then it clicks. "We should throw her a party!"

"I don't think Jacks is in a partying mood."

"Not like a *party* party, a little one. Invite some of her friends over. You can grill. It'll be good."

"You know what?" Dad asks. "That does sound like a good idea."

"I've been known to have them every now and then."

He grins. "This is true." He rips off another piece of toast, then says, "Maybe you'll meet some of your mom's old friends."

My stomach drops. I hadn't thought about that. It's a small suburb. It makes sense Aunt Jackie would still be friends with people she's known her entire life. But I've never thought of my mom as having friends because when she leaves a place, she leaves its people too.

"Have you, um…heard from her?" I ask, feeling a bit guilty I still haven't told him about the postcard.

Dad studies my face, then softly says, "No, I haven't. When I heard about Jacks, I did the usual send out." Email to an address she never checks, letter to a place she's already left, call to a number that's inevitably disconnected. "But I haven't heard back from her."

"*Asshole,*" I mutter under my breath. Dad stiffens at the word. "You think she'd at least check in every once in a while to make sure we're all breathing."

"I'm sorry, Anise. I wish she wasn't like this. Jacks wishes she wasn't like this. But your mom is complicated, and coming home for her…well, it's more difficult than leaving home for you. The last time she was here was for Jacks's wedding. It was a miracle we got in touch with her, and she still missed the ceremony and only showed up for part of the reception. We just have to accept your mom for who she is. We'll never be happy otherwise." He leans over and kisses me on the head. "Come on, let's go plan that party."

But I can't leave it at that. "How can someone be so selfish?"

Dad pauses. "Sometimes it's hard to see outside of yourself…" He pulls off another piece of toast but doesn't eat it. Instead, he looks at me. "…especially when you don't want to."

━━━

Aunt Jackie is against having a party at first, but once we convince her that we'll only invite a few people and Dad will grill his famous garlic smashed burgers, she gives into the idea. We spend the rest of the day and the next prepping, so when the doorbell rings, and I'm doused in chocolate and powdered sugar, and Dad is outside busy with the grill and the boys, and Emery is hiding upstairs, and Aunt Jackie is not adept at using her wheelchair yet, I'm the one who answers the door.

I stand there kind of shocked because instead of one of Aunt Jackie's friends on the stoop, I find Lincoln and Austin. Lincoln is wearing a tight, white T-shirt, which hugs his hard stomach, where my eyes land for a solid three seconds.

"Hey," he says. I draw my eyes to his face. He's smiling— like *really* smiling, like *I know what you were staring at* smiling.

"Hey. Hi. Umm…" I pause. "What are you guys doing here?"

"See?" Lincoln tells Austin and nudges his shoulder. "Didn't I tell you Anise was the most hospitable person in the world?"

"Ha-ha." I shift on my feet. "But really, what are you doing here?"

"Emery invited us," Austin says. *Good. At least she's still talking to someone.* "Well, she invited me, and then I asked if Lincoln could come, and she said you'd like that, so I—"

"She did?" I flush.

Lincoln nods. "She did. So can we come in?"

"Uh, yes. Come on in."

I wonder if Emery invited Austin because she likes him or because he was the only friend she could invite. If she and her friends are even half as tight-knit as my group of friends, maybe the incident was more serious than I've been telling myself. If Emery's still upset tomorrow, I need to press her to tell me what happened.

"Thank you, gracious host." Lincoln half bows, and then they both step inside. I point them toward the backyard, and Austin heads that way, but Lincoln lingers next to me. He bends slightly, and for a second I think he's going to kiss me. But he just brushes his finger across my cheek and whatever chocolate or powdered sugar is there and then licks it off his finger.

He grins as I stand there blushing. "Delicious."

An hour later, about a dozen of us are congregated in the backyard, all piling our plates with food from platters of burgers, hot dogs, grilled veggie kabobs, and tilapia. Not to mention coleslaw, homemade potato chips sprinkled with paprika and pepper, and our favorite summer salsa chock-full of onions, black beans, tomatoes, pineapples, and lime. Lincoln and I make our way down the line of food. I hold our two plates so Lincoln can use his hand to pile them with a bit of everything. "Have I mentioned I'm in love with your dad?" he asks.

"If you finish everything on that plate, he'll probably be in love with you too," I say.

"Everything on this plate?" He raises his eyebrows. "Darling, this is only round one."

He walks off to join Austin and my cousins around the lip of the pool. Emery and Austin are chatting quietly. Maybe she's confiding in him like she used to confide in me when she was younger, sharing my bed on their family vacations and whispering secrets under the blankets.

Before joining them, I walk over to the grown-ups. Aunt Jackie, her friends, and Dad sit around the large table. Aunt Jackie already looks happier, a slight flush on her cheeks. Though, the flush might be from her cup of sangria. "Hey, kiddo," she says as I stand behind them. "Have you met everyone?"

I shake my head and get introduced around the table. All the faces and names blur together, but I smile like I'll remember each and every one. One of the women, I think Claire, wearing a light blue cardigan, looks at me and then Jackie and then says, "Goodness, Jackie, you were right—she looks exactly like her. Spitting image."

Her. Blue Cardigan Claire must know my mom—must *have known* my mom. I wonder if they were close before she left, if they've seen each other since my mom was my age. I wonder how many friends my mom has made over the years only to move on and leave them behind.

I take her comment as my cue to leave. "Nice to meet you guys." I rush the words and head toward the pool.

Spitting image. You remind me of her.

Even though my mom is never with me, I can't escape who I came from, how I look, and now, with being gone all summer, perhaps how I act too. It's like no matter what I want, bits of my mom cling to me. My skin crawls at the thought. I wish I could scratch it off.

───

A couple hours later, the kids have all migrated into the front yard. Parker and Nash skateboard up and down the driveway, Austin and Emery dribble a basketball against the pavement, sometimes throwing it into the rusted hoop, and Lincoln and I sit on the grass, making our way through the entire plate of Parker and Nash's specialty cookies, which turn out to not be disgusting so much as delicious. Blue Cardigan Claire's comment aside, for the first time in days, I'm relaxed; Aunt Jackie is home and healthy, all the kids seem happy, and I'm eating cookies next to the best-looking guy in Nebraska.

"I'm going to be sick," I mutter, biting off another piece of the chewy, candy-filled cookie. "Like *sick* sick. Like C-grade zombie flick sick."

"Right there with you." Lincoln rubs his stomach like he has a beer belly instead of washboard abs. "I've got to get this recipe. Maybe my dad will bake them."

"Is your dad the chef of the family too?" I ask.

"I don't know if I'd go so far as to call him a chef, but he definitely does most of the cooking. Mom is the definition of a workaholic."

"What does she do?" I ask.

"I told you we used to move around a lot, right?" I nod. "She's one of those people companies bring in to fire other people. Say some giant corporation needs to get rid of three hundred employees? They'll bring her in to assess who's integral and then fire everyone else. The jobs usually take about six months, which means—"

My mouth drops open, probably exposing chocolate-coated teeth because I enjoy embarrassing myself. "Moving every six months? Seriously?"

"Seattle, Atlanta," Lincoln counts off the cities on his fingers as he names them, "Detroit, Vegas, St. Louis, Tucson, Boston, oh—and Baton Rouge. That was a good one. Awesome Cajun food. And that was all before middle school. Dad homeschooled us in the beginning, but he couldn't keep up as we got older, so when I started seventh grade, we took it down to one move a year tops."

I can't imagine moving even once as a kid, much less

dozens of times. The idea of starting over like that, pulling up roots again and again, having to make new friends sounds exhausting and terrifying. "Did you hate it?" I ask.

"No." He pauses. "I think it's hard to hate what you're used to. I mean, it's the only life I've ever known. And I love new places. So I never had a reason to hate it."

"So, like…" I pull apart another cookie. "If you move that often…is anywhere really home?"

"Look." Lincoln nudges me, then nods at Parker and Nash. They're trying to ride on the same skateboard, balancing by holding each other, giggling and falling and trying again. "Home isn't a place. It's people. And I've always been with my people."

The words should comfort me, but most of my people are in Santa Cruz. If I'm not with them, where am I? *Who* am I?

"You okay?" Lincoln asks, his voice gentle.

I pluck a piece of grass from the yard and shred it into tiny strips. "Yeah." I clear my throat, then shove his shoulder. "C'mon, let's go play basketball."

I jump up from the grass and head toward the hoop before Lincoln can push further. I remember what I told Emery— "It's okay to be not okay."

But as the words echo in my mind, I think maybe I was wrong.

After everyone has left and the kids have gone to sleep, I head to the kitchen for a glass of water. Someone is already in there—Dad's alone and talking tensely on the phone. I watch him pace from the doorway. He's saying something about "Wasn't in the plans," and "Someone will have to deal with this," and then "Fine, fine" before hanging up.

He does not look happy.

"Uh, Dad?" I ask. "Everything okay in here?"

His startles, then sighs and runs a hand through his hair. It's strange to see him stressed. When I was really young Dad was constantly frazzled by the single parent thing, but he's been a pillar for years now. "Everything *will* be okay," he says, "but my guys screwed up big time on that three-story oceanside project, and I've got to fly home to fix it."

My mind spins. Back home. Back to Santa Cruz. Back to surfing, back to Tess, back to…Eric. Eric, who seems so far away, it's as if he's in not another state but another plane of time. I can't even remember the last conversation I had with him. Distance has chipped away at our communication. I glance out the kitchen window at where I was sitting with Lincoln earlier this evening. His image is so much clearer than the one of the guy I left at home. Home is fading—has faded enough my constant want for home suddenly turns into a painful need.

"Anise," Dad says.

"What?"

"You can't come with me. You know that, right? Jacks just

got home, and she can't walk. I hate to leave you like this, but I have to. We can't afford to lose this job. I'll call one of Jacks's friends to ask for help while I'm gone."

My stomach drops. "Why can't one of her friends come and take care of everything? I need a break. I need—" I struggle to keep my voice steady. "I need to see my friends. I'll come back. I mean, you're going home. I should get to go too. It's only fair, right?"

"Anise, I'm sorry, but no," Dad says, his voice quiet. "Even ignoring flight costs, Jackie's friends have jobs. I'm not going to ask them to take off work when you're here and capable. And think about her feelings. You don't want to make her feel like an obligation, a burden."

I'm not going home yet. The thought hits hard and something cracks.

"But she *is* a burden. And she knows it." The words are harsh. I wince as they come out.

Dad looks angry, but he takes a quick breath, and his words come out gentle. "No, she's not. She's family, not a burden. Family isn't a burden. It's a gift."

He's right. I look down. "I'm sorry. I know."

"I wouldn't be going back to Santa Cruz unless I absolutely had to. Aunt Jackie needs all the support she can get, and that includes emotional support, and I'm depending on you for that. Not to mention, if you haven't noticed, the kids are attached to you. Don't you want to be here for them? Wouldn't you want them to be there for us if we needed them?"

I want to say I care about surfing and my friends and reclaiming home before it's no longer mine to claim. But then I think about how upset Emery has been, about when Nash fell into the pool. These kids do need me, and I'm not going to be like my mom. I'm not going to be the fuck-up who leaves town when someone needs her because what I want matters more.

"Okay," I finally say. "You're right. I'm sorry. Again."

Dad sighs, puts a hand on my shoulder, and meets my eyes. "I know this is not the summer you had in mind for yourself. But it's the right thing to do, and you'll be glad you did it. I promise."

"I know, you're right," I say. But inside my stomach twists because not only have I been torn away from home this summer, but now home is tearing Dad away from me too.

ELEVEN

"YOU KNOW, SWEETHEART," Aunt Jackie says, "You don't have to keep checking on me every five minutes."

"It's not every five minutes," I mumble.

Aunt Jackie sits propped against, like, eighty pillows, a book in one hand and her phone in the other. "True. Much closer to every seven."

What else am I supposed to do? Dad left me here alone with an aunt on the rebound from a near-fatal accident. Well, not technically alone, but Emery's still hiding out in her room, Nash can't do anything without accidently breaking something, and Parker just discovered a three thousand-piece jigsaw puzzle of Mount Rushmore hiding in the garage, so unless you're looking for the three-pronged piece of Abe Lincoln's nose, he's not interested.

I wish I could have gone in Dad's place. Handle the construction complaints and see my friends. I know he's right. I need to be here for my family. I want to be here for my family, but that doesn't ease the growing pain of seeing picture after picture of my friends. It's like I'm disappearing from their lives, like if I scroll down their feeds far enough, I'll have even vanished from the pictures I know I'm in.

Plus, it wasn't until after Dad left for the airport that I realized I still hadn't told him about the postcard. He has no clue my mom might show up at the house. Not that she *normally* sends warning anyway. But I left that note on the bathroom mirror... What if he sees it and knows I've been hiding this secret from him all summer? I hate being dishonest with him. Even in her absence, the power of my mom's destructive forces are immense.

Aunt Jackie says, "If I need anything, I can always call." Then she waves her phone at me. "Or *call*."

"I know, I know. I just like checking in." Aunt Jackie is markedly happier since her party, but she's still anxious from being cooped up for so long. Literally. I sit down on the bed and run my hand over the comforter, so much smoother than the tattered edges of Tess's quilt. If I'd had more time to pack, I would've put it in my suitcase so I could curl up with it at night while reading a Detective Dana novel. "Can I get you anything?"

"Healed legs." She cocks a half grin. "Kidding. I do miss running, though. Your mom turned me on to running—did you know that? It was her favorite sport. She turned your dad on to it too."

The irony doesn't escape me that my mom's favorite sport is running.

"One time," Aunt Jackie continues, "I think it was my spring break freshman year, I went to visit your parents in Santa Cruz. They'd been dating for a while then, about nine months. It was a miracle. It was the longest she'd stayed in one place since leaving home. Actually, I think she was already pregnant with you at the time, but she didn't know it yet. Anyway, we all went for a run on the beach. It was one of those perfect nights, cool and still, just the lightest breeze coming off the water. So we started running, and we're all a bit competitive, family trait, so no one wanted to be the first to stop. So we kept going and going. Every now and then someone would slow to a jog so sluggish it was basically a walk, but then we'd pick up the pace again. We ran for miles and miles down the beach.

"It wasn't until the sun had long set that we all gave up and collapsed in the sand. I can't remember ever being so exhausted in my life. It knocked me out more than those painkillers do. Well, next thing I knew, I was waking up to the sun rising and the tide washing over us. We watched the sunrise together and then walked home along that perfect blurred line, you know, where the water meets the sand.

"Took us about six hours to walk back, and the only food in the house was a loaf of bread and those orange cheese slices, the Kraft ones, so we ate grilled cheese sandwiches and then promptly fell asleep. When I woke up later that day, I found your mom in the living room blasting Stevie Nicks on the stereo and dancing. It's like she was born with this extra cosmic energy. Maybe she—"

Aunt Jackie stops speaking midsentence and reaches forward, brushing my cheek with her hand, and I realize I'm crying. Not *crying* crying, but a few tears drip down my face. Chances are I'll never get to run down the beach at night with my mom, and I know plenty of people in the world have it a lot worse than that, but the truth is, deep down, I think it'd be nice to wake up to the sunrise and eat grilled cheese sandwiches and dance to Stevie Nicks with her.

"I'm sorry, sweetheart," Aunt Jackie says. "I didn't mean to upset you."

I tilt my head down and scrub my face. "It's fine." I clear my throat. "You didn't. I'm just tired."

"Of course you are. And you miss home and your friends. Those painkillers have me rambling again. Your mom puts us through hard times, but I want you to know about some of the good ones too."

She says this as if a moment of my mom's presence can counteract years of her absence.

As if a grain of good can negate a field of bad.

"Look," Aunt Jackie says, "why don't you leave the kids here and take some time for yourself? It's a beautiful day out. Call that new friend of yours. Lincoln, right? He's not so bad looking, you know."

Calling Lincoln *not so bad looking* is like calling the Pacific Ocean damp.

"I don't know… Are you sure?" I'm kind of uneasy leaving Aunt Jackie alone, but I guess the kids are here if she needs something. And the next door neighbors are home too, and like she said, she can always use her phone. Not to mention, she just got released from being monitored by doctors 24/7, so besides her legs, she probably couldn't be any healthier if she tried.

Aunt Jackie reaches over the comforter and squeezes my hand. "I'm sure."

Half an hour later, Lincoln picks me up in a Jeep Wrangler with a bit of rust and nicked paint. When I texted him using the number he'd put into my phone and asked if he maybe wanted to hang out and skate or grab lunch or something, he responded saying it must be fate because his shift at work just got canceled. Then he asked if I could be gone for approximately nine and a half hours.

In true Lincoln style, he refused to tell me anything more, and though I felt uneasy about being away that long, I said yes.

"Bring us back presents!" Nash shouts as I head out the front door.

I turn toward him. He's in the living room, sitting on the floor and playing video games, next to Parker who is still piecing together the giant puzzle. "How do you know there'll be presents where I'm going?"

Parker looks up and furrows his brow. "There are presents everywhere if you look hard enough."

"Okay there, Confucius. I'll see you later."

As I head out to the car, I glance at the house and the closed curtain of Emery's room. If there are presents to be found, one for her is at the top of the list.

———

I learn three things driving in the car with Lincoln:

1. He owns all eighteen Bruce Springsteen albums and refuses to listen to anything else until *I've* listened to all eighteen Bruce Springsteen albums.
2. He uses something called a spinner knob, this little black device attached to his steering wheel, to help him make turns one-handed. On straightaways, he grips the wheel with four fingers and idly touches the knob with his pinky.
3. He cannot drive farther than ten miles without providing at least one "fun fact" about a plant we pass.

We're shooting down the highway, about two hours into our apparently three-hour drive, "State Trooper" blasting from the speakers, muffled by the heavy wind thrashing through the open-top jeep, when Lincoln swerves to make the upcoming exit.

I yelp and grab onto the metal frame of the car for support. "You know a family member of mine *was* recently in a near-fatal car crash?" I ask. "What are you doing?"

"Food!"

As he says the word, my stomach grumbles. I hope he's planning on pulling into a fast food drive-thru because it's been many hours since my four eggs, two bowls of cereal, and Pop-Tart. But he doesn't pull into a drive-thru, he pulls into an almost-empty parking lot of an almost-empty grocery store that looks like it's half a century old. The sign reads "Grocery" in chipped, faded green paint, and exactly one cart sits outside on the curb.

"Okay," Lincoln says. He turns off the ignition and climbs out of the car. "We're going to play a little game."

"What game is that?" I ask, getting out of the car.

He slips two ten-dollar bills from his wallet. He passes one to me and stuffs the other into his pocket. His eyes light up as he explains the game. "We both have ten dollars and five minutes to find the best food we can, check out, and meet back at the car. Please keep in mind that there will be zero cooking facilities at our final destination, unless you have a permit to build a campfire on government property."

"Unless I what?"

"Go!"

Instead of answering me, Lincoln shoots off into the grocery store, and since I don't like losing—ever—I shove my questions aside and rush off after him.

I burst through the *not* automatic double doors and into an employee wearing a red apron, who stares at me like the devil herself just came in for some light grocery shopping. "Sorry, sorry!" I call out, rushing past him.

I pace in front of the tops of the aisles and scan. Lincoln is down one of them. He presses his basket into the shelf with his hips, while quickly throwing in items. I don't have time for pacing. Too bad Spinner isn't here. He's got a nose for awesome food. But I'm on my own, so I pick an aisle at random, speed down the worn linoleum floor, and happen upon the perfect thing.

We check out separately, and Lincoln insists we keep our bounties hidden in their brown paper bags until we get to our final destination. My growling stomach disagrees with this, so he tells me to open the glove compartment. Inside I find a few granola bars in different flavors, little bags of Skittles that look suspiciously Halloween-themed, and an apple with more squish than any apple should ever have. I chuck the apple out the window and smile because this messy glove compartment proves that Lincoln has at least one flaw and is therefore human.

"Almost there," he announces, two granola bars and a bag of hardened Skittles later. In the last three hours Nebraska has turned from suburbs to commercial highways to this flat expanse of road and empty land and little else, exactly what I always imagined Nebraska to look like.

"And where exactly is here?" I ask as we pull into a small lot filled with a few cars, mostly SUVs and trucks.

"Definitely the coolest place in Nebraska." He shuts off the ignition and adjusts his black-framed glasses. "And I would know since I've made it my life's calling to find the coolest place in each and every state I've ever lived in."

"Cooler than the river?"

He gives me a pitying look. "Compared to what I'm about to show you, that river is a speck on the galactic spectrum of super cool shit."

Despite Lincoln's assertion, I'm doubtful. There's nothing here but baked dirt and grass, and a short walk from the car, two structures—one that looks like a giant airplane hangar and the small, squat building in front of it.

"Come on." Lincoln hops out of the car. I start to grab my purse and the bags of food, but he glances at me and says, "Leave the food for now. You'll want to see this first."

⸻

The smaller building has wood siding and a sign that reads *Ashfall State Historical Park Visitor Orientation Center.*

"A historical park." I turn to Lincoln as we walk toward the glass doors. "For our grand adventure, you're taking me on a school field trip?"

"Have faith, surfer girl."

The inside of the building is freezing. My skin prickles. I tell Lincoln I'll wait for him outside while he buys our tickets. I grab for my wallet to offer him some money, but I must have left my tote bag with my phone and wallet in the car. I consider going back to grab my phone, but maybe it'll be nice to spend a couple hours without it, without my fingers unconsciously pulling up another slew of pictures of my friends.

Lincoln comes back outside a few minutes later and guides us toward the airplane hangar-like building. We pass a few people on the concrete path that connects the two buildings. Everyone looks like they live on the road—sunglasses, fanny packs, worn-out shirts featuring American flags and bald eagles. They take their time walking the short path, pointing out hills and sparse trees in the distance like they're noteworthy sites.

As we near the hanger, I read a sign. *Hubbard Rhino Barn*. A barn? Did Lincoln take me all the way out here for just some glorified petting zoo?

Before I have a chance to ask, he pulls open the tall door and says, "After you."

I step inside.

"Oh shit," I say.

"Whoa," I say.

"What?" I say.

It takes a while to comprehend what's in front of me. Light pours in from large, rectangular windows, sun-flooding the enormous room. A short, fenced-in walkway keeps everyone on an elevated path above a giant, dusty pit that takes up the majority of the space. Inside the pit are life-sized animal molds. No, not animal molds—animal *bones*. Hundreds and hundreds of animal bones poke out of the ground like they tucked in for an afternoon nap and woke up eras later.

A few people with badges crouch inside of the pit, brushing dust away from the bones with cautious, gloved hands.

I turn to Lincoln and find him already looking at me. "What is this place?"

"Didn't you read the sign?" He grins. "Ashfall Fossil Beds."

My hairs rise at the sight in front of me and the story Lincoln tells.

Twelve million years ago a volcano erupted in Idaho.

The eruption spread ash and powdered glass, far and wide—all the way to a watering hole in northeastern Nebraska. The animals grazed on the ash-infused grasses and drank the ash-infused water and breathed the ash-infused air and died an ash-infused death. The ash continued to blow, covering their bodies and preserving them in a twelve million-year-old ecological bubble. This site was founded decades ago when someone discovered the skull of a juvenile rhinoceros peeking out of a cornfield.

"Pretty cool, huh?" Lincoln finishes. I continue to peer out over the 3-D fossilized remains, the rib cage of an ancient rhino tucked against the hoof of a three-toed horse. I've never seen anything like this. Maybe if I'd taken up Dad on that DC trip offer, I would have seen some dinosaurs at the Smithsonian. But not like this, not animals in their natural habitat, still preserved in the ground millions—*millions*—of years later.

"When we moved here, I was sixteen and actually really upset about a move for the first time," Lincoln says. He keeps his voice low, and our shoulders press together as we watch people cautiously brush ash off the unmoving animals. "I loved traveling and discovering, but I'd finally settled down in Raleigh. I'd made some great friends, and I wanted to graduate with them. Mom felt awful that I was so upset, so she did her research and brought me here. And I fell in love with the place. Kind of hard not to."

I wonder what it must be like to have a mom who cares you're upset and tries to make it better.

He points at the remains of one of the rhinos, leaning a bit closer to do so, providing more heat than the twenty-foot windows baking us with afternoon sunlight. "Some of these guys still had grass in their mouths. Just up and died midchew. This part of Nebraska used to look like the East African savannas. It's surreal. There's so much of the world I want to see. But here—here, I can see the past."

As Lincoln says this, I imagine myself back in Santa Cruz, out on the water, surfboard beneath me when a storm of ash sweeps in, a thick cloud of choking gray dust, suffocating me, sealing me in my own giant watering hole so that millions of years from now aliens will stare at my skeleton and talk about how amazing it is that I've been preserved so well.

The immense power of the ash, the power to stick and unstick time and place—if I could harness that kind of power, I could do anything. If I wanted to, the next time my mom drops in town, I could bury her in it. Preserve her in powdered glass, mold her by our sides so she could never leave again.

My own little fossilized Santa Cruz family.

The air feels cooler outside as I settle at one of the large, wood-planked picnic tables. Lincoln runs back to the car for our bags of food, promising not to peek at mine until we're together. I glance at the rhino barn and think how odd it is that a few feet and some aluminum siding separates me from twelve million years ago, like if I blinked I could slip back to another time entirely. Did my mom know about this place? Probably not. If so, she probably would've tried to free the bones from their eternal homes.

Lincoln returns and places the brown paper bags on the table. "You okay?" he asks.

"Um, yeah," I lie and then pause. I'm not okay. I was okay. At the beginning of the summer, I was great, but now I'm here in Nebraska, without my friends and in a place that constantly pulls my thoughts to my mom like a cruel geographical magnet. "Actually, no—I'm kind of..."

"What is it?"

It's weird. I've never had to tell this story to anyone. Everyone in my life knows about my mom, how she left and came back and left and came back, how each time I was more upset and less interested in talking about it. I mean, I didn't even tell *Tess* about the postcard.

But Lincoln knows nothing about my mom and all she's done to me and all she hasn't done for me. I don't know if it's the centuries old animal bones or the way I feel when Lincoln locks eyes with me, but suddenly I want to tell him.

So I do.

I tell him about her many disappearances. The hurt, the

disappointment, the anger. I tell him things I don't even like to admit to myself—the way I still let her back in every time, the way I hate myself for doing so. How much I hate being here because an invisible piece of her hides around every corner. I tell him about the postcard, how my stomach tightens each time I get home from the park because there's the slight chance I could find her watching TV in the living room.

"I'm sorry, Anise," Lincoln says when I finish.

The three simple words make me want to cry, but I force those tears away. I'm a lucky person. I live in the most wonderful place in the world. Dad loves me. I have everything I need. I don't *need* her.

"I wonder what's harder," Lincoln says.

I look at him. "What?"

"I wonder what's harder," he repeats, thoughtfully. "Having a biological mom I'll never know or having a mom who comes and goes without warning, like yours."

I chew my lip. I'm not sure which is harder either. I guess it's impossible to know unless you've experienced both. All I know is how bad I feel for the woman, who for whatever reasons, never got to experience what a wonderful person Lincoln is.

We sit in silence with our thoughts for a few minutes. I let the wind calm me, listening to the way it whistles through the dry grass. Then my stomach growls and completely evaporates the intense mood. Lincoln laughs, his dimple popping out. "Are you ready for our challenge?" he asks.

"I'm always ready to win."

"Losers first." He coughs. "I mean, you first."

I'm so confident in my food choices that I don't even argue. I open my bag and place five items on the table—a baguette, cilantro, jalapeño, some chili sauce packets I may or may not have stolen from the fresh-made deli section, and though it makes my stomach churn—

"SPAM!" Lincoln snatches the can from the table and stares at it and then the rest of the ingredients. "Bánh mì Spam! Okay, you won. You definitely won. How did you—"

The only thing I love more than Lincoln's smile is being the cause of Lincoln's smile. "Well, obviously I didn't have enough money for all the ingredients, but I saw the Spam and remembered your road trip story and figured I might as well give it a shot."

Lincoln glances at his bag and looks a bit deflated. "Now I'm ashamed of my purchase. Let's just eat bánh mì Spam sandwiches for the rest of forever."

"I don't think so." I grab for his bag. "Let's see… Oh my god." I look up at him. "How did you—"

"Your cousins shared your particularly eclectic taste in breakfast cereal combinations. Our mom was horrified when she found Austin eating it last week."

Inside the bag I find boxes of Cap'n Crunch, Lucky Charms, and Cocoa Puffs. My heart flutters like it does when I see a good wave forecast, and I can't pull the smile from my face. I open the Lucky Charms and lift the box toward him. "Cheers, Lincoln."

He lifts his can of Spam and taps it with my cereal. "Cheers, Anise."

––––––

It's not until we've been back on the road for a few miles that I remember it's been hours since I've checked my phone. I push aside my bag of souvenirs (fake animal bones made out of white chocolate for the family, postcards for my friends, and a little plush rhino for myself) and grab my tote. I pull out my phone. My mouth goes dry and my stomach churns.

Ten missed calls.

I might throw up my Cap'n Lucky Puffs.

Ten missed calls and ten voice mails—six from Emery, two from Dad, and two from unknown callers.

I press play and listen.

And listen.

And listen.

Aunt Jackie...infection...where are you...hospital...emergency surgery...where are you...call us...where are you...where are you... where are you...

"Anise? Anise, are you okay?" Lincoln asks.

My phone shakes. No, my hand shakes.

My throat is tight. "Hospital," I manage. "We need to get to the hospital."

TWELVE

— — —

—

SURGICAL SITE INFECTIONS apparently strike one to three percent of all surgical patients. Warning signs include tenderness, swelling, and pain—all symptoms you might consider normal if you've been in tender, swelling pain for more than a month. Emery checked on Aunt Jackie while I was gone, noticed she was flushed and disoriented, and took her temperature: it was 103.

The good news is she panicked and called for an ambulance right away. An hour later Aunt Jackie was in emergency surgery for a deep incisional infection. The doctor told me if they hadn't caught it in time, it could've permanently damaged her leg—or worse.

"Emery, is that you?" Aunt Jackie asks, her voice muffled.

"It's Anise," I say and lean forward in the armchair. "The others went home to rest."

I spent last night in the hospital waiting room with Emery, Parker, Nash, and two of Aunt Jackie's friends, piled on armchairs, using sweatshirts and hoodies as blankets. Lincoln stayed until almost two in the morning, going to the cafeteria on coffee and food runs, trying to nudge a smile out of my cousins, an impossible task since Aunt Jackie still hadn't woken up from the surgery.

He offered to come back this morning, once Aunt Jackie had woken up, and take the kids home and watch them all day. I accepted so Aunt Jackie's friends wouldn't have to take off work and since Dad couldn't get a flight back until tomorrow. His worried phone calls kept me on the phone all night and morning. I think he blames himself that he wasn't here…but I wasn't there either. Just like my mom, I left home, left someone who needed me for something more exciting on the horizon. My eyes threaten to well every time I think of Emery going into Aunt Jackie's room, taking her temperature, fingers trembling to call the ambulance. In that moment, with no information and Aunt Jackie incoherent from the high fever, Emery probably thought she was losing her mom, even faster than she lost her dad. I flew here to help her this summer, to take care of her, to protect her, and when she needed me most, I wasn't there.

I try to mask any shaking in my voice and ask Aunt Jackie, "How are you feeling?"

I move over to her hospital bed, uncomfortable at how normal the scene feels. Aunt Jackie already spent a month here.

She smiles weakly. "Guilty, mostly. Can't believe I didn't

notice the fever myself. Emery…" Her voice cracks. "…She was so scared. I don't remember much once the fever hit, but I remember those scared eyes."

"Emery is okay now," I lie. I don't want to put more stress on her when she needs to recover.

In reality, Emery shut down last night, not even yelling at Nash when he tried to start a talent show in the waiting room. She just sat and stared at the wall—at the *wall*, not even her phone. I tried to talk to her, hug her like I kept hugging the boys, but she stayed unresponsive.

Maybe I'm fucking this up. I should tell Aunt Jackie that Emery is hurting a lot more than she's letting on. And yet, every time I go to do so, the words stick in my mouth. The doctor said Aunt Jackie needs a low-stress environment. I can handle this on my own. I don't need to give Aunt Jackie a reason to worry.

"You'll be back home in a few days," I say. "And everything will go back to normal."

I say these words with conviction, even though at this point, I'm not sure what normal is.

———

I end up dozing on the extra hospital bed in Aunt Jackie's room. And by dozing, I mean I knock out for a solid two hours until Aunt Jackie's friend, Blue Cardigan Claire, shows up to take over. "Let me give you a ride home," she says.

I nod, blinking with sleep-weighted lids, then crawl out of my hospital sheet cocoon.

In the car, I press my head against the cool glass and watch the empty suburban streets slip by. It's nine o'clock. Most people are probably in their beds, TVs and tablets softly glowing.

When she drops me off, I thank Claire for the ride and mentally thank her for not bringing up my mom. The house looks silent. Almost all the lights are out. Are the kids already asleep? My phone battery died a bit ago, so I haven't been able to text Lincoln for an update.

I unlock the door. The living room light is on, but I don't see anyone. "Hello?" I call out. "Emery? Lincoln?"

No response.

My heart thumps as a dozen scenarios flash through my mind:

They went out to get ice cream at that little store a couple miles away.

An axe murderer came into the house and killed them all!

The stress exhausted them, and everyone went to bed early.

Aliens abducted them and they're never coming back!

Then I notice light coming from the backyard. I walk through the living room and pull open the sliding glass door. Soft music thumps from portable speakers. The outdoor lighting basks the concrete in an artificial glow. A few people who are definitely too tall to be my cousins stand around the edge of the pool.

What the hell?

I step outside and count about ten people in the backyard, hanging out, skating around the pool, and skating *in* the pool like it's the bowl at the skate park. Then I focus in on the music. It's an old song made recently familiar to me.

Bruce Springsteen. I narrow my eyes. "*Lincoln.*"

And then he's in front of me, wearing jean shorts as always, a straw hat, and an unbuttoned Hawaiian shirt with nothing underneath it but his dark, defined abs. He pulls me into a hug, his chest hard and warm, and tempting, but I shove him away. "What the *hell* is going on?"

Anger rattles through me. My aunt is sick, and he took that as an opportunity to throw a party? This is so unlike him. I mean, not that I *know* him. I met him a month ago. And you can't *know* anyone in a month. And yet, I would have never expected this from him. This is the guy who spent ten minutes consoling Parker after Nash nailed a kickflip better than him. That guy doesn't throw parties at other people's homes when they're in the hospital.

But—I guess he does.

Before he has a chance to respond, I snap, "Get these people out *now*! And where are my cousins? What the hell were you even—"

"Anise, calm down." He tries to put a hand on my shoulder, but I back away.

"Don't patronize me. My aunt just had emergency surgery, and you're throwing a fucking party in her backyard instead of watching my cousins. Where are my—"

"Anise!" Nash bounds up to me and hugs me around the waist. A bit of chocolate rings the corner of his mouth, probably from the cookie in his right hand.

Before I can respond, Parker runs up to wave at me and tug Nash away, saying, "You *have* to watch this guy."

"Don't worry," Lincoln says. "They're strictly forbidden from going into the pool. No more broken limbs in the family, I promise."

"And Emery—"

"Right there." Lincoln points toward the back corner of yard, where Emery sits on a pool lounge, talking to Austin.

Lincoln speaks again, quickly, probably so I can't interrupt. "Look, they napped for a while and woke up in bad moods, like really bad moods." He lowers his voice. "Like *my mom almost died again* moods, and so I brought them out here, and we cleaned all that sludge out of the bottom of the pool so I could show them a few tricks, and then Emery asked if Austin could come over, and then one thing led to another. I texted you to let you know, but you weren't responding, and Parker and Nash were loving it so much, so a few more friends showed up. I'll send everyone home now if you want. Maybe I fucked up, but they were upset, and I was trying to—"

"It's fine."

"It's what?"

"It's fine." I take a second to think it through, then nod. "Yeah, I mean this was pretty irresponsible and don't think

I'm still not totally pissed at you…but the kids seem happy."
Even Emery looks okay—maybe not happy but okay, a stark
contrast to earlier at the hospital. "So it's fine."

"Okay. And I'm sorry. I won't do it again." Lincoln's worried look transforms into a mischievous one. "Moving on
though, I only have one question for you. Ever skate in a
pool?"

An hour later, bruises, tiny scratches, and not-so-tiny scratches
splatter my body, but I can't wipe the smile off my face.
Adrenaline pumps hard and fast as I balance on the lip of the
pool, shout, "Dropping in!" then lean forward and plummet
into the rutted cement bowl. Air slaps me as my wheels rattle
against the uneven terrain, my pulse accelerating with every
bump and jolt. The pool has less length than the bowl at the
skate park, but I have enough room to ollie before I gear
down, kick hard against the pavement to regain speed, and
burst out over the rim. I land in a tangle of my own limbs, but
at least I'm outside of the pool, a giant success in itself.

"You okay there?" Sofia leans down to lend me a hand.
Her long hair flows over her shoulder, falling over her sleeveless white T-shirt.

I grin and take her hand, standing up to assess the damage.
Just more bruising. "Most definitely okay."

"Awesome." She grins with infectious eagerness. "Watch

this." She turns and launches off into the pool with all the grace of someone who's been skateboarding since birth.

"I kind of hate her." Lincoln comes up behind me, speaking so close to my ear that I can barely think of anything but how near his lips are to my skin.

"Why?" I ask.

"Because talented people make me look less awesome in comparison."

"Oh, I still think you look pretty awesome," I say, trying to concentrate as Sofia lands trick after trick.

"Oh, you do?" Lincoln asks. I turn to find a roguish—yes, *roguish*—smile playing on his lips. "I think you look pretty awesome too."

I don't think we're talking about skating any more, especially as Lincoln's gaze flicks over me, making me all too conscious of my flimsy cotton shorts and tight-fitted tank.

"Come on." He nods at the house. "Let's see if we can scavenge up some of your cousins' old pads, otherwise when your dad gets back, he's going to ask why his daughter is completely black and blue."

I hesitate. My heart races again, this time with a different type of adrenaline. I should probably still be pissed at Lincoln for throwing this mini-party, but of the many things I feel right now, anger is not one of them.

I scan the yard to make sure my cousins are still occupied and safe. When I respond, the words sound louder than they should. "Okay, sure."

We scavenge through dusty boxes that fill most of the two-car garage, finding an elbow pad here and a kneepad there, all of which are too small for me. My heart jolts every time I see a box with worn-out tape, and I wonder if something of my mom's is inside. But nothing ever is.

Eventually I give up, exhaustion hitting me hard and fast after the past twenty-four hours. I sit down on the small flight of stairs that leads into the house. After digging through a few more boxes and coming up empty, Lincoln walks over and joins me.

His shoulder touches mine. I wonder if he's thinking about my shoulder touching his.

He breaks the silence. "This place is wild."

"What place?"

"This garage. There's so much stuff. Years and years and years of stuff."

"Aren't most garages like that? Mine sure as hell is." I think of the generations of beach gear, decades and decades piled on top of each other.

"I guess we move around too much to collect many things." His arm rests behind my back. And though he's not touching me, I can almost feel his fingers, close to the exposed skin below my tank top.

"I can't imagine what it's like moving around all the time like you guys did. I've lived in the same place my entire life."

Lincoln laughs. "Yeah, it shows."

I look at him, narrowing my eyes. "It does?"

"That first day I met you the park. It was so obvious that you were out of place." He shoots me a goofy grin. "A literal fish out of water."

He lifts his arm, scratching his neck, then lowers it again, I swear this time even closer to my back. "That's why I like skateboarding so much. Before I developed my spectacular social skills, it was really hard to make new friends. But once I started skating, I realized wherever we moved, I could always find some kind of skate park, some kind of community."

I try to imagine what life must have been like for Lincoln. Moving so many times. Always having to make new friends. It must have been doubly hard since he looks different. But his personality—okay, and his looks—are infectious. It's impossible *not* to gravitate to him.

I think that's what I like the most about him. His confidence in his own skin. Like he carries his home with him.

The silence stretches between us for a few long moments. "Lincoln?" I say.

"What?" he asks.

"I'm going to kiss you now."

"You're going to wh—"

I answer by leaning forward and pressing my lips to his.

He responds immediately. And then my body starts working two steps ahead of my thoughts. I wrap my arms around him, pulling him closer, letting my hands explore the top of his strong back. As he presses against me, I nip the bottom of his lip. He inhales sharply, pumping my body with more adrenaline than any wave or skate bowl out there.

Kissing Lincoln makes me wonder why I've never kissed Lincoln before.

For the last month, I've been searching for some relief from this taxing summer, and here it was, right in front of me—a pair of soft and skilled lips.

My hands wander down the hard muscle of his back and up again, his heat escaping through the thin cotton of his shirt. As my hands continue to wander, I brush against his nub.

I startle and break away. "Crap, sorry." His eyes stay shut for a long second.

Dread washes through me. Why did I freak out like that?

He opens his eyes and meets my gaze. "Anise." His voice is soft, yet solid. "I only have one arm. You know that, right?"

"Umm, yes," I say, voice meek.

"And the other side—it's just the beginning of an arm, mostly shoulder really." He pauses and reaches for my hand, holding it in his. "Does this weird you out?"

His touch does the opposite; it calms the ebb of dread, restores my pulse to stasis.

"No."

"Okay, so this shouldn't either." He takes my hand and raises it to that rounded end below his shoulder. "It's just another part of me."

The skin is soft, warm. I trail my hand along it slowly and then up to his collarbone, his neck, and then his cheek, and then brush my fingers across his lips for just a second, his eyes flicking quickly to mine when I do.

I blush. "Sorry. I just...umm...got distracted."

Lincoln grins. "I've been told I can be quite distracting."

In that moment I realize I'm probably not the first person to kiss Lincoln. And more likely, not even close to first. There's probably a connect-the-dots line of people all over the country who have kissed Lincoln. And that sparks my competitive nature.

"Anise?" Lincoln narrows his eyes. "Why do you have that look on your—"

Before he can finish speaking, I move (okay, lunge) toward him because the thing is, if I can't be the only person to kiss Lincoln Puk, I'm sure as hell going to be the best.

———

Everyone heads home (or to cooler parties with alcohol) around eleven o'clock, so then it's my cousins, Austin, Lincoln, and me sitting together at the bottom of the empty pool. It's a cool night, and as I lie on my back against rough cement, pressed close to Lincoln, the breeze ruffles over me, tickling my skin in an oddly comforting way, like if I closed my eyes I could smell the sharp salt of the ocean breeze.

I tilt my head to peek at Emery and Austin sitting next to each other, their hands splayed on the cement, their fingers centimeters from each other, and I think of my first crush—the way I was aware of every eyelash, every freckle running up and down his arms, the way he'd always brush back his shaggy hair before speaking. Every detail about him memorized in innocent, yet obsessive, infatuation.

My feelings for Lincoln are different, broader.

It's not the way he pumps his fist every time Austin lands a trick but the fact that he triumphs in his brother's victories.

It's not so much his deep dimple but the way it pops out whenever he sees me.

"Watch out!" Nash shouts. I pull my arm out of the way, escaping the crush of Nash's sneaker as he and Parker sprint around the pool, pretending to be on skateboards, calling out the names of tricks as they jump into the air with full force energy and no fear. Their gleeful shouts relax me, like a raucous thunderstorm comforts after a long drought.

"Whatchya thinking about?" Lincoln asks. We both tilt our heads toward each other. Just a few inches closer and I could brush my lips against his.

Instead, I say, "You."

"I was thinking about me too." He grins.

I roll my eyes. "Ha-ha."

"You look tired."

"What a charmer."

"Maybe I should tuck you into bed."

I eye him with suspicion. Is Lincoln the type of guy who thinks one quick (okay, rather long and heated) make out session equates to me jumping into bed with him? I've never had sex before, and although I'm not against the idea in theory, I'm sure as hell not about to after one kiss.

Lincoln, probably noticing my look of distaste, continues, "That wasn't supposed to be a come-on. I literally want to tuck you into bed. You look like hell, surfer girl. I'm thinking you could use some sleep."

"Really, your flattery skills are top-notch."

"Come on." He stands and stretches in the way that only lean, six-foot-three boys can, and then offers me his hand. "Let's get the heathens in bed too."

We all caravan upstairs, a weird, patchwork family. Austin brings the boys to their room and Emery slips into ours. I stand in the dark hallway with Lincoln. He takes my hand and leans close, so my back presses against the wooden edge of the doorframe. "Sweet dreams," he says and grins as he leans in to kiss me.

I return the kiss, long and languid and warm.

As he breaks away, he whispers, "Okay, and maybe a little savory too."

I give him a soft shove. My hand lingers on his chest. "You're so weird."

He grins and closes his hand around mine. "You love it."

THIRTEEN

THE NEXT COUPLE of weeks fly by with disconcerting speed. Dad landed back in Nebraska the day after the party. He might have noticed a couple red Solo cups in the back-yard, but he didn't say anything. He also didn't mention my mom or the note I left for her in Santa Cruz, and since Dad likes hashing out feelings, I'm assuming it's because he didn't see her or the note. Aunt Jackie came home from the hospital a couple of days after that, and from there, time has melted by in a never-ending rotation of park visits, skateboarding, and games of Monopoly and Scrabble. And Lincoln. And Lincoln's kisses—snuck behind trees at the park, in the living room late at night while everyone else is asleep, at the riverbed after jumping off the rope swing, in the dark outside his house after dinner with his family.

We haven't talked about *us*, our relationship, or even called it a relationship. Sometimes, after spending a long day with Lincoln, my thoughts will flick to Eric, and I'll wonder if he's also found someone else. My communication with friends has stalled because every time I pick up my phone to message them, I see evidence of the memories they're creating without me. Sometimes I think the day I left home that universe closed behind me, and everyone and everything there continued to exist as if I were never there in the first place. The thought makes my stomach twist, so I push it away.

Thinking about *us* with Lincoln makes my stomach twist too because I know it can't last. I'm going back to Santa Cruz and staying there, and Lincoln is going to hike the PCT and then explore the rest of the world after college. Putting a name to what we have will only make me more aware that I won't always have it.

I tell myself not to think about it because I see him at the park every day. And when I tug his hand, his lips press against mine. For now, that's enough.

"Anise, your phone won't shut up," Emery says, entering the kitchen, where I'm eating a bowl of Cap'n Lucky Puffs. She's started to warm up to me—barely—but freezer burn is better than frostbite. Her mood lifted when Aunt Jackie came home again, but she joins us at the skate park every day instead of going to see her friends. Much to the twins' annoyance, Austin takes frequent skating breaks to hang out with her.

I'm still tempted to say something to Aunt Jackie, but I'm keeping a careful eye on Emery, and she seems a bit happier each day. We restarted our nightly binge of *The Office* routine, and she doesn't even roll her eyes at me when I say, "Oh my god, you're going to laugh so hard at this prank!"

"Can I have it?" I ask.

"It's in the living room."

"So you came to tell me my phone won't shut up, but you didn't actually bring me my phone?"

"Yup." She shrugs and then leaves the room.

"Right," I mutter. "Thanks so much."

I shove away from the table and head into the living room. I have about ten million messages from friends informing me that a slew of famous surfers have been added to the Surf Break roster last minute and that if I don't make it home, I'm basically the worst person ever.

We know you've wanted to get that poster of Fitzgibbons signed since you were like eleven

Hey stranger! If you stay in Nebraska any longer, you're going to turn into a cattle herder (okay, still not sure what exactly is in Nebraska)

Wright is going to be there! Wright AND his abs!

Where the hell have you been? Get back NOW

Literally I don't care if you have to hitchhike—you'd better be here

As I scroll through the many messages, I spot three from Eric.

Did you hear about the new roster?
Are you going to make it?
Hope your summer is going well...

Those three dots cut deep. Eric's been one of my best friends for seventeen years, and we haven't spoken for weeks. Unless you count the occasional *like* on Instagram and Facebook. It's been so long I'm not sure what to say. At first there wasn't anything interesting to share about my trip, and now the stretched silence feels awkward. Plus, there's Lincoln. Do I tell Eric about him? Would it hurt him? What would I even say?

But Eric's image, the image that was so grainy before, flashes sharp and clear. Blond curls falling into his always-squinting eyes because he refuses to wear sunglasses like a normal person. Strong arms that pick me up and toss me into the water with ease. That smooth, easy laugh.

This is what leaving home does—rips you from your friends, your life. Forces you to start new.

My phone beeps again with a message from Tess:

Dear best friend who fell off the face of the earth, are you planning on coming home to me?
Like ever?
Please send proof of your existence.

If you'd asked me a year ago—no, even three months ago—if I'd ever go a single day without texting Tess, I would have laughed. But as I scroll through our most recent messages, I see that most recent equates to more than two weeks ago.

Dad and I are scheduled to fly home in three weeks.

But in three more weeks, will it even feel like home?

I start to type a response but stop because for the first time ever in our friendship, I don't know what to say.

———

It's too hot for the park today, so Lincoln and Austin come over, which has become a somewhat regular event. We all play an endless game of Monopoly. Aunt Jackie wheels herself out of the guest bedroom and sits at the folding table we put in the living room so she can play with us. She sneaks money from Emery's stash and gets caught on purpose, probably because she enjoys that loud gasp of, "*Mom!*" every time she does it.

I sit at the end of the table, watching instead of playing, toying with my phone. The unanswered messages sit heavy in my palm. All I want to do is assure my friends I'll be home in time for Surf Break. But of course, I won't. And the longer I wait to reply, the longer I can postpone that reality.

Lincoln nudges me. He went bankrupt early on from buying Nash's Park Place card for an outrageous price. "You okay?" he mouths.

I shrug my shoulders.

He stares at me for a second longer, drumming his fingers in quick raps against his leg, and then stands and tugs my hand. "Come with me."

"Why?" I ask, a little louder than I meant. Everyone looks over, but their attention is drawn back to the game when Parker pulls a Community Chest card and gets to collect fifty dollars from every player.

We head into the kitchen. Lincoln sits at the table, but I stand, pressing my back against the kitchen bar. "Obviously you're not okay," Lincoln says. "What's going on?"

I hesitate. It's probably rude to tell Lincoln how badly I wish I could be in Santa Cruz, like saying I'd rather have *it* than *him*. But the thing is, as much as I like Lincoln—like skating with him, laughing with him, kissing him, especially that spot on his neck, right beneath his jaw that always produces this little gasp—I know I'll have to give him up soon. Even if I weren't going back to Santa Cruz, it's not like we could stay together forever. He wants to travel, and I refuse to spend my life not knowing when he'll come back.

"Anise?" he asks again.

"I—" I pause to string the words together first. "You know that Surf Break thing I was telling you about?" Lincoln nods. "Well, this morning, a bunch of amazing surfers were added to roster last minute, and so now I want to go more than ever."

"So why don't you go?"

I eye him, confused. "What?"

"Just go."

"Umm, first of all, plane fare is expensive as—"

"So we'll drive."

We. "And I have to help watch my cousins."

"They seem fine to me. And your aunt is doing great."

"I mean, I guess—but there's no way my dad would be okay with this."

Lincoln shrugs. "Can't hurt to ask."

⸻

I can't sleep that night. All these weeks and I still haven't adjusted to the stillness of Nebraska—no hum of the ocean to smooth out the world's creases. Emery's light snores help cut the quiet, but then they remind me she's getting rest while I'm wide awake. Sighing, I push off my covers and climb out of bed, being careful not to wake Emery.

I make my way downstairs. The kitchen light is on, and there's a faint chopping sound. I find Dad slicing thin strips of peppers and onions. "Umm, Dad?" I ask. "You know it's like three in the morning, right?"

He turns to me and shrugs. "I have trouble sleeping some nights. Too silent." Oh, of course. If it's hard for me, it must be even worse for him. The ocean has lulled him asleep for forty years now. "Making some veggie fajitas. Want some?"

"At three in the morning?"

He grins at me. "I'll take that as a yes."

As Dad prepares the food with calm and measured hands, I drift back to my earlier conversation with Lincoln—Surf Break.

My nerves tighten despite all logic. This is Dad, the person I'm most comfortable with on the planet. The person who made me chocolate chip pancakes when I lost my first surfing competition. The person who slathered me with oatmeal and calamine lotion when I had the chicken pox. The person who let me skip school that one time because the surf forecast looked *that* good.

"Anise?" he prompts. "You okay?"

"Umm, yeah." I scratch behind my ear. And then I scratch my forehead. And then I scratch my arm. "I have a question. I know the answer is probably no, or definitely no, but *canLincolnandIdrivetoSurfBreaktogether?*"

Dad picks up the knife and continues to slice vegetables, the sharp chop against the wooden cutting board synching with the thumps in my rib cage. I expected him to say no. I was okay with no. Of course it's a no. I'm asking to abandon my responsibilities and to go off, chaperone-free, with a guy for days. But I wasn't expecting silence.

I disappointed him. It was selfish of me to even ask.

I'm about to apologize when the chopping stops and Dad says, "Okay."

"Okay, what?"

"Okay you can drive to Surf Break with Lincoln."

"Oh," I say. And then it sinks in. "*Oh.*" A week from now

I'll be back in Santa Cruz, back to the waves, back to my friends, back *home*. And then it sinks in further. "Wait, why?"

Dad wipes his hands on a dishcloth. "I was thinking about letting you go back early anyway. Jacks is healing faster than expected. We'll be able to manage fine without you, and you deserve it. You sacrificed a lot this summer."

I know I should feel happy. And I do. But I also feel guilty, like I'm getting a reward for helping my family.

"Not to mention," Dad continues. "I'm happy you're doing something out of your comfort zone, going on a road trip, seeing some new places. You're such a thrill seeker—you always have been, ever since you were a little kid, going for the biggest wave, always ready to challenge anyone. But, I was getting worried you'd be too scared to leave home."

I twist the bottom of my shirt. "I'm not home now."

Dad sighs. "You know what I mean. I'm happy you're opening yourself to new things."

I don't tell Dad that the main reason I want to go on this trip is to get back to the familiar, to get back home. I want ocean sunrises. I want Tess's quilt. I want my surfboard.

I'm thinking that's the end of the conversation, but then Dad continues, "Now, I'm trusting you and Lincoln to make responsible sexual decisions and be safe, okay?"

My cheeks flame. Sometimes I *really* hate how comfortable Dad is with communication. Any other father would get fidgety and horrified at discussing sex with his teenage daughter, but not Dad. He gave me the condom and birth control talk in excruciating detail when I was fourteen. Thankfully we've avoided the topic since then, but I guess going on a road trip with a guy you've been sucking face with all summer justifies a second round of the talk.

I clear my throat and focus on breathing. "Yep, sure. Absolutely." I want to escape the kitchen and this conversation, but damn Dad's cooking smells good.

"Not so fast," Dad says. He points to one of the kitchen chairs. "Sit."

"Dad, look I'm not planning to…you know." My cheeks burn even more. Thank God no one else is around to hear this conversation. "Look, I can't even say the word, so if that's not a clear enough indication that I'm not planning on, well, doing it, then I don't know what is."

"That's fine," Dad says. "And I believe you. But teenagers change their minds very quickly. So we're going to go over safe sex practices one more time, just in case."

I groan. "That's *really* not necessary."

"Neither is letting you go to Surf Break."

We stare at each other, but we both know he's won and I'm just postponing the inevitable. I place my head on the table. "All right then," I say. "Get on with it. But I deserve an *extra* large serving of those veggie fajitas."

"Yes, you do." He turns back to the stove. "Now when you're picking out condoms, it's important to remember…"

When I call Tess to tell her I'll be at Surf Break, I'm pretty sure she squeals for two minutes straight. We then launch into a mass of exciting details.

"Wait, wait, wait," Tess interrupts me midsentence. "*We?* As in you and Lincoln?"

"Well, yeah," I say. Tess and I have been so out of touch that she only knows the bare minimum of my new…whatever-ship. I told her about our first kiss and something after that, but I haven't updated her thoroughly. And although she mentioned she's met a summer fling, I don't even know his name. "If we split gas, it'll be cheaper than me flying, and well, you know…"

"So, like, you two are *banging*? Holy shit! Dude, you were supposed to tell me when you had sex so I could send you a *you had sex* congratulations card. I can't believe you'd do this to me."

"Why does everyone think we're having sex?" I ask. "Tess, we are *not* banging." I pause. "We are making out on a some-what regular and enthusiastic basis."

"And you're only telling me this now? Darling, best friend, you've got to keep me updated. And you're going to drive halfway across the country together? *Alone?*" She pauses, and even though we're miles apart, I can see her eyes narrow as the gears of her mind turn. She doesn't know Lincoln like I do. He's not driving halfway across the country to have sex with me. He's driving halfway across the country because he likes adventure. He won't stop talking about how excited he is to be on the road again and to visit his friend Wendy from middle school. Apparently their parents were friends too. Wendy's mom is Vietnamese, and she used to have "best bánh mì" competitions with Lincoln's dad.

"So um, what are you going to tell Eric?" she asks.

"What?"

"Eric, your other best friend, whose face you made out with before ditching us all for Nebraska?"

The words sting. Everything stings more when it comes from your best friend. "I didn't *ditch* you guys," I mutter, my throat tight. "I came to help my family. You know that."

"You're right." She breathes out. "You're right, I'm sorry. I've just barely heard from you. I miss you." She pauses, and those gears turn again. "But you're finally coming back, and Eric will see you toting some hot piece of man along with your luggage. Where did you guys leave things? We haven't really talked about that either."

Probably because Eric and I haven't talked about it. I don't know where we left things. After that first text message, we haven't mentioned the kiss at all. When I think of the kiss, I remember *liking* it more than I actually *remember* it. I'm with Lincoln now. And Eric is a best friend from back home. I haven't told him about Lincoln, but we haven't talked at all, so it's not lying. It's...well...it's not lying.

"Anise?" Tess prods.

"Yeah..." I say slowly.

"You made out with your *best friend*. Okay, your second

best friend. And then you started dating another guy without telling him. And now you're going to bring the new guy home with you. Don't you think you should give Eric a heads up?"

"No," I say, quick and stubborn. "I wouldn't care if Eric hooked up with someone else. It's not like we were dating. It was *one* kiss." But even as I say those words, I know they're bullshit. I'd be thrown, maybe even hurt, if he found someone else to wrestle into the water this summer. My cheeks burn as I cast my pride into the flames. "*Did* he hook up with someone else this summer?"

"God, Anise, you are truly amazing. No, he did not. You know, he told me you weren't talking to him. I tried covering for you, said you were busy with family stuff, but I think you hurt him falling off the face of the earth like that."

"Well, why didn't you tell me that?"

A long pause. Her voice isn't as solid when she speaks again. "Because you weren't really talking to me either." A pause. "I love you Anise, but you've been shitty about communicating."

I think about the unanswered texts, the missed FaceTime calls. I've been blaming it on the distance, the never-ending babysitting duties, the time difference. I've been blaming it on everything except myself.

Did I fuck up?

Did I take off and leave everyone behind?

Did I—am I—doing *exactly* what my mom does? Was it inevitable that I'd end up like her, giving zero shits about the people I'm supposed to care about? I've spent so much of my life swearing I won't be like her, and without even realizing it...

Panic makes me light-headed. When was the last time I called Cassie? Texted Marie? Why didn't I ever send those postcards from Ashfall? How many unanswered messages do I have online? As the thoughts connect, my breathing strains, like I'm wearing a shrunken wet suit and can't find the zipper.

"Anise, you still there?"

I manage a tight, "Yeah."

I'm about to say I'm sorry and ask how I can fix things, when she says, "Look, I've got to go. My parents need help with the dinner rush. I'll keep the Lincoln thing under wraps until you figure it out. I can't wait to see you, okay? I'm seriously so excited, but I've got to go. Bye!"

I stare at the screen.

Call ended.

"Bye."

————

"What the hell are you doing?" Emery asks.

Emery's standing in the doorway of her room, and I'm standing in a pile of clothes and magazines and hangers. My conversation with Tess unleashed all my anger and frustration. I had to leave my friends behind and spend the summer here, in the home of the woman who abandoned me—and now I can't help but realize, despite my hatred of everything she is and does, I'm just like her.

I want my own piece of destruction, a bit of that satisfaction Aunt Jackie felt by ripping my mom's stuff apart at the seams. So I pulled out drawers and checked for notes taped to the bottom of the old furniture and plowed through the closet, hunting for a loose panel or some piece of my mom I could ruin. But I found nothing.

She's never here.

"Sorry," I say. "I'll clean everything up."

I pick up clothes and begin to fold them. Emery turns on a Beatles' album then joins me in cleaning, even though she doesn't have to. "Seriously, um, what were you doing?"

I almost laugh. I almost cry.

"I'm an asshole friend," I say. "A shitty, terrible, fuckup, asshole piece of crap." I whip my head toward her. "Don't curse."

She grins. "But you set such a shining example."

"I was…well, you know how you said this was my mom's room?" Emery nods. "I guess I was looking for something of hers."

"Did you find anything?"

I shake my head. Of course I didn't. She hasn't lived here for more than two decades. What was I expecting? But I'm exhausted and aggravated and frustrated, at my mom, at myself, and at Emery. And I just need to *do* something. Emery is making the same mistake I did, putting distance between her and her friends.

"What's your problem?" I ask, ditching the tiptoeing tone I've used with her for weeks. She spins toward me. I can't tell if she's scared or pissed. "No, really," I continue. "What the hell is going on with you? Everything is fine, and then you go to the lake and come back in this terrible mood. You stop hanging out with your friends. And you won't tell me why, no matter how many times I ask. And you made me promise not to tell your mom. But here's the thing—your time is up. Either you tell me what's going on, or I'm telling your mom and letting *her* worry about it. Whatever happened, you can't keep it all bottled up inside or you'll—"

"Explode?" Emery asks, eyebrow raised.

I pause. "If you don't talk to me, I *will* talk to your mom."

"You wouldn't do that."

"Watch me."

We stare at each other. "I Am the Walrus" plays in soft tones from her computer. Emery sets her jaw. "I don't want to talk about it."

"Too bad."

"Fine."

"Fine."

"*Fine.*" The song switches to "Strawberry Fields Forever." Emery fiddles with a sweater, toying with its hem. "You're going to think it's ridiculous."

"Try me."

"Like really ridiculous."

"Emery, when I was twelve I tried to scale our roof using

one of those back massagers as a grappling hook. Seriously, try me."

For a second, she looks like she's going to laugh. But then her face shifts back to anxiousness. "So remember how I was invited to the lake last minute?"

I'd actually forgotten about that, but now I remember Dad mentioning it. "Yeah?" I ask.

"Well, apparently everyone else had been invited, like, weeks in advance. I thought I was part of the group, you know? It wasn't until the end of the weekend that Ashley, who I'm not really friends with, told me the truth. I was basically leftovers. Charlie wanted exactly thirteen girls at her thirteenth birthday party, and when Natalie couldn't come last minute, Charlie asked me. So basically she only invited me because I was the only person she knew pathetic enough not to already have weekend plans."

My stomach sinks. Back home, our group is tight-knit. But this summer I've experienced being the odd person out, and it doesn't feel good. I'm glad the situation isn't more serious, but I understand why Emery feels as if she can't show her face around her friends. It's got to feel miserable to think your friends don't want you.

"I'm sorry," I tell her. "That sounds terrible." I try to think of something hopeful to say. "But you're making new friends. You and Austin seem really close."

"Yeah…" She still seems tense.

I'm not sure if our talk has actually changed anything.

Saying a problem out loud doesn't fix it...but maybe, just maybe, it starts to help.

"I'm sorry I snapped at you," I say.

She's quiet for a moment before responding, "It's okay. You were only trying to help. Hey, after we finish cleaning up your mess, we should stay up and watch as many episodes of *The Office* as possible so we can finish before you leave town. If you want to or whatever."

"Sure." I smile at her. "You know, whatever."

The next week rushes by in a blur of planning and packing and overwhelming excitement mixed with more than a tinge of dread. I'm going home. Finally. But Tess's phone call weighs heavy in my mind. I should text all my friends and apologize for losing touch, but Dad always tells me it's better to apologize in person, so I ask Tess to let them know I'm coming back for Surf Break. I'll apologize to them all in person when I'm home.

Today is my last day in Nebraska, and I'm spending it at the park. As my cousins and I ride down the tree-lined paths I've come to know so well, Emery says, "I'm going to go to the basketball courts."

I grind my skateboard to a halt. Parker and Nash do the same. "Can we go ahead?" they ask.

I nod. "Yeah, I'll meet you guys there in a minute. Be

careful." They rush off down the path, Nash almost knocking into a Great Dane and its owner. I turn my attention back to Emery. "The courts?" I ask. She just told me how cruel her friends were. Why on earth would she want to go back to them?

She shrugs. "Well, I thought about it some more and realized I don't know the whole story. I figured I should find out. When I went last time I just stood there and didn't say anything. Now I'm going to ask why they did that to me."

Don't do it, I want to tell her. I think of the many times I've forgiven my mom, how I've convinced myself that maybe she did care and maybe she wouldn't leave. It was always a mistake. I always regretted pushing away that gut feeling of *she just doesn't care.*

But I don't tell Emery any of this because her friends aren't my mom. Maybe it was a simple misunderstanding, and Emery is brave enough to find out. "Just—I love you, okay?"

She rolls her eyes and smiles at me. "I know. I love you too. I'll be okay." She sticks her tongue out at me and then pedals off. I watch her disappear down the winding paths, and I believe her; no matter what happens with her friends today, or with her mom, or with anything, I know she'll be okay.

———

"No more," I pant. There's nothing like glorious exhaustion to get your mind off of stress. Sweat drips down my face and trails onto my neck. This is what four hours of nonstop skating will do to you. I collapse onto the concrete and dangle my legs over the edge of the skate bowl.

Lincoln collapses next to me, our heated bodies pressed close. I lean my head on his shoulder, not caring that his shirt is damp with sweat, and let my pulse return to normal, which is challenging as his fingers trail lightly up and down the bare skin of my thigh. We sit in peaceful silence, watching his friends, *our* friends, drop into the bowl and land trick after trick. Those hard thwacks that sounded so alien weeks ago are now a comforting clatter.

"I want to try! *Pleaseeeee.*" I turn and squint into the sun to find Parker standing over me.

"Try *what?*" I ask.

"The bowl!"

I'm so used to Nash being the daredevil that I don't automatically say no. But then my brain kicks in. "That doesn't sound like a good idea." Aunt Jackie has banned them from the bowl until they turn ten, but tons of kids their age and younger skate in it.

"Pleeeassssse." He pouts. "I'll wear my helmet and knee-pads and elbow pads. I'll even borrow Nash's pads and wear those too. Pleeeeeasseee."

I should listen to my aunt. Their mom. But it is my last day here, and Parker really wants to get in that bowl. Isn't indulging their want for adventure the least I can do for my cousins? Didn't I break Dad's surfing rules a thousand times as a kid and turn out fine? This summer has been tough on everyone in some way, and I have no idea when I'll be with my cousins and a skate bowl again. Maybe a little rule breaking is exactly what we all need to end our time together on a perfect, exhilarating note.

I turn to Lincoln and raise my eyebrows. He doesn't know about Aunt Jackie's rule. "What do you think?" I ask him.

"Oh, no," he says. "You're not putting any Sutter blood on my hands. This is your decision."

"How old was Austin when he started in the bowl?" I ask.

Lincoln glances up at Parker with a sly smile, sunlight reflecting off his glasses. "Younger than him."

═══

I've made a lot of bad decisions in my life, but today I discovered there's a difference between making a bad decision that only affects me (like eating an entire carton of ice cream before getting into the water) and a bad decision that affects others. A big difference.

After about thirty minutes of Parker learning to ride in the bowl, there was a sharp *crack* followed by the most gutwrenching scream I've ever heard. It was worse than when I found Nash in the pool. Time stopped as I rushed into the concrete pit. Parker was crying and screaming and clutching his arm, which was definitely at a weird angle. Then time sped up, and we were all at the hospital once again, only this time without Aunt Jackie. Dad met us there and kept her updated on the phone amid all the chaos—Parker crying in pain, me crying at Parker crying, Nash and Emery crying in laughter when Austin impersonated the doctor's squeaky, rubber duck voice.

By the time we get home, everyone is exhausted, especially Parker who is doped up on low-grade painkillers and wearing a green, pink, and blue striped cast from his shoulder to his wrist because he just couldn't choose a color.

Aunt Jackie holds back stubborn tears as she dotes on Parker, or at least dotes as much as one can in a wheelchair and straight cast. They're a matched pair, all bandaged up. She runs a hand through his hair and mumbles, "My poor baby. Why couldn't you be obsessed with chess?"

I glance around the room and only see people who need my help. Parker is in pain. Aunt Jackie is in pain for him. Nash is confused about how to help. Emery is silent and grim. In all of the rushing to the hospital, I didn't get a chance to ask how it went at the basketball courts, but the look on her face tells me it probably didn't go too well. As I take this all in, it hits me—I can't leave them worse off than they were at the start of summer.

"I'm not going," I mumble.

Dad, standing beside me, asks, "What did you say?"

"I said I'm not going," I repeat. "I'll stay here and fly home with you like we planned."

This time I say it loud enough for everyone to hear. Aunt Jackie whips her head in my direction. "Oh, no you're not."

"What?" I ask.

Oh, god. She's mad at me. I broke her rule. I let Parker get into the bowl. Her child got hurt, and it's my fault. Just like I was the one who wasn't watching Nash when he hurt himself in the pool. And I'm the one who still hasn't said anything about Emery and her friends.

Aunt Jackie wants me out of here before I damage them more.

"You're leaving tomorrow," she says.

I feel queasy. I wrap my arms around my waist and stare at the floor, trying to figure out how to apologize, when Aunt Jackie continues, "You've worked your ass—sorry kids, *butt*—off all summer taking care of this family, and you're not going to miss out on your festival because Parker went and broke his arm. Not happening. Tonight is the last night you're sleeping under this roof."

It takes a second for my brain to register that I'm not under attack. She's not mad at me. She's trying to say thank you. "Umm…" I say. "Okay."

"She's right," Dad agrees. "Parker will be fine without you. He has two very caring siblings to look after him, doesn't he?"

Nash and Emery nod.

"In fact, those two siblings were going to make ice cream for everyone, isn't that right?"

Nash and Emery nod again, this time with half smiles, which manages to ease my tight chest. They dash for the kitchen, where I hear cupboards slamming and silverware rattling. I settle down onto the couch next to Parker and push back his hair so that he can look up at me. "You sure *you* don't mind me leaving?" I ask.

"It's okay. As long as you promise to teach me to surf like you next summer." He looks really worried for a second as he glances back and forth between Aunt Jackie and me. "My arm will be better by then, right?"

We both laugh. "It'll be better in about a month, dude. But it's a deal. Next summer, it's you, me, and the ocean."

———

"Anise, will you come in here for a second?" Aunt Jackie calls from the guest room as I'm heading upstairs. It's past midnight, and after finally finishing packing, I rewarded myself with my third bowl of ice cream for the night.

"Yeah, of course." I pad into the dark room, which is only lit by the small reading light attached to Aunt Jackie's paperback book. "Do you need something?" I ask. She's gotten pretty independent during the day, but once she's out of the wheelchair and in bed, it's easier for us to get her a glass of water or Advil or whatever else she needs.

"No, no. I'm fine." She sets the book on the bed and pats the comforter. "Come sit for a second. I wanted to talk to you before you left."

"Um, okay." I sit on the edge of the bed instead of next to her. I've always been pretty comfortable around Aunt Jackie, but something about her tone makes me think I might not be comfortable with this particular conversation.

"I wanted to thank you."

"What?"

"Thank you for everything this summer. You did such a great job with the kids. It means a lot that it was you looking after them and not some stranger. I know…I know I'm not your mom, of course not, but I think of you as a daughter, and so I wanted to say thank you. I know three kids are a lot to take care of, and I never saw you flinch once."

"Oh," I say, throat suddenly tight. "You're welcome."

She takes my hand and squeezes it, her eyes warm. "I'm proud of you, Anise. I just wanted you to know I'm really proud of you."

Dad has told me he's proud of me a million times, but this feels different. In the dim light, Aunt Jackie's features are barely visible—I can't see the color of her eyes or hair. In the dark, she could almost be my mom telling me she's proud of me, which is even better than telling me she loves me— because it would mean she took the time to notice I've done something to be proud of.

FOURTEEN

MY ALARM GOES off at five in the morning. I quickly silence it, not wanting to wake Emery. I packed and said all of my good-byes last night so I wouldn't have to rouse my cousins when they could be in the throes of very important growth spurts. I ease out of bed and slip into my jean shorts. My legs prickle, protesting being out of the comforter's warmth. A quiet voice breaks the predawn silence. "Anise?"

Emery rolls over in bed. A slice of moon lights her face as her sleepy eyes focus on me.

"Hey," I whisper. "Go back to sleep."

But then I realize I never found out what happened at the courts yesterday because of Parker's accident. "Wait! Wait!" I say, more than a bit too loud. "What happened with your friends?"

After rubbing her face and exerting a few sleepy yawns, Emery relays the story in quick, hushed words. Apparently the reason Emery only found out about the last minute invite at the end of the weekend was because the other girls were purposefully trying to keep it a secret so they *wouldn't* hurt her feelings. And she wasn't *not* on the invite list—it was Charlie's mom who had insisted on thirteen friends to celebrate Charlie's thirteenth birthday.

"They felt really bad about it," Emery said, "Well, except for Ashley. But whatever."

I smile in the dark. "I'm glad you made up with your friends."

"Me too," she says.

Emery rolls over after that, pulling her blankets tight around her as her breathing grows even. Relief floods through me that it was all a misunderstanding. Hopefully my friends will accept me back into their fold as easily. More likely than not, I'm blowing my fears out of proportion like Emery did with hers.

I finish getting dressed and kiss the top of Emery's head before leaving the room, flashing back to when I'd spend hours on my back porch, holding a young Emery in my lap and brushing her soft hair. My eyes flicker across the dim room. At first, living in this house, I'd expected to have to tiptoe around the ghost of my mom. But this isn't the house of a person who always disappoints me—it's the home of people who always amaze me.

I head downstairs and past my luggage piled by the front

door. I find Dad in the kitchen with a cup of green tea in hand.

He grins at me. I give him a smile that breaks into a yawn. "Breakfast?" he asks.

My stomach says yes, and suddenly I have a craving for *supoesi*, a coconut cream and papaya soup served at Tess's family restaurant. But I'm still in Nebraska, and Dad doesn't have any papayas.

"Santa Cruz specialty omelet?" I ask instead.

"Good call. Coming right up."

Instead of sitting at the table, I join Dad at the counter, helping chop the sweet red peppers, jalapeños, celery, and squash. "You sure this is okay?" I ask him. "Me going away?"

He turns to me. "I'd be lying if I said I was completely comfortable with it. But let's think of it as a test run for the both of us. We won't be able to keep eyes on each other forever."

I want to ask *why not?* If I go to the University of Santa Cruz, I'll only have to stay in the dorms for the first year, and then I can spend the rest of college at home, on the beach, like it should be.

Why do so many people equate *growing up* with *leaving*?

I press back from the counter, leaving Dad to finish the omelets. The chances of them burning are high if I continue to participate once they hit the stove. One more reason to stay home forever—I'll never have to cook for myself.

I ease my phone out of my pocket and flip it back and forth in my hand. Lincoln will be here in less than half an hour, and then we'll spend the next two days road tripping across half the country, stopping midway to sleep at his friend Wendy's house. The thought of spending so much time with Lincoln is unnerving. I'm not sure what to expect—the best time of my life or catastrophe. So instead I focus on going home, but that only makes my nerves worse since my friends might be mad at me or, as doubtful as it is, my mom could be there.

I settle at the table while Dad finishes the omelets and sift through my faded tote bag, making sure I have everything I need for the trip. My fingers brush against my wallet, toiletries, a change of clothes, tampons, books, and then something small and smooth. My throat tightens as I pull the object out of the bag—the sea marble Eric gave me on my last night in Santa Cruz. I'd forgotten I'd slipped it in my bag. Just like that, memories rush back full and fast—his scent, his smile, the feel of his lips. In a few days I'll see him again, but so much has changed...

Will he ever give me a sea marble again?

Maybe I should text him saying I can't wait to see him and I'm sorry I was so out of touch, but then Dad is sitting down with our plates of food. "Here you go," he says. I fork out a large chunk of the omelet, but my stomach churns. "Anise," Dad says, looking at me with concern. "I know this isn't easy for you. But I think you'll look back and be glad you did it."

"This is kind of twisted, you know, the father persuading his seventeen-year-old daughter to drive cross-country with a very handsome boy?"

"Ah, so you think he's handsome."

"I'm not one to contest factual evidence."

"Do you think you guys will stay in touch after this summer?"

Why are parents so good at pinpointing the one thing you don't want to talk about? Though, to be fair, there are a few things I don't want to talk about right now.

I hug one arm to my waist, while my other hand toys with my fork, cutting the omelet into progressively smaller pieces. "I don't know," I mumble. Keeping Lincoln at arm's length has become harder these past few days, and voluntarily putting myself in a car with him for twenty-four hours isn't exactly going to make it any easier.

"Not everyone runs away," Dad says.

I look at him sharply. "I know that."

"Lincoln doesn't seem like the type to disappear."

"I know."

But after this summer, after falling off the grid, ignoring my friends, I can't help but think *Lincoln might not be the type to disappear, but what if I am?*

———

Twenty minutes later my phone beeps, announcing Lincoln's arrival. I text him back, telling him I'll be outside in a second. Dad and I head to the front door.

"Here." He pulls a small folded envelope from his back pocket and hands it to me.

"What's this?"

"A little emergency money...or, if there aren't any emergencies, a little 'have a great trip money.'"

"Thanks, Dad." I hug him. It lasts longer than usual and takes a bit of willpower to pull away.

"Drive safe and text updates. Hourly." He scratches his thick hair. "Actually, make that half hourly."

I nod in agreement. "Promise."

I turn to open the front door, and as I do, two figures hurdle down the stairs. "Slow down, Parker!" Dad and I warn at the same time.

"Is he going for a set of broken arms?" I mutter.

The boys get to the bottom of the landing and stare at me with agitated eyes. "You were going to leave without saying good-bye," Nash accuses.

"Yeah, not cool." Parker agrees.

Instead of pointing out that I *did* say good-bye last night, I say, "Very not cool of me. I agree." Then I bend down to hug both of them, being extra careful of Parker's broken arm.

It'll be strange to wake up tomorrow morning without these shaggy-haired nuisances trailing my every step. I've gotten used to having three shadows instead of just the one.

"We got you something," Nash says.

"Yeah, give it to her." Parker nudges him.

"Wait, I don't have it. You do!"

"No, I don't! You do!"

"No you—"

"Guys, seriously," another voice cuts in. Emery emerges at the top of the stairs, carrying a small, square package in hand. "I have it."

She trots down the stairs and passes the package to me. The boys chant, "Open it! Open it!"

I tear at the newspaper wrapping to find a CD labeled ANISE AND LINCOLN'S AWESOME ROAD TRIP MIX. The illustration features Lincoln and me rushing down the highway in his open-top Jeep. Most of the songs are road trip themed, like Halsey's "Drive," but halfway down the list I notice "No Night to Sleep," my favorite Motel/Hotel song.

"They helped pick out the music," Emery says.

"When you'd let us," Nash says in a dark tone.

"Oh," I say, my throat tight, and not in that I-just-woke-up-and-need-water kind of way or even in the Dad-put-too-much-jalapeño-in-the-omelet kind of way.

Parker and Nash stare up at me expectantly. Emery toys with the cotton ties of her pajama bottoms, but I know she's waiting for my reaction too.

"It's perfect. It's really, really perfect. Thank you guys."

"We'll miss you." Parker and Nash jump forward and hug me again.

"You will?" I ask, my voice muffled by their hair.

"Yeah," Emery says, and I catch her eye and a small smile. "We really will."

I stuff my luggage in the back of Lincoln's Jeep. He put all the windows and roof panels back on, probably so we don't get caught open-topped in a torrential downpour as we speed down the highway. I climb into the passenger seat and hand Lincoln the CD. "Does this mean we get to listen to something besides Bruce Springsteen?"

"Absolutely." He grins, dimple popping, and I think of the first time I saw that dimple and how it was attached to a cute stranger, and now only weeks later I'm driving halfway across the country with that same dimple. Lincoln inserts the CD. The Beatles' "The Long and Winding Road" plays.

"How appropriate," Lincoln says, then frowns. "Though it's more like the long and very straight road." He grabs a mug from the cup holder, takes a sip, then offers it to me. "Want some?" he asks.

"What is it?" I ask.

"Tea."

He hands it to me, and I take a sip. "Fuck, that's delicious." Even better than the green tea Dad made me this morning. "What is it?"

Lincoln smiles. "Remember our first adventure? The wild bergamot I grabbed?"

I take another sip and let the flavor wash through me. That first day at the river seems so long ago; it makes me realize how much I've settled into this new place. As Lincoln pulls out of the driveway, I lean my head against the cool window and stare at the houses we past. When I first arrived, they all looked like cookie-cutter homes, but now I can spot the differences in each one of them.

"You okay?" Lincoln asks.

"Just tired." I know I should be bubbling with enthusiasm, sneaking a kiss to Lincoln's smooth cheek, rambling on about all of the amazing things we're going to do at Surf Break, but I can't muster the enthusiasm. Because the thing is, as we pull out of the neighborhood and toward the highway, I can only think of Parker, Nash, Emery, Aunt Jackie, and Dad.

My thoughts keep going to my family.

Is it possible to leave a place without leaving anyone behind?

"Why don't you take a nap?" Lincoln suggests. "I'll wake you when I get bored. Or more likely, when I get hungry."

"Okay." I don't resist. I close my eyes, not really intending to sleep. But as the car rumbles over the textured pavement and the engine hums beneath us, I slowly drift off.

⎯⎯⎯

My body senses the car's deceleration, and I wake with bleary eyes, glancing at the time—it's almost eight in the morning. I shift in my seat. Lincoln says, "Driver needs some fueling. Also, look where we are."

I check the sign as we pull off the highway—Lincoln, Nebraska.

"Ah, an ego-pumping pit stop."

He grins. "Something like that. Do you mind if we eat in? Driving and eating with one arm—not exactly safe."

"Of course." I nod. "No problem."

Lincoln pulls into the lot of a chain diner. The early-morning air is muggy and still. My legs are already cramped after a couple of hours. I can't imagine how stiff I'll be in two days. My muscles demand motion, and I won't be getting much of it until we hit the Santa Cruz shores.

We head into the diner, where a few people in baseball caps and reading glasses and shirts with sequins sit over heavy plates of greasy breakfast food. We slide into the sticky seats of an open corner booth and peruse the thick, plastic-coated menus. Lincoln rambles about some story where he and his friends were chased out of a diner for coordinating a large-scale paper plane invasion. I try to nod and smile and say, "Mhmm," and "Oh, shit," at the appropriate points.

He quiets once breakfast arrives. We both ordered the special—steaming plates of waffles, hash browns, bacon, sausage, grits, eggs, and toast—enough food to feed an entire family. It's weird that Parker and Nash aren't here to pick at my food before I have a chance to get to it.

Despite my growling stomach, I barely make a dent in my breakfast. We pay the check and head back to the car. I'm fully aware that I'm soaking in my bad mood, yet I can't seem to turn it around. Lincoln must notice too because as we click in our seat belts, he turns to me, a set look in his dark eyes. "Do you want me to take you home?"

Home. I know he means Aunt Jackie's house.

Against all reason, I'm tempted to say yes.

Instead, I slump down in the seat and stay quiet.

Lincoln turns on the ignition and asks again, "Anise, do you want me to take you back to your aunt's house? I don't know why you're upset, and I'm really sorry you are—I really am—but I'm not going to drive twenty-four hours like this. If you don't want to go to Santa Cruz, we don't have to go. Just tell me now before we waste more gas."

His words are logical, though they feel harsh. But when I glance at his face, I only see hurt there. He probably thinks my bad mood has something to do with him, like I'm second-guessing spending so much time alone with him. I mean, let's be honest, Lincoln thinks highly enough of himself that he might assume he's the cause of many of my emotions.

"I just..." I fiddle with the seat belt strap. "I don't want to leave them."

"Your cousins?" Lincoln asks. I nod. His eyes soften as he leans toward me. "Anise, I know this might be hard to believe, but your cousins were fine before you arrived, and they'll survive now that you're gone."

Survive. I hate that word.

Survive. Get by. Scrape through.

I don't want my cousins to just *survive*.

Like survival has anything to do with happiness.

"Anise?" Lincoln asks. "You're doing that quiet thing again. Let's talk about it."

"God, you sound like my dad." I manage a small smile. "Look, I know they'll be fine without me, but…I don't want them to think I've abandoned them for something better. Like, *Hey, Parker, sorry you broke your arm, but I want to go surfing now, see ya!*"

"They're not going to think that," Lincoln says.

"How do you know?"

"Because you're not abandoning them. You're not their parent. You're their cousin, and you live halfway across the country. They understand that concept."

"I don't know…"

"Anise, I don't want to push you on this, but we have a long drive ahead of us. *I* have a long drive if we want to make it to Wendy's house tonight. I'm sorry you're worried about your cousins, but they'll be fine, and we'll have a great time in Santa Cruz. Just think of the pure joy of watching me eat it my first time surfing."

The thought does seem promising.

And the thing is, even if we turned back now, Dad and I would be flying back to California in a week. What's the difference between leaving my cousins now and leaving them then? It's the same thing, except in one scenario, I'll miss Surf Break and create more distance between me and my friends.

"Okay," I say. If I say it maybe I'll believe it. "You're right. Let's go."

"You don't sound convinced," he says.

"I am."

"No, you're not." He pauses. And then he turns off the car. "I have an idea."

"What are we doing?" I ask.

"Making sure you don't abandon the cousins you are definitely not abandoning. Now follow me."

I have no idea what Lincoln is planning, but given his past surprises, I figure he deserves the benefit of the doubt, so I open my car door and follow him into the humid parking lot. A small gas station and convenience store sits next to the diner where we just ate. I follow Lincoln inside. We weave through the aisles of the store, passing pork rinds and ibuprofen and playing cards.

"Here we go." Lincoln stops in front of a wire rack of postcards. He picks through the variety with agile fingers and then holds up two cards. "Pick one."

The words LINCOLN, NEBRASKA scrawl over both cards in heavy font, but one shows a map of the city and the other shows the capitol building. I pick the one with the map. Lincoln puts the other card back and then walks to the register.

"Excuse me," he asks the cashier, a small and balding man with more wrinkles than my shirts when I do the laundry. "Do you have a pen we can borrow?"

The man eyes Lincoln with suspicion but then hands over a blue ballpoint. Lincoln thanks him and turns to me. "Okay, turn around," he commands.

"Umm, what?"

"And bend over."

"Excuse me!"

Lincoln sighs. "Just a little. I'm going to lean on your back to write."

To be fair, various displays of candy and knickknacks cover any foreseeable counter space in the store.

"Fine." I turn and bend a bit at the waist.

"Wonderful." Lincoln presses the card against my back. "Now what would you like to tell your cousins about our trip so far?"

"Oh," I say, finally getting why Lincoln got a postcard. "Tell them...tell them that I miss them already and that I hope Parker is feeling better and that diner food really does taste better when you're on the road."

Then I think of the postcards my mom sends me and why I hate them so much.

"And then write my address and tell them they can write or text me whenever they want. Make sure to include that, okay?"

As I feed him that information, the slight pressure of Lincoln's writing tickles my back.

"Mhmm, okay. Yeah. Got it."

A few seconds later, the pressure relieves, and I straighten up.

Lincoln takes the card back to the front counter. "I'd like to purchase this and one stamp and..." He grabs a giant bag of beef jerky. "...and this."

I raise an eyebrow at him. "Dude, you literally just ate, like, twelve thousand calories."

The cashier rings up Lincoln and even says he'll send the postcard for us when the mailman comes. We thank him and head back to the car.

"Better?" Lincoln asks.

The air is still humid as hell, and I'm still miles from home—any home—but my entire body feels lighter. "Much better."

―――

When you spend twelve hours in a car with someone, you find out a lot about them. Here's what I've discovered about Lincoln:

1. When he was a kid he had a recurring nightmare of going to his mom and dad for help in the middle of the night and lifting the covers on their bed to find snakes.

2. He really was serious about making me listen to all eighteen Bruce Springsteen albums.

3. From ages five to seven his family got so tired of constantly packing up and moving into new houses that they decided to live in a really nice trailer for two years.

4. He knows Latin—but only for plant names.

It's almost eleven o'clock by the time we pull off the highway for Wendy's house. I guess the good thing about moving around a million times when you're a kid is that you have friends all over the country. What I don't understand is how he stays in touch with all of them. If I've started to lose contact with my friends after a couple months, wouldn't a couple years completely evaporate a relationship?

I'm a little uncomfortable about staying at a stranger's house. Okay, I'm a lot uncomfortable. I barely adjusted to Aunt Jackie's house. I know humans used to be nomads, but there must be a reason we evolved past that.

"You're going to love Wendy," Lincoln tells me for the tenth time. I'd be jealous if he hadn't spent the day kissing me every time we stopped for gas or food. "She's one of the coolest people I've ever met."

"Can't wait," I say, trying not to sound nervous. Maybe I'll love Wendy, but will Wendy love me? Over the summer, Lincoln's friends welcomed me, but I always felt a bit like a tagalong, accepted because Lincoln was accepted. I shouldn't worry. I'll know this person for less than twenty-four hours. It doesn't matter what she thinks of me.

Wendy lives in a suburban neighborhood that looks uncannily similar to Aunt Jackie's. For a second, I'm convinced we spent the last twelve hours driving in a circle on the highway, rather than heading directly west.

We pull up to one of the older-looking houses on the block. It's a one-story home with a flat yard of short, dry grass. The house is pitch-black except for a single light over the small front porch. Maybe we're at the wrong place, or maybe they forgot we were coming, or maybe Lincoln doesn't really have a friend in Utah and this has been one summer-length con to abduct and kill me.

Lincoln seems confident as he shuts off the engine. "Ready?" he asks.

It's a silly question. What could I possibly say?

No?

Let's sleep in the car.

Let's get an overpriced hotel room.

Let's keep driving.

Of course not. Instead I manage a nervous smile. "Sure thing."

Lincoln pops the trunk and we grab our bags. I take out my tote that I packed with the necessities. My duffel bag and old suitcase, stuffed to the brim with random items I collected over summer, like my helmet and skateboard and plush rhino from Ashfall, are too bulky and stay in the car. As we walk toward the front door, it opens, and a girl rushes out. Before I have a chance to register what's happening, she sprints across the yard and leaps, arms opened, at Lincoln, slamming into him with a hug that almost topples his tall frame; this is a particularly impressive feat since the girl, presumably Wendy, can't be more than five feet.

She has a chopped, pixie haircut. Her pink-striped pajama bottoms and blue cotton T-shirt hang loosely over her small frame. After hugging Lincoln for another second, she releases him and then punches him on the arm. "I cannot believe you waited this long to visit!"

Lincoln holds his arms in the air in submission. "I know, I know, I'm the absolute worst, as you've told me thirty-six and a half times, but it's not like you've visited either."

"*I* don't have a car." At this point, she turns to me, and before I have a chance to say anything, she hugs me too. "Hi! Sorry for being rude, I'm Wendy! Welcome! Lincoln's told me so much about you!"

"He has?" I ask.

"I have?" Lincoln asks.

Wendy steps back and rolls her eyes. "Okay, not exactly. But it's the polite thing to say when you meet someone's girl-friend, right?"

My skin flushes. "Umm, not his girlfriend," I mutter. I expect Lincoln to agree, but he just stands there with an unusually uncomfortable expression.

"Oh, right. Sorry." Wendy says. She rocks back and forth on her feet. "Anyway, let's get inside. It's muggy out here. Sticky, gross! Um, we just have to be extra quiet. My parents go to sleep at, like, six because they wake up at the crack of dawn. They own a bakery and, as my dad says, *the pastries won't bake themselves.*"

We follow Wendy inside the house. Lincoln places his hand on my lower back for a moment. I lean into the touch, com-forted. I'm in a new place, but Lincoln is still right behind me. The house is dark, lit only by small plug-in night-lights and the glow of the moon through the windows. It's quiet too. For a moment I think I've plunged straight into one of those horror movies Eric loves so much. But thinking about Eric starts to feel like a horror movie in itself, so I push away the thought. The closer I get to home, the more daunting home feels. I should be thrilled to get there—it's all I've wanted since leaving in the first place—but each mile we get closer to the coast, my nerves increase.

Wendy's room reminds me of my own. Not because of the posters of shirtless teen heartthrobs or the stacked shelves of fashion magazines or the many stuffed animals, but because it looks so lived in. I bet this room hasn't been cleaned out since Wendy was born. It makes me yearn for my own drawers, stuffed with years of junk, walls plastered with posters I've outgrown but still haven't taken down, Tess's worn quilt spread neatly on my bed.

"Feel free to sit." Wendy jumps on, grabs a stuffed animal, and hugs it in her lap. I hesitate for a second, but it's a queen-size mattress, and there's plenty of room for all three of us. Lincoln climbs on, leaning against the far wall, and I follow, perching on the edge beside him.

Are we going to be sleeping here too? Three pigs in a blanket?

"Sooooo…" Wendy says. She tosses the stuffed animal aside, pulls out a ball of bright yellow yarn from her bedside table, and starts knitting. "How was the drive? Get any speeding tickets? Rob any banks?"

Lincoln grins. "Much less eventful than that. It's easy to follow the law without your influence."

I raise my eyebrows. Not to judge a book by its fluffy pink color, but with all the boy band posters, stuffed animals, and knitting, I wouldn't have counted Wendy as a rule breaker.

Lincoln glances at me. "Wendy here is quite the rebel."

"Really?"

Wendy nods in confirmation. "It's true. I am. Lincoln lived here during the eighth grade, and I'm pretty sure I was in detention half that time."

"For what?" I ask. I almost never break the rules. Detention equals more time at school, which equals less time surfing.

"Oh, you know, the usual." She waves her hand in the air. "Talking back to teachers, being late to class, freeing the mice in science lab, leading a strike on the mystery meatloaf in the cafeteria, impersonating a teacher for a whole period, you know, same old, same old."

I stare at her open-mouthed, and she and Lincoln break out laughing. Wendy smiles. "Okay, maybe not the usual." Her smile widens in excitement. She sits up, putting her knitting to the side. "That reminds me! I didn't tell you about the senior prank we pulled! Dear god it was epic. Six months of masterminding. Hardest plan I've ever worked on in my life…"

As Wendy tells us about her prank in vivid detail, I become more comfortable in the warm room. I crawl further onto the bed, leaning against the wall with Lincoln, our shoulders pressed together, fingers idly touching. As Wendy talks about water guns and rigged alarms and farm animals, my exhaustion hits in that satisfying cozy way. I lean against Lincoln's shoulder and fall into an easy sleep.

FIFTEEN

I WAKE TO the clanging of pots and pans and possibly the most delicious scent that's ever existed. The room is dim with only a dusting of dawn light. I don't know if I've ever been so flat out exhausted, but that scent entreats me to pry open my eyes. I'm exactly where I fell asleep on Wendy's bed. Lincoln is on a trundle bed on the floor. And Wendy herself is nowhere in sight.

"Lincoln," I mumble, my voice thick with sleep. "What's going on? What time is it?"

He rolls over in bed. I can barely see his shadow in the dark room, but I can tell he's looking in my direction. "What?" he mumbles in sleepy confusion. Then he sits up and says, "Oh my god. Yes. Yes. Yes!"

"Umm...what?" I ask.

Lincoln launches himself up from the trundle bed to where I'm resting in a pile of warm blankets. His face is so close to mine I think he's going to kiss me, which normally I wouldn't mind, but I probably have middle-of-the-night breath, which isn't exactly attractive. But he doesn't kiss me, he just says, "Miller Breakfast!"

"What?"

He tugs my arm, dragging my sleep-heavy limbs out of bed. "Come on. Get ready for the best experience your stomach has ever had."

"Wait, what time is it?" I'm still in my clothes from yesterday, so I slip my phone out of the pocket of my jean shorts. It's four in the morning. Who eats breakfast at four in the morning?

Lincoln guides me through dark hallways he seems familiar with. A flood of light comes from the same direction as that heavenly scent. We step into the kitchen. It's older like mine in Santa Cruz but equipped with dozens more pots, pans, and appliances, which is saying something considering Dad's rather large collection. Wendy is at the stove, along with her parents. They're both fully dressed like it's the middle of the day, not the middle of the night. Music plays from a radio. I think it's a Temptations song. Wendy and her parents sing along, occasionally pounding spatulas and whisks to the beat, reminding me of Tess's family in their restaurant, singing along with the radio at top volume while prepping dishes for the day.

"Hey guys!" Lincoln yells over the music.

Wendy whips around and smiles. "Hey! Figured I'd let the bacon wake you up."

"Mission accomplished," I say, forgetting my shyness and stepping close to the sizzling skillets. "That smells amazing."

In addition to bacon, I spy pans of eggs, sausage, and hash browns. There are also trays in the oven, and an assortment of pastries on the counter. Wendy's mom greets us. She's the same height as Wendy, but has long hair almost down to her waist. It's tied back in a braid, probably so one of the many burners doesn't set it on fire, and a hot pink streak threads through it.

She hugs Lincoln and then me. "Please, call me Lisa. So nice to meet you."

I smile back but have trouble saying anything but, "You too."

This is all a bit overwhelming, especially since part of my brain is still asleep. Wendy's dad, white and almost as short as Lisa, also turns from the stove and introduces himself as Sam. Then he says, "Please, please sit down."

"You sure we can't help?" Lincoln asks.

Everyone bursts out laughing. "I think not," Lisa says. "Remember when we let you cook the bacon last time? You ate it all before it made its way to a plate."

Lincoln has the decency to look a bit sheepish. "I was hungry. Fourteen and growing."

"Who's to say you're not still growing?" Sam asks.

Lincoln already towers over everyone in the kitchen. "Sit, sit!" Sam repeats, ushering us toward the kitchen table.

I settle into one of the wooden chairs. They all have soft seat cushions in different fabrics, like scraps bought from the bargain bin at a craft store. I like the look. It feels homey. Lincoln takes my hand under the table and idly rubs his thumb against my skin. Here I am, half-asleep, in the middle of who knows where, salivating over a strange family's breakfast, and through all of that, I'm suddenly turned on. Like, what is that even?

I keep my eyes on the action in the kitchen, where the entire family is too busy cooking to pay attention to us, but that does nothing to deter Lincoln. He leans forward and nuzzles his head into the crook of my neck, planting half a dozen soft kisses on the sensitive skin. *Middle-of-the-night breath, Middle-of-the-night breath*, I chant to myself. But that doesn't keep me from kissing him, a kiss that lasts half a second but keeps my lips buzzing long after.

"Hungry?" he asks, smiling deviously.

My cheeks flame. "Shut up." I turn back toward the kitchen and catch Wendy watching us. She winks, then goes back to cooking. I'm embarrassed. I hate PDA. And PDA in someone else's kitchen while they're cooking you breakfast is worse than average.

Ten minutes later, we're all sitting around the kitchen table digging in. This seriously puts yesterday's diner breakfast to shame. Bacon, turkey bacon, sausage, veggie sausage, eggs (fried, over easy, and scrambled), roasted potatoes, hash browns, veggie casserole, bagels, biscuits, muffins, whole grain toast, scones, and so on.

I pile my plate with a little of everything. My stomach growls loudly since I was barely able to eat yesterday. I let everything combine so that every forkful is a mix of the feast. "Thank you for doing this for us," I say between bites. "Seriously this is above and beyond."

Everyone stares at me for a long, silent second—and then they break into laughter. Why does this keep happening to me? "This is like a regular occurrence," Wendy says. "Since my parents work such weird hours, we try to do a giant breakfast at least once a month. You know. Bonding time and all."

Lisa leans over and ruffles Wendy's chopped hair. "Won't be the same without you next year, sweetie," she says.

"Next year?" I ask.

"Wendy's going to school in Miami."

"Whoa," I say. "Isn't that scary to go so far away?"

"Not really. I mean, it's college, right? Isn't moving away half the point?" Wendy forks a giant glob of eggs into her mouth.

No. "I guess…"

"You're a senior this year, right? Where are you applying?" Wendy asks.

I shrug. "Probably just a safety school and USC—University of Santa Cruz. It's a pretty good school and all."

The conversation shifts, but despite my deflections, it keeps coming back to me. I know they're trying to be nice, but it makes me uncomfortable to talk about myself.

"Will your mom be in Santa Cruz?" Sam asks after I tell him about Surf Break. "I know you mentioned your dad is still in Nebraska."

I pause midbite. Lincoln takes my hand under the table and squeezes it once.

"I don't know. It's...complicated," I say.

"You don't know?" Lisa asks, concerned.

Lincoln cuts in, "Mr. Miller—Sam—you have to tell me what you put in these eggs. Take pity on me, please."

Sam smiles and shakes his head. "That's a trade secret," he says but then proceeds to launch into a lengthy recipe anyway. I quietly zone out of the conversation. I know I should be better at answering questions about my mom by now, but it's still so difficult. There's no easy way to say my mom likes to run away for months, sometimes years at a time, without a word to anyone and then show up on our doorstep like everything is fine.

Once I told someone she was dead because it seemed easier.

Lincoln's phone beeps. He pulls it out of his pocket. "Crap. That's the alarm. We should get going soon if we want to make it to Santa Cruz at a decent hour."

"It's already six?" I ask.

We spent two hours eating and talking?

"We should get going too," Lisa says. "We're already more than an hour late, but you know, special occasion and all."

Lincoln and I stand and start to clear the table, but Wendy shoos us away. "Guests don't clean," she says, "especially guests who are here for less than twelve hours."

"Speaking of which, where'd you sleep last night?" Lincoln asks.

Wendy smiles covertly, shrugs her shoulders, and mumbles something about *pranksters never sleep*. I think her parents pretend not to hear her.

Lincoln and I hurry to get ready. There's only one bathroom, so we skip showers and quickly brush our teeth and wash our faces. I pull out fresh clothes from my tote—athletic shorts, underwear, and a soft V-neck shirt—and put them on. Lincoln changes after me, and when he walks out of the bathroom, I can't keep my mouth from gaping.

"Umm…no," I say.

Lincoln grins widely. "Umm…yes."

He's wearing his Hawaiian print shirt.

"I'm just trying to get into the California spirit," he says.

I shake my head, but don't say anything else. There's no way I'm going to let him wear that when he meets my friends.

"Man, I wish I could come with you guys," Wendy says as we walk back outside, the early morning sun already heating the air. Even though I've known her less than twelve hours, I wish she could come too. I really like her. Plus, she'd give Lincoln company for part of the drive back to Nebraska.

"Umm…do you want to come?" I ask.

Lincoln and Wendy both look shocked by the invitation.

Maybe I need to make an effort to be nicer.

Okay, I *definitely* need to make an effort to be nicer.

"There's plenty of room at my house. You're totally welcome."

Wendy lets out a big sigh, actually more of a grunt. "I totally wish that I could, but I'm leaving for Miami in T minus five days, and if you didn't notice last night, I'm kind of the opposite of packed." Wendy gives me a tight hug and then does the same to Lincoln, telling him, "You know, it wouldn't be the worst thing ever if you came and visited me next year in Florida."

Lincoln laughs. "Considering that drive is about twice as long as this one, I don't know if that's going to happen any time soon."

"You could always fly."

Lincoln shifts uncomfortably. I stare at him and then Wendy and then back to him. "Oh my god," I say. "You're scared of flying! Lincoln Puk is actually scared of something!"

"Okay, okay. So I'm scared of flying. What's the big deal? Lots of people are scared of flying."

"So you'll fling yourself off of a ten-foot ramp, but you won't get in an airplane?"

"An airplane goes a lot higher than ten feet."

"An airplane also crashes infinitely less often than you do."

"I do not crash often."

"Really?"

"Really."

"Woah, okay you guys," Wendy says. "Maybe you should continue this conversation on the road. In private. Where I don't have to listen to it. Because it's really annoying."

"You're right," Lincoln says. "We really do need to get going."

"Yeah, time sure is *flying* by," I say.

Lincoln shoves me in the arm. I shove him back. And then we grin at each other.

"You guys sicken me," Wendy says. She gives us hugs again. Lincoln and I climb into the car as Wendy calls after us, "Text me when you get there so I know you're alive and shit!"

"Will do!" Lincoln says.

As we start to pull away from her house, Wendy stands in the yard, waving. I would have enjoyed staying at her house longer and hanging out. I guess new places aren't all so bad.

———

"Do you want me to drive for a bit?" I ask. We've only been on the road an hour, but I've spent most of that hour napping. I figure Lincoln deserves some sleep too, and it'd probably be safer for both of us if he didn't get that sleep behind the wheel.

"Isn't that…how do I say this…illegal?" Lincoln asks.

"As your dear friend Wendy would say, it's only illegal if you get caught."

The car ahead of us keeps slowing down, so Lincoln shifts

his grip to the left side of the wheel, bracing his hand against it, while flicking the turn signal with his fingers. I've watched him do this dozens of times now, the ease of the movement showing impressive dexterity.

"I'll tell you what," Lincoln says. "Instead of driving, why don't you keep me awake by telling me a story?"

"A story?" I ask. "What about music instead?"

"I like your sunshiny voice better."

I roll my eyes but smile. "I can't think of a story. I'm not the *creative type*. Too bad Parker isn't here." Just saying his name makes me miss him. And Nash. And Emery. If they were in the back of this car right now, no one would *ever* have to worry about falling asleep.

"So read me something," Lincoln says.

I reach into my tote and pull out one of my Detective Dana novels. It's the third in the series, my personal favorite. I've read it at least five times. "*The Zebra Zodiac*," I read the title. Then I pause.

"Keep going," Lincoln says.

I open the book. The pages are so well-worn that I can fold the spine open from page one. "The call came at five in the morning," I begin. "Detective Dana rolled over in bed, her left arm sore from sleeping with it tucked under her head, and picked up the receiver. 'Hello. This is Detective Dana. What did you say? A dead zebra on the subway? *Again?*'"

I read thirty pages. Thirty *slow* pages because reading to Lincoln is frustrating. Every page or so he interrupts with a question, and every page or so I remind him that it's a *mystery* novel, and the whole point of reading a *mystery* novel is to have your questions answered at the end.

"But *you* already know what happens," Lincoln says. "So why can't you tell me?"

"Because!" I say. "I'm not going to ruin the book."

"It won't ruin the book."

"How could solving the mystery for you thirty pages in not ruin the book?"

"Because then I get to mock Detective Dana every time she takes a wrong turn."

"You're infuriating."

"You're pretty."

"Ugh!"

"Okay," Lincoln says. "No more reading. Why don't you tell me about your friends?"

My friends. My friends who I'm about to see in less than a day. My friends who may or may not currently hate me.

My throat feels tight. "I've told you about my friends."

"Not really. You've told me their names, but tell me what they're like."

I hesitate. Of course I want to tell Lincoln about my friends, but at the same time, thinking about them makes me shift uncomfortably in my seat. I hope I didn't mess up too much. I missed a few phone calls and texts, but lifelong friendships don't end over that, right? So I start talking, working through the tightness in my throat and the uneasiness in my stomach until the words slip out like I'm reading them from the pages *The Zebra Zodiac*.

I begin with Tess, of course. I ramble about our friendship for a solid half hour, from a description of our never-ending sleepovers during the summer between third and fourth grade to that time we ordered one of everything from the Shak, spending two months of allowance each on our meal. Then I dive into describing the rest of my friends—Cassie and her excitement about joining the navy. Spinner and the time we tried to scoop little fish from a shoal and sell them to tourists. Eric and—

Oh. Should I tell Lincoln about Eric? Tell Lincoln there's this guy who happens to be one of my best friends who I kissed less than twelve hours before leaving for Nebraska? Tell him this guy might be mad at me for ignoring him all summer, which means he might no longer be one of my best friends? Tell him—

"Food?" Lincoln asks.

He saves me from my internal tailspin. I nod in gratitude. We have hours left to drive. I can tell Lincoln about Eric later, once I've found the right words. "Definitely food."

All the talking dried out my throat. The sun is high, and my stomach is grumbling.

We are smack dab in the middle of nowhere without any of those helpful highway signs that tell us which town has what food, so we get off at a random exit and hope for the best. At first, our attempt seems like a fail. We drive past two miles of empty land, minus a storage complex and what looks like a dilapidated airplane hangar, which reminds me of Ashfall. But then, as we're about to give up and turn to go back to the highway, I shout, "Look there!"

A log cabin style restaurant sits off in the distance. A single white sign with black lettering reads, "Cook House." A few cars arc in the parking lot, the only evidence that the place hasn't been closed for decades.

Lincoln pulls in, tires bumping over the gravel. The windows of Cook House are old and dusty, so we can't really see the inside. As we get out of the car, I have second thoughts. What if this is some kind of mafia drop bar like in Detective Dana's *Bloody Money?* Or worse, what if it's just a local restaurant filled with unfriendly locals? We should probably get back on the highway and find something familiar, like a McDonald's or Subway.

Lincoln looks at me and holds out his hand. I hesitate, then take it. He threads his fingers through mine. He keeps doing that. Like he has an internal alert system that says, *Anise is freaking out. Touch her and she'll feel better.* I glance up at him, and he smiles. "Come on," he says. "I'm level eighty hungry."

Inside, the first thing that hits me is the sound of three squeaking overhead fans. Otherwise, the restaurant is silent. That's probably because the handful of customers are all staring at us. I squint in the dim interior. The two small booths by the door are already occupied, and a heavyset woman sits at the front counter.

I want to tug Lincoln by the back of his shirt and hit the highway. Before I can do so, Lincoln swaggers over to the counter like he's been coming here every day since he was born and plops down onto one of the wooden stools. He turns to the woman next to him, extends his hand, and says, "Hey there, I'm Lincoln. What's good to eat?"

If this were Detective Dana's *Wicked Feast*, the lady would grin maliciously, say *you*, and then proceed to murder and cannibalize us. But this isn't a novel. This is the middle of nowhere, and the woman smiles and says, "Hi there, Lincoln. I'm Marybeth. Y'all passing through?"

I approach the counter. Clearly Lincoln is here to stay and eat. I sit next to him, grateful that his bulk hides most of me. But then Lincoln pulls out his stool so we're both sitting more side by side, and I'm very much in view of Marybeth. He wraps an arm around me and pulls me close. "Sure are," Lincoln says. "On the way to Cal-i-for-nia from good ole Nebraska."

I have no idea why he's putting on this ridiculous accent. But it does make this unfamiliar place a little less daunting and a lot more ridiculous.

"Ah, I miss the traveling days myself. Used to be a bit of a vagabond after growing up in the South. Up and down the East Coast, then shot straight out west, dillydallying all over these here states for a decade or so."

The story reminds me so much of my mom that I bite my lip and look away. I wonder if my mom is also sitting in some diner in the middle of nowhere, telling a pair of teenagers her own wild vagabond tales. I hate that it's easier to imagine that than imagine her sitting on our own living room couch, telling me about her most recent adventures.

"Really?" Lincoln asks and leans forward in interest. As he does, the waitress, a squat woman wearing what looks like a hand-stitched uniform, enters from the kitchen.

"Know what you want?" she asks.

I'm about to ask for a menu when Marybeth interjects. "They'll take two Tuesday specials, extra slaw on the side, fizzy lemonade, and a slice of pecan and boysenberry pie."

I'm curious what the Tuesday special is and why you're allowed to order it on a Thursday, but my mouth stays shut. "Sounds great," Lincoln says. "And if you don't mind putting a bit of a hurry on it, we'd appreciate it. We need to get ourselves to that big ole green state by tonight."

The waitress nods without interest and moves away. "Why you in a rush?" Marybeth asks. "Wandering the country ain't fun when you can't do any wandering."

"Well," Lincoln says. "This beautiful gal of mine has an engagement she needs to make. I keep telling her to stop and smell the roses, but you know how feisty gals can be."

Marybeth laughs. "Oh, that I do. The men I've tucked under my thumb." Marybeth gives us a wink, then goes on for five minutes about a string of interesting men in her life. Lincoln starts to ask her where exactly one guy had that dolphin tattoo when Marybeth says, "Ooh! Here comes the food!"

The waitress emerges from the kitchen with two steaming

plates of Tuesday Special. As the plates get closer, I recognize the fare—meatloaf, mash potatoes and gravy, and corn soufflé. I wonder if the meatloaf has been sitting around since Tuesday, but I decide that's still relatively fresh considering the expectations I came in with. Marybeth stares at us expectantly, so I grab a fork and dig in.

The flavors hit me hard and fast. Sweet and spicy and tangy all at the same time. The whole spice rack must have gone into this one dish. I take another bite and then another and then spear some of the corn soufflé and scoop up some of the potatoes and finally try a bite of crunchy slaw. It's all equally delicious.

I turn to Lincoln. He's shoveling in food at the same pace as me. "Looks like we picked the right exit," I say.

Mouth half-full, he grins and says, "Looks like it."

"Now Marybeth," I say, feeling more comfortable with a steaming plate of food in front of me. "I'm sure you have some more interesting stories to tell."

She winks at me. "Oh, where to begin?"

SIXTEEN

BY THE TIME we're done with our lunch (which was the opposite of a quick pit stop), we've heard Marybeth's full life story and exchanged numbers and promised to keep in touch. "Let me know if you're ever in Santa Cruz!" I tell her.

"I'll definitely do that," Marybeth says. Before we leave, she asks the waitress to pack us two extra slices of pie for the road. As we go to pay, she shoos away our money. I try to insist, but she says, "You youngins in love traveling the country need to save every penny you can. Besides it's my treat to treat people."

We finally relent, grab our to-go bags, and head back out to the warm parking lot. I know we're running behind schedule and will probably get to Santa Cruz late, but it doesn't really matter. I'll sacrifice an hour of waves for the Tuesday Special any day of the week.

It's hard not to doze after a meal that heavy, but Lincoln

and I play marry, bury, screw, which might be weird to play with someone who's lips have been on yours on a regular basis for the past few weeks, but coming up with combinations like the Loch Ness Monster, Springsteen circa *Born to Run*, and the tooth fairy makes it so weird it's not weird at all. For the record, I would marry Springsteen circa *Born to Run*, bury the tooth fairy, and screw the Loch Ness Monster, and Lincoln would marry the Loch Ness Monster, also bury the tooth fairy, and screw Springsteen circa *Born to Run*, which neither of us found the least bit surprising.

We play the game until we feel a little delirious and a little too familiar with each other's obscure predilections, then turn on the stereo and listen to Emery's road trip CD on repeat, at which point I discover another rare Lincoln flaw—he can't sing. Like at all.

But that sure as hell doesn't keep him from doing it.

An out-of-pitch person belting out Rihanna's "Shut Up and Drive" at the top of his lungs is quite the experience, especially when it takes place in a moving vehicle in which, for all intents and purposes, you are trapped.

"Make it stop," I moan as the song switches to "500 Miles," and Lincoln starts singing with even more enthusiasm.

"Never." He grins. And sings. And grins. And sings. "I'm the driver, and the driver gets to make all the rules, and this driver says I'm allowed to sing as much as I want even if Anise is staring at me like she's devising the five best ways to murder me and get away with the crime."

"Honestly, going to jail would be worth it at this point," I mutter.

Lincoln laughs. "Oh you're just as sweet as honey."

I laugh back. But really. I do need a break from this car. With the exception of a quick fuel and bathroom break, we've been driving for five hours straight since lunch. My cramped legs protest. I need a surfboard or a skateboard or at least a little walking to stretch them out. I glance out the window at the signs whipping past and spot one that says "Reno: 12 miles."

Reno.

My mom's postcard. The bar.

I close my eyes and try to visualize the name. I think it was called Kelsey's or something. "Let's get off here."

Lincoln furrows his brow. "Really? Not sure we can do much gambling until we're twenty-one."

"Let's just look around. I need to stretch my legs." I pull out my phone and Google "Kelsey bar Reno." Sure enough the bar pops up. I look up directions. "Actually I have somewhere specific in mind. Take a right off the exit."

"Have you been here before?" Lincoln asks even though he knows very well that I've never been anywhere but California and Nebraska and now a string of highway between the two.

"I've just heard of this bar. It's famous or whatever."

"A bar? You do realize I'm only eighteen, and you're still shy of that. You packing fake IDs and didn't inform me?"

Actually I do have a fake ID back in Santa Cruz. I used it once to buy beer for one of our bonfires, and even though I didn't get caught, I still had a near heart attack using it. From that point on, I always let Tess buy our booze since the possibility of getting arrested doesn't seem to faze her.

"It'll be fine," I say. "I think they serve food there too. They probably only ID you if you want to drink."

I continue to give Lincoln directions, and he follows them quietly for a few minutes. But I know that quiet won't last. Eventually he asks, "Anise, how have you heard of a bar in Reno?"

I don't answer. Maybe if I just keep giving directions instead, he'll let it go.

"Anise?"

"Take a right after the next light."

"Anise? I do have the power to get back on the highway if you don't answer me."

Lincoln knows the basics about my mom—terrible mother, runaway, abandoner. But he doesn't know exactly how much all of that has eaten away at me over the years.

Lincoln doesn't have his birth mom either, but it's different. For whatever reasons, she left his life for good. He's not haunted by the possibility that she'll crash back into his world at any moment…or that she'll never crash into his world again. He might not understand this magnetic pull I'm feeling toward this place solely because she might be there, or at least was once there.

My instinct is to lie, like how I always hide thoughts of my mom from my friends. But no lie comes. And even if one did, would I really tell it to Lincoln? Lincoln who has been nothing but honest with me since the day we met and he called my eyes seaweed green.

I stare out the window. "My mom sent me a postcard from there earlier this summer, so I...you know..."

I'm waiting for the onslaught of questions. *Why do you care? Why does it matter? What's the point? What do you expect to find?*

An onslaught of all the questions I'm asking myself.

But all he says is, "Okay." And then. "A right up here, yeah?"

My throat feels even tighter than my chest. I manage to say, "Yeah."

It's barely six in the evening, but the Reno strip is already lit up. Huge billboards, flashing lights, an illuminated sign arching over the street that reads, "The Biggest Little City in the World." It's like a miniature version of Vegas—or what I assume Vegas looks like from the movies. Casinos and clubs line the roads. We pass a 24/7 marriage chapel, and Lincoln turns to me and asks, "Want to get married?"

"I'm going to have to take a pass on that," I say, but I wonder what it'd be like to marry Lincoln. I envision us twenty years down the road, raising a brood of surfers, the fifth generation in my Santa Cruz house. But then that image blurs and sparks. Because Lincoln isn't the type to settle in Santa Cruz. He's the type to take twenty-four-hour road trips halfway across the country because it sounds like a fun idea. The type to hike the PCT for months. The type to fly—okay sail—around the world.

Lincoln has grown up on the road. I would never ask him to go sedentary for me.

"Where next?" Lincoln asks.

I continue to direct him, past the main strip and down a few side streets to an alarmingly darker and more abandoned side of Reno. The lights here flicker accidentally instead of on purpose, and no crowds of tourists snap pictures. My stomach clenches uneasily.

"There it is!" Lincoln lurches the car to the right and pulls into a gravel drive-thru. A wooden sign with the word "Parking" in red paint directs us toward an unpaved parking lot. The lot is surprisingly full considering the early hour. But then again, this seems like a city that appreciates a bar at all times of day.

I bite my lip as I watch a man and a woman step inside, leaving their large motorcycles in the lot. Both of them are dressed in jeans and black leather. Both of them look at least twice my age and twice my size. "Maybe this was a bad idea," I say.

Not just a bad idea. A pointless idea.

What am I trying to achieve anyway?

Do I think I'll find my mother sitting at one of the barstools, sipping on a piña colada, twirling the toothpick umbrella? Do I think she wrote that postcard and never left? Just sat and sipped one fruity drink after another? This isn't a Detective Dana novel. She didn't leave me clues. She doesn't want to be found.

For all I know she's in Santa Cruz. Or on the East Coast. Or in another country entirely.

For all I know she hasn't thought of me once since she wrote that fucking postcard. "Let's go back to the highway," I tell Lincoln.

"Oh no," he says. "That sign there clearly states 'country's best burger and fries for five dollars.' We're not going to pass up an opportunity like that."

I know if I really wanted him to, he'd turn the car around. But at this point, we're here, *right here*, and later I'll be mad at myself if I don't at least look inside.

"Fine," I say. "Let's go."

⸻

No bouncer checks ID or bans us from coming in. Neon beer signs pierce the dim interior, creating an almost alien atmosphere of shadowed faces and disjointed movements. I search for a slim figure with wild hair—but there are about a dozen people in the bar, and in less than a minute, I know none of them are my mom.

I shouldn't be surprised. It's been months since that postcard, and since when has my mom ever stuck around anywhere for that long? I hate the bitter disappointment washing through me because it says I was actually holding on to some kind of twisted hope.

"Come on." Lincoln tugs on my hand. "Seats by the bar."

I want to leave. This was a terrible idea. But it was my idea, and Lincoln might as well get his hamburger. We sit down on two tall, vinyl stools, the kind that spin round and round. Tess would love it here. She'd twirl in her seat and make friends with the guy with the shaved head and Mickey Mouse tattoo in the corner slinging back shots.

A bartender comes over to us. Her hair is teased with hairspray, her face bare of makeup, save dark red lipstick. She looks like she's been working here as long as I've been alive.

"Get out." She points a thumb toward the exit.

"We just want some grub," Lincoln says. "Heard you guys have great burgers. And we'll sit right here at the bar where you can keep an eye on us."

The bartender stares at us skeptically. "Who the hell says I want to keep an eye on you?"

Lincoln digs into his pocket and pulls out a twenty. "Two burgers, two fries, two cokes, and then we're gone."

I don't know why the hell he's pushing so hard to stay. Lord knows we could get back to the main drive of Reno and eat at a dozen different places. But the bartender relents, takes the money, and says, "You're not getting any change back."

She walks the length of the bar to a small window opening to what must be the kitchen. "Two burgers and fries!" she shouts.

As she walks back to fill the order of someone at the bar, she catches my eye and mouths, "One hour."

One hour is more than enough time for me. Hopefully the burgers will be out soon, and we can scarf them in a couple of minutes. Next to me Lincoln drums his fingers on the wooden bar to the beat of "American Girl" playing from the Jukebox. I feel him watching me, but I focus on his fingers tapping out the bum-bap-bap of the song.

A few seconds later, the bartender slides two Cokes across the counter. They come in chilled beer steins with skinny cocktail straws. I take my drink and sip. Maybe it's the chilled glass, but it's the best Coke I've ever had. The sugar revives me, speeding through my system. I take a sip, and then another, and then I turn to Lincoln. "How much driving time do we have left?"

"Oh, I'd say about three hours give or take. Should get in around ten."

Home in three hours. Back to my room with the tangled surfing medals on the wall and Tess's quilt on the bed. Back to my kitchen with the cracked tile floor and bay window. Back to the ocean.

My ocean.

"Anise?" Lincoln asks.

"Hmm?" I respond as I take another sip of Coke.

"Maybe you should ask someone if they know your mom."

I thought we'd somehow miraculously moved on from that topic. I wish he wouldn't do that, bring her up, especially after knowing me for so short of a time. But maybe that's why he can do it—because anyone who's known me all my life knows *never* to bring up my mom.

The Coke doesn't taste good anymore. It's sickly sweet. I feel nauseous as the scent of grilling hamburgers wafts from the kitchen. Coming here was enough. Looking was enough. There's no need to drag this out.

"There's no point," I say.

"Sure there is," Lincoln insists. "Maybe they'll know where she is."

"So? So I'll just—" My thoughts have trouble forming. "I'll just find out where she is and what? Chase her down? Drop everything and—"

As I say the words, I realize that is what I'd want to do. Part of me at least. I'd run straight to her. Crumble in her arms and bury us in volcanic ash so she can never leave me again.

But instead I tell Lincoln, "I'm not going to run around the country hunting down someone who obviously doesn't want to be found."

Lincoln's voice goes soft, gentle. Yet there's still that urging. "I'm not saying you should. I'm only saying it doesn't hurt to ask. Maybe it'd be nice to have a choice in the matter."

Of course it would. Because that's the problem, isn't it? My mom has always made the decision for us, and even worse, I've never known why. At the end of all my Detective Dana novels, all of the questions of a case are always answered. The doctor did it because she was in love with the patient's husband. The fisherman did it because someone had stolen his prized catch. Again and again the motive is explained.

I want to know my mom's motive. What makes you abandon your own kid, not once, but over and over again? If I knew where she was, I could ask her.

There's always a motive.

"Fine," I say.

The bartender comes back around, this time carrying two red plastic baskets filled with burgers and fries, and I say, "Can I ask you something?"

"No, you can't drink," she says.

"I don't want to drink. I want to know if you've ever seen my mom in this bar."

The bartender looks at me blankly, so I ramble. "Hair my color, green eyes...probably drinking something that comes with fruit around the rim."

"Do you have a picture?"

"Oh, right. Yeah, a picture."

I slip my phone out of my pocket and scroll and scroll and scroll. The last time I saw her I had a different phone, but amid the endless photos of beaches and friends and waves and skateboards and cousins is a picture of a picture, one that Dad keeps tucked in the drawer of a side table. The photo is of my mom and me when she came back for that long haul when I was seven, the last time I was convinced she actually might stay for good.

I pass over the phone, and as the bartender stares at the

screen, her eyes soften. Or maybe it's the lighting. "I'm not sure, sweetie," she says. "I don't recognize her. A lot of people come through here. She wasn't a regular, I can tell you that."

Of course not. Regular connotes a period of stasis that my mom has never been capable of. Lincoln leans forward on the bar. I'd almost forgotten he was there. "Are you sure?" he asks. "Just think a bit harder on it, please."

She half frowns, the wrinkles around her lips exaggerating, and shakes her head. "Sorry, I've got nothing."

"Right," I say. I can't believe I did this. I promised myself I wouldn't get my hopes up, but then tricked myself into believing for even a few moments I could have an active part in our relationship. "Never mind. Thanks for the burgers."

She nods. "I'll get you guys some refills on those Cokes."

As she walks away, I turn to Lincoln. "I'm not hungry. I'll meet you out by the car."

Before he has a chance to respond, I slip off of the stool and leave this place I should have never come to.

―――

I'm leaning against the car, arms crossed, when Lincoln comes outside. He's carrying a white paper bag, probably with our food in it, because he's the type of guy who would bring me my food even after I stormed out of a restaurant. I kick the gravel with my foot.

"Anise?"

I snap my head up. He looks startled. My expression must show the fury boiling inside me.

"Let's go."

"Look, I'm sorry I made you ask, but—"

"You didn't *make* me do anything. I was the one who asked to come here. It's *my* fault we wasted time on her. Now let's go."

"It's not your fault—"

I throw up my hands. "Fine! Then it's your fault! You dragged me inside, you got my fucking hopes up, you made me ask that waitress about my mom, and now you get to watch me deal with it. It's fine. I just want to go home."

But part of me doesn't want to go home—doesn't want to go to yet another place my mom *might* be. It's exhausting tiptoeing around my life, both hopeful and terrified she could appear at any moment.

Lincoln stares at me, so I turn and yank open the car door. I slide inside and slam the door shut behind me. After a minute, Lincoln joins me in the car, wordlessly handing over the food. The greasy smell makes my stomach churn, so I stuff the bag by my feet and cover it with my sweatshirt.

Lincoln starts the car, and we pull out of the gravel lot. I sink into the seat, curl up my legs, and lean my head against the door. Anger pulses through me.

I hate her. I hate her for making me hate her.

I hate that she probably doesn't care that I hate her.

"Do you want some music?" Lincoln asks after we drive in silence for a few miles.

I shrug my shoulders and mumble, "Sure."

"Do you mind?" he asks.

"Right," I say. Adjusting the stereo is difficult when your only hand is busy driving the car. I glance over at him. Moonlight bathes his dark skin. His jaw is tense. It's an unfamiliar sight. He looks tired, grim. Like a different person entirely. I know I should apologize, but the words stick in my throat. Instead, I lean forward and flip on the stereo, flicking through the songs and watching Lincoln's expression as I do. At the sound of Springsteen's "Jungleland," his face softens the slightest bit, so I leave the CD there and lean back in my seat.

———

Stars speckle the dark sky. Overarching lampposts light the highway. The roads by home look different driving in from the west. My limited traveling has only ever taken me north and south, never out of or into California. We pass a sign that reads "Santa Cruz 9 miles," and I grip my seat belt. Home. In minutes I'll be home.

Surf Break begins tomorrow. I'll spend all day on the beach, with Tess and everyone else. Unless they're mad at me. God, please don't let them be mad at me.

As we get off the highway, I barely recognize the roads in the darkness, like a world I lived in many years ago. And yet

I turn off the GPS and give Lincoln directions by memory. I still owe him an apology, but we've settled into a subdued silence.

We pass my school. A few lights are on, probably for security. In less than two weeks I'll be back in class for my senior year. I've had the same classmates for twelve years; I know every face I'll see on that first Monday back, every name, every personality.

And then a year after that, they'll all be gone. Off to San Francisco, or Hawaii, or New York, or wherever else people go to college when they're too dense to realize what they already have is so great.

Slowly we pull down my street. It's long and has a slight curve along the coastline. As I text Dad to tell him we made it here safely, we pass Tess's house, and then further on we pass Eric's. His bedroom light is on. I wonder if he's looking out the window, watching cars pass, wondering which one I'm in. Even Tess doesn't know specifics about my arrival time, so maybe he's been there all day, watching, waiting for me. Or, maybe he doesn't care at all. Maybe he's night surfing with someone else. In an alternate universe, he'd be next to me right now, and we'd be running out to the water together. If Lincoln and Eric had both lived in Santa Cruz, who would I have ended up with? If a nature-nerd skater with a perfect dimple had approached me at home, would I have even noticed him?

As we near my house, a different anxiety presses in. Will

there be an unfamiliar car in the driveway? Some run-down piece of crap with a thousand bumper stickers or a shiny BMW, borrowed from my mom's latest *friend*?

I tell Lincoln, "Up on the right. Green paint. Well, green-ish. Faded green paint."

He inches down the road and then asks, "This it?"

Only Dad's truck sits in the driveway.

"Should I park in the driveway, or is there room in the garage?" Lincoln asks.

"Driveway," I say. "No room in the garage. It's all filled with gear."

My gear.

My surfboard.

And then it hits me. I crack the window and inhale that sharp salt scent. I'm home.

I yank the car handle and push open the door. "Come on!" I press in the code for the garage, and it opens, reveal-ing a mess of gear. My surfboard is at the front. I grab it and head back to the driveway where Lincoln is just getting out of the car.

He's yawning, which makes sense since we drove twelve hours after only sleeping three, but I still yell, "Hurry, fol-low me!"

Before waiting to see if he does, in fact, follow, I race around to the old wooden boardwalk connecting our house to the beach. The familiar planks feel odd against my sneak-ered feet, so I hastily kick off my shoes and socks and leave them behind. My body relaxes at the feel of the dusted sand and worn wood.

I hear Lincoln behind me, mumbling something about, "Twelve hours of driving, Jesus Christ." But his mumbling stops as soon as we climb past the sandy dunes and approach the ocean, glowing in the light of the moon. "Whoa," he says.

I turn and grin at him. "Welcome to my backyard."

And then I run, surfboard tucked under my arm, right into the tide. The salty water drenches my shorts and tank top, but I don't care—wet fabric can't weigh me down. Nothing can. I climb onto my board and paddle out to meet the tide. The strain pulls on my arms.

But I push through, because I know I can. A wave pulses forward—a huge one. I know I should probably wait for a milder one since it's been so long, but I can't reject the ocean's first offer, so I paddle around on my board and press to my feet as the water comes hurtling toward me. I falter for a second, but then a lifetime of experience takes over, and I balance perfectly on my board as the wave seamlessly carries me along with it.

Despite the exhaustion, the stress, the worry, exhilaration courses through me. My lungs fill with air. My heart fills with relief. I'm home.

SEVENTEEN

I STAY OUT in the surf for half an hour, then pry myself from the water, only because I know it'll be here when I wake up tomorrow. As I head back to shore, I notice all the signs of Surf Break in the distance, the temporary stages, the food trucks, the line of portable toilets. Tomorrow thousands of people will flood the beach, but for tonight it's still just my backyard.

I find Lincoln on the shore, lying on his back, arm tucked up under his head. My board falls to the ground and I collapse next to him. I rest my head on his chest so that we're crossed perpendicularly. My heartbeat calms as I stare at the expanse of stars above me, the same ones that blinked above me nights ago in Nebraska.

Then Lincoln shifts beneath me, and his hand reaches out to take mine.

"I'm sorry," I say. "You know, for earlier. You were only trying to help."

"I forgive you." His chest hums when he speaks. "Feel better now?"

"I think so. Maybe. I—" I continue to stare at the stars and wonder if they can feel my gaze, wonder if they ever watch back. "I mean, I hate that she's not here, but I think what I hate more...what sometimes scares me more...is that no one really remembers her, like she's not even real...and maybe that's why..." I trail off.

"Why what?" Lincoln asks, his thumb idly rubbing my palm.

"Maybe that's why I was so scared to leave home, why I'm so scared to be back. What if my friends don't remember me either? What if I'm just like her, and I disappear into nothing?"

Even now I feel like I'm floating in this half existence. I was too scared to tell my friends exactly when I'd be back. I couldn't handle the pressure of them being on my doorstep the second I arrived. So I'm home, but Dad isn't here, or Tess, or any of my friends. Home isn't really home without your people.

"You know that's not true," Lincoln says.

I roll over so my cheek presses against his chest and I can peer up at him. "How?" I ask. "How do I know that? People move away all the time, and people forget about them all the time. I lost touch with almost everyone this summer. I'm *exactly* like her." The knot of dread constricts again.

"No," Lincoln corrects. "People move away all the time,

and people remember them all the time. Where do you think we just were?"

"Umm..." I tick off the states, "Wyoming, Utah, Nevada."

"No, we were at Wendy's house. My friend who I haven't seen for what, five years? And we remembered each other perfectly fine." He pauses. "I think some people choose to be forgotten...or maybe don't care whether or not they're remembered." He meets my gaze. "No one is going to forget you, Anise Sawyer. Not if you don't want them to."

He leans forward and our lips meet.

The kiss is slow and soothing, like the lapping of the waves before us.

My mom isn't here. The house is pitch-black when we enter, and she always leaves most of the lights on, dirty dishes in the sink, hemp clothing on the floor.

In the darkness, I realize how well I know my own home. I drop my keys into the porcelain bowl that sits on our entry-way table, and the clatter rings through the empty house. I'm tempted to open the junk drawer, check if the postcard is still there. Maybe it was all some early summer hallucination.

But then Lincoln bumps into me, and we both trip and almost fall on the uneven floorboards. "Ow!" I say, then steady him, hands reaching out to his strong form. "Way to be clumsy dude."

"I wouldn't call tripping in a pitch-black house I've never been in before clumsy," he mutters.

"I'll take what I can get. Gotta keep your perfect athlete ego in check."

"Could you turn a light on maybe?"

"Okay, okay." I take us a few more steps down the hall and into the kitchen. The moonlight creeps in through the bay window. I'm not sure I'm ready to see Lincoln standing in the full artificial brightness of my kitchen. Out of place. Like a famous actor making a cameo on a RV show or Dad showing up at school.

So I walk over to the stove and flick on the dim overhead light. It illuminates the room enough to prevent Lincoln from tripping. Suddenly I'm having trouble looking at him. I'm in my house alone with a guy. A guy I *really* like. Growing up on the beach has provided plenty of relatively secluded opportunities to be alone with a boy. But there's a big difference between being alone on the shore where technically anyone can walk by, including Dad, and being alone in an empty house where there are empty beds, and Dad is sleeping many states away. I had no intention of having sex with Lincoln—I *have* no intention of having sex with Lincoln— but that doesn't keep me from being aware of how easy it would be.

Lincoln's stare is on me. I look away and pull open the fridge door. The light spills out, and I blink twice. "Hungry?"

There's a pause. Or at least it feels like a pause, enough time for Lincoln to choose words instead of just say them. "I could eat. Is there anything in there?"

"Good question." The fridge is almost entirely bare, save some of those orange Kraft cheese slices and half a loaf of bread. It's not stuff we normally keep in the fridge. Maybe Dad had some weird food cravings when flew back alone. "Grilled cheese?"

"Sure," Lincoln says. "Want help?"

"I've got it."

I've never actually cooked grilled cheese before, but after all that driving, Lincoln deserves to rest. Besides, I'm not sure I'll make responsible choices if he stands close to me right now.

Behind me, I hear him settle at the kitchen table. The chairs drag against the floor as he rearranges them. I keep my eyes on the stove as I heat up a pan. Move back to the fridge for butter. Drawer for a knife. Slice off the butter. Sizzle. Bread in the pan. Peel the plastic wrapping off the slices of cheese.

My heart thumps. When did it start doing that? My hands shake the slightest bit as I carefully settle the slices of cheese onto the bread. I hope the bread doesn't burn. Why did Dad put bread in the fridge in the first place? We never put bread in the fridge. I guess so it wouldn't go bad.

I turn around to ask Lincoln how toasty he likes his grilled cheese and find him draped across two chairs, legs propped up, head nodding off to the side, snoring lightly.

"Right," I say to myself. "Okay then."

The grilled cheeses look kind of lonely sitting there in the pan, so I eat them both myself.

―――――

I wake up completely disoriented. The light slants into the room at the wrong angle. I reflexively turn over and startle when I don't see Emery in a bed beside me. *Oh. I'm home.*

Last night after finishing the sandwiches and staring at a sleeping Lincoln for a solid thirty seconds, I woke him up and led him to the guest bedroom, where I was able to avoid all questions of sex when he climbed onto the bed and passed out. Apparently after twenty-four hours of driving, cuddling up with a down comforter is more appealing than cuddling up with me. The vast size of the West defeated Lincoln and his infallible energy.

After dropping him off in bed, I stripped out of my salt-crusted clothing, dropped them outside the washer in the hallway, and zombie-walked to my room. I pulled on an old cotton T-shirt, comforted by the scent of my own detergent. Then, I promptly collapsed on my bed, curled up with Tess's quilt, and fell into a deep sleep.

I now grab for my phone on the nightstand. My jaw drops when I see it's half past noon. I never sleep this late. Waste of wave time. Crashing past ten is an absurdly rare occurrence. This is just ridiculous. I also have about twenty texts and missed calls, most of them from Tess saying something along the lines of: WHERE THE HELL ARE YOU I WANT TO SEE YOUR FACE.

The most recent text message reads: Fuck it, I'm just coming over. That one was sent more than half an hour ago...

And then I hear the muffled voices. "Oh fuck." I rip off my tangled sheets and jump out of bed, yanking on a pair of shorts under my sleep shirt. I hurry down the hallway toward the sound of voices. In the kitchen, I find Tess and Lincoln casually chatting like they're already best friends.

Midday light sweeps in from the windows. Lincoln cooks at the stovetop, presumably more grilled cheese since that's the only food we have. Tess sits on the counter, book abandoned beside her, and chats with Lincoln. The scene is so surreal that I wonder if maybe I'm still dreaming. Two parts of my life intersecting over melted cheese. She looks different. Hair a bit longer. A new piercing in her left ear. Her skin its deep end-of-summer bronze. Before I have a chance to truly comprehend the moment, Tess spots me standing there and stops midsentence.

"Holy fucking shit! You asshole!" She leaps off the counter and bounds over to me, wrapping me in a tight hug. And I was worried she might be mad at me. Maybe I freaked out over nothing. I hug her back, and my entire body relaxes, comforted by the familiar smell of her coconut aloe shampoo.

As soon as we release the hug, Tess takes a step back and shoves me. "But seriously. Asshole move. You've been back for like, what? Twelve hours? And you're just seeing my shin-ing face now?"

"I was tired?"

Tess gives me a no–bullshit look. "Sure, too tired to see me but not tired enough to resist the water."

"How did you—"

She points down the hallway. "Shouldn't have left out those ocean clothes."

"Right." I shift on my feet. "Sorry. But I'm seeing you now!" I smile and move to hug her again.

"All right, all right, I get it. On Anise's scale of all things important, everything comes after surfing. But you could've texted me so I'd know you didn't die in a fiery crash of fire."

"Sorry," I repeat, then hug her again. "Oh my God, I can't believe I'm here. You're here."

Tess hugs me back, then pulls away and nudges her fore-head to mine. "Best friends together again."

It really is hard to believe there can be bad in the world with her by my side. I hug her one more time for good measure.

"Anyway," Tess continues, "While you were sleeping this beautiful day away, I was busy getting to know your new...*friend*."

Lincoln looks up from the stove, where he's sliding the sandwiches onto a plate. "I like her," he says. "She also scares me a little."

"Exactly the aesthetic I'm going for," Tess says.

"Yeah," I say, drawing the word out slowly. "What exactly were you guys talking about?"

"You," they say at the same time. It makes me think of Parker and Nash and their twin timing. I miss them. I wonder if they'll get my postcard today.

"Right. I don't know how I feel about that." I wait for either of them to expound, but neither of them volunteers more information, which is maybe for the best. "So, Surf Break?"

Tess grins. "Surf Break."

Lincoln brings the sandwiches to the table. We all sit down together, and again I'm hit with how strange this situation is, but I must be the only one who finds it strange, because Lincoln and Tess both start digging into the food and chatting away without me.

"So you're the only one who doesn't surf?" Lincoln asks.

Tess nods. "I prefer to cha e literary pursuits, not waves."

I cut in. "By literary p ...s, she means thinly veiled erotica."

Tess rolls her eyes. "Like your Detective Dana books are great works of American literature. Don't be a snob, dude. A good book is a good book."

"Very cool." Lincoln nods. "I always mean to read more, but I have trouble staying still for that long."

"You should totally try audiobooks," Tess says. "Listen to them while you skateboard or whatever."

Lincoln grins. "I'll definitely do that. Do you have any suggestions?"

Tess starts to respond, but I cut her off. "SO," I say loudly. "Surf Break."

"Right," Tess says. "Surf Break. Marie's party isn't for

hours. You sure you don't want to meet up with everyone before then?"

I shake my head. As excited as I am to see my friends, I'm also overwhelmed and nervous at the prospect. For this afternoon I want to enjoy Tess and Lincoln in solitude. Besides, Tess told me she accidentally slipped up on the Lincoln secret, so now everyone including Eric knows about us, and I don't know how to handle that.

"*Okay*. We'll see everyone tonight then."

Everyone. My nerves churn. Tess isn't mad at me, but Tess is my best friend. She's prone to be more forgiving than everyone else.

"Motel/Hotel is playing near there, so we're going to meet around eight, pregame some, go to the show, and then wander around and watch drunk people do irresponsible shit."

"Also be drunk people doing irresponsible shit," I say.

"Yes, that's a legitimate possibility."

"So what do we do until then?" Lincoln asks.

Tess and I exchange looks and then we start laughing.

"What?" Lincoln looks bewildered.

Tess leans forward on the table and takes Lincoln's hand in her own. "Lincoln, darling, sweetie. Anise just got back to her beloved Santa Cruz after a two-month separation. What do you think she's going to do?"

"Oh," he says. "Right."

I grin. "Hey Lincoln, want to learn how to surf?"

"You disgust me," I say as Lincoln trudges through the shallow water and back to shore, surfboard tucked under his arm, ocean water beading down his dark abs, that infuriating self-assured smile pinned to his face.

"No, I don't."

I grab Dad's surfboard from him, and his smile widens. "There's no way you learned to surf that well in one afternoon."

Lincoln inches closer to me, sweeps down, and plants a quick kiss on my lips. The taste of salt is sharp. "I have a really good instructor. Plus, having one arm gives me eighteen years of off-center superhero balance. Come on, give me the board back. I want to go again."

"No, you're not allowed. At this rate you'll be better than me by then end of the weekend."

"I've seen you out there. We both know that's not true. Come on." He reaches for the board, and I step away. He follows, and I step back again. Then he gets this look in his eyes, and he smiles, that dimple popping out.

"What are you—"

He leaps forward, and I yelp, struggling to get full control of the board while turning and breaking into a sprint down the damp shore, feet pounding on the packed sand, little splashes of water kicking up behind me. "I'm faster than you!" Lincoln yells.

I'm not sure if that's true, but he's definitely faster than me when I have a heavy surfboard in my arms. He gently tackles me from behind, and we both fly to the ground, the surfboard cast to the side as Lincoln pins me, his body flush against mine. "Hi there," he says.

"I hate you," I say.

"Okay," he says.

And then he kisses me.

———

Five hours later, I'm lying on the beach between Lincoln and Tess, our backs pressed into damp towels, the early evening sun stalking us between scattered clouds. I know I'm home because with closed eyes I can identify each familiar sound.

Bark, a dog racing down the coast.

Crash, the waves rolling onto the shore.

Squawk, the seagulls circling overhead.

The sounds mingle with each other, and yet I can pick out each distinct one. My fingers twist idly in the sand, every so often brushing up and against the warm skin of Lincoln's nub and then away again. He sleeps soundly next to me. Surfing exhausted him. Teaching him surfing exhausted me because I ended up competing more than teaching.

Tess is on my other side, a paperback open across her stomach, sunglasses over her probably closed eyes. Even asleep, her presence is unspeakably comforting. I wish I could freeze this moment. I wish Lincoln wasn't going back to Nebraska, wish Tess wasn't going to leave in a year. I wish here and now would just stay here and now.

―――

Later that evening, while Lincoln naps more and before Tess comes over, I'm organizing my room because, somehow, it's already a giant mess. I move my tote bag to sort a pile of unfolded clothing, but then I pause. The weight doesn't feel right. I rifle through the bag until I find my copy of Detective Dana's *The Last Stop on the Train*. A sticky note from Emery is on the cover.

Found this after we cleaned up your mess. Didn't want you to forget it.

But I don't remember bringing this to—I glance up at my bookshelf. I have the same exact book there. This isn't mine. Unless I have two copies. But I don't think so…

My fingers tremble as I open the book. There's a signature and a personalized note from the author to my mom.

May your travels take you further than the last stop.

Aunt Jackie's words echo in my mind. "Your mom was terrified to end up like our mother, to live and die in the same place without seeing the world…so she left."

It's odd. My mom was terrified of ending up like her mom, so she left home, and I'm terrified of ending up like my mom, so I was scared to leave home.

And in an hour I'll discover if my fear was justified.

I hear the front door open. "Anise!" Tess calls out.

My heart races. This entire summer, I was so eager to discover something of my mom's, but now it feels like I'm about to get caught with contraband. I stuff the book and thoughts of my mom in the back of a drawer. When Tess bursts into my room moments later, she declares we're going to go all out for Motel/Hotel tonight. She drops a pile of neon and spandex clothing on my bed. Where and when she acquired all of this clothing is beyond me; she's definitely never worn a bright orange spandex jumpsuit to school.

After picking through all the clothing, Tess ends up in a black tube skirt and multi-colored neon midriff shirt, and I end up in neon purple leggings and a bright aqua sports bra. Lincoln, with limited wardrobe available, wears his trusty jean shorts and borrows a tie-dye T-shirt from Dad's collection. It's not exactly the right fit for an EDM show but decidedly better than his dark flannels.

After getting dressed, we spend a half hour tracing our skin with neon and glitter paint. Lincoln seems more fascinated by the paint than Tess or me, and he spends a solid twenty minutes in front of the mirror perfecting the swirling neon mask around his eyes.

"I didn't know you had an artistic streak," I say.

He puts down a tube of glitter and wraps his arm around me. "I have an everything streak."

I roll my eyes. "My turn. Stop hogging the mirror."

However, my own attempts at the paint are so terrible that

both Tess and Lincoln have to fix it for me. We then crack glow sticks and slide them on our wrists and necks. "All right, all right," I finally say. "We're properly decorated. Can we go now?" My nerves have kicked into high gear. I just want to see my friends and get whatever will happen over with.

"Oh, almost forgot!" Tess says. She opens the freezer door and pulls out a bottle of chilled liquor she must have put in there this morning. "Shots!"

I wince. I hate shots. When I do occasionally drink, I mostly stick to beer. However, before I can mention this, Lincoln says, "Hell yes," and sidles up next to Tess at the counter.

"Come on," Tess says. "You're not getting in the water tonight. You're not driving a car—not that you ever do that anyway. Your dad is in another state. And, most importantly, you're about to have the most awesome night ever with your most awesome best friend ever."

"And me," Lincoln says.

"And him," Tess agrees. She holds the bottle out to me. "Also, this is Bacardi Dragon Berry, and I promise you've never tasted anything so delicious."

I take the bottle from her. This night could be the best night ever, or the worst night ever. Either way, a little liquor won't hurt.

I unscrew the metal cap and fill the three shot glasses.

— —

Thirty minutes and three shots each later, we're all walking (stumbling, giggling) down the beach toward Marie's house. The beach is ten times as crowded as usual, filled with Surf Break attendees. Unfamiliar faces pass, not just strangers but out-of-towners. I can always recognize when someone isn't from Santa Cruz, and Surf Break always flips the ratio of natives to visitors.

My body is warm and fuzzed around the edges. Dragon Berry doesn't exactly taste good, but it doesn't exactly taste bad either, which is probably why I ended up taking three shots and why I'm feeling quite drunk. But there's nothing to worry about—I'm buffered by Tess and Lincoln. Nothing bad can possibly happen with a net so strong.

We approach Marie's house, and there are about thirty people on her back deck. Just a little further down the coast I see the main stage and hundreds of people already milling in front of it. The quick and low beat of the preshow music is loud enough to reach us. "Come on!" Tess waves Lincoln and me forward as she climbs the stairs to Marie's deck.

I hesitate, thinking of all my friends up there. Cassie, Spinner, Eric—oh fuck. I never told Lincoln about Eric, our kiss, our start of nothing. It's not like I did anything wrong, but still, I should have told him. It's one thing not to tell Eric about Lincoln—but Lincoln, I'm dating or whatevering him. I would've wanted to know if he'd hooked up with Wendy before we'd arrived at her house. I drop Lincoln's hand. "Are you okay?" he asks. I've stopped in the shadows at the bottom of the stairs.

"Anise?" Lincoln asks again.

I play with the three glow sticks on my wrist, twisting them round and round. I shouldn't be nervous. This is Lincoln. Lincoln is calm. Lincoln is reasonable. And it's not like I lied to him. I simply forgot to share information.

"Anise?" he asks again.

I take a deep breath, wishing I could have one more shot of Dragon Berry to help me through this, and then tell him in quick words about Eric and the start of summer and that one kiss. Lincoln watches me the whole time, though it's hard to see his eyes in the shadows, the enclave of the stairs blocking the light from the moon.

After, I'm so nervous part of me wants to duck under his arm braced against the wooden railing and sprint down the shore, away from him and toward home. I'm nervous because I realize how much I care what he thinks. How much I care about him, his feelings. How much I care if this information will make him mad, or worse, hurt him. When I finish speaking, I want to grab for his hand, close the gap between our bodies. Instead I wait for him to speak, worried that he won't.

But then he lowers his arm, and his fingers thread through mine, and he nudges his forehead against mine so that we're looking into each other's eyes, and he says, "Don't be nervous. It'll be fine."

And I realize while I've been worrying about his feelings, he's been worrying about mine. And that soothes me, cradles me like the water does on a tranquil day. I have this sudden urge to explain exactly what I am feeling, but I've never been good at that, so I lean forward and kiss his left cheek, and then his right, and then his lips.

"What's taking you guys so long?" Tess asks. I look up and find her halfway down the stairs.

"Coming!" I say.

With renewed confidence, I head up with Lincoln, my hand wrapped in his. He's right. Everything will be fine. I have nothing to worry about. It's not like Eric and I were in a relationship. We kissed once, and maybe if I'd stayed it would've happened again, but I didn't stay, and that's the end of it. And you can't destroy years of friendship with a couple of unreturned texts, right? I've been psyching myself out for no reason.

As we climb onto the deck, someone I don't recognize hands Lincoln and me red Solo cups that are filled to the brim. I take a small sip. It tastes like vodka with a side of pink lemonade and burns going down. I spot two girls, arms wrapped around each other, black and white, short and tall—Cassie and Marie. My friends. Their backs are to me, and they're talking in a group. I take a deep breath, wishing Lincoln would put his cup down so I could hold his hand again.

I thread through the crowd and then stop right behind them. "I'm back!" I say. Okay, maybe I scream it. There might be a little more Dragon Berry in my system than I'd thought.

I wait for them to turn, jump on me, and scream with equal enthusiasm.

But they don't. Cassie turns, gives a big smile that seems

forced, and a hug that seems even more forced. "Tess told us you were coming, but we didn't know if you'd make it. It's good to see you. I missed you," she says, voice subdued.

"Welcome back," Marie adds, the words chopped. She doesn't hug me or smile at all.

The warm air turns cold on my skin. This isn't how my close friends should greet me. This isn't right. Are they mad or is this just awkward since so much time has passed? Maybe we don't know how to act around each other anymore. Or maybe I had reason to worry.

I take another sip of the vodka lemonade, wincing at the burn, and force myself to soldier on. They've returned to talking to each other, so I have to speak over them. "So, um, this is Lincoln. I think Tess mentioned him."

Lincoln steps forward and grins wide, his dimple popping out. "Hey guys!" he says brightly. "Love the tie-dye," he says, gesturing toward Cassie's bandanna and then his own shirt.

"Thanks," she says. "You too!"

I swear she gives him a warmer smile than she gave me.

Lincoln, either sensing the tension or genuinely curious, then says, "I'm going to have Anise introduce me to everyone else. It was nice meeting you guys."

Cassie nods and gives another smile without meeting my eyes. Marie turns away from me. My stomach clenches. I'm not overreacting. Something is definitely wrong. My friends hate me. Should I apologize? Maybe, probably. I hurt my friends, abandoned them, like my mom always does to me.

I take another sip of my vodka lemonade and then another and another as we weave through the crowd. The reunions with my friends continue to be tense, off-balance, not as icy as with Marie, but like talking to strangers and not close friends I've skinny-dipped with a dozen times. And I haven't seen Eric. I keep Lincoln close to my side and scan the crowd for Tess since they're the only two people I know for sure want me here.

"ANISE!" someone shouts with actual enthusiasm.

I whirl around to find Spinner running up to me, his hair loose around his shoulders, twenty glow sticks wrapped around his neck. He gives me a huge hug. "So good to see you! Shit, dude, it's been way too long." Then without pause he turns to Lincoln and hugs him too. "Nice to meet you man!" Spinner ushers us forward. "Come on, we must celebrate with shots."

I'm not sure if that's such a great idea. I already drained my cup of vodka lemonade, and that combined with the Dragon Berry from earlier is more alcohol than I've ever consumed at once. But I'm just so glad—so relieved—that at least one of my friends is actually happy to see me that I nod and follow him through the crowd.

"I'll be there in a minute!" Lincoln shouts. "I think that guy has glow-in-the-dark face paint."

I almost say *wait, stay with me* because I'm nervous to be left alone.

I wonder how fucked up it is that I'm nervous to be left alone at a party with my own friends.

Everything blurs. One second I'm at the folding table with Spinner taking shots of something that tastes a lot worse than Dragon Berry, and the next second I'm in the crowd for Motel/Hotel, surrounded by unfamiliar faces, eyelids dipping closed then open, moving to the rapid electronic beat of "Sparkflash," head and stomach swirling, sweat dripping. Someone passes me a cigarette, no a joint, and I take two long puffs, coughing afterward and taking a sip of—oh, the beer in my hand. Not sure where I got that, but it's helping with the cough, so I take another sip, and then decide I don't want to hold the can while I'm dancing, so I chug the rest and drop it to the ground, dimly guilty about littering my own beach.

The song switches to one of Tess's favorites, and I spin around to find her, but she's nowhere in sight. Lincoln isn't here either, and my heart races from more than the dancing. Spinner is to my right but dancing close with a girl I don't recognize. Where is everyone? I push through the crowd, but the crowd pushes back. It won't let me leave, a million hands coming toward me and holding me in place. I shut my eyes and count to three.

When I open them again, the hands aren't coming for me. I make my way through the crowd more forcefully now.

When I get to the edge of the fray, I spot Marie and run up to her, stumbling in the sand, forgetting her anger from earlier tonight. "Have you—" My tongue feels thick, "Have you seen Tess or Lincoln?"

"*Are you fucking kidding me?*" she speaks so softly that I swear I don't hear her right.

"What?"

"I said," her voice louder now, "are you fucking kidding me?"

"I don't—" I feel queasy, the Dragon Berry mixing with the vodka lemonade mixing with the beer and pot. "I don't understand."

But I do understand. She hates me. Everyone hates me. And I don't blame them.

"Jesus, Anise, I don't know where your *friends* are. Do you even really care? You'll probably just ditch them too."

"What are you—"

She steps forward, her eyes hard. "Look, I get it. It's not your fault you had to go to Nebraska, but Cassie leaves for boot camp in a couple of days, and then she'll be shipped off to who the fuck knows where and won't be able to talk to us for who the fuck knows how long, and you ignore her all summer? She's one of your best friends, and she's freaking out, and you go MIA because picking up the damn phone is inconvenient? I can't believe you even showed up to my house tonight. Look, I can handle you ignoring me. Whatever. You were busy. I have thick skin. But you hurt my girlfriend, and I can't forgive that."

Her words hit hard, piercing my drunken haze. Cassie is scared about the navy? I thought she was excited. My eyes sting with tears. I can't think of anything to say as Marie pushes past me, so I say nothing.

And then I run for home.

—————

"Anise!"

I'm running through the sand.

"Anise!"

The grains hit my calves and stick.

"Anise!"

I stumble to the ground, hands braced in front of me.

"Anise!"

I right myself and keep running. But I've lost my lead.

"*Anise Sawyer!*" Someone collapses onto to me, her arms around my shoulders. I feel her strained breathing. "*Fuck you.*" The breathing calms a bit. "You *know* I can't run for shit."

Tess and I stand there together catching our breath.

My pulsing thoughts relax to a dim, inflamed hum.

Then Tess takes my hand and walks me to the water. We sit in the damp sand and let the tide wash over our feet. Surf Break is in the distance, the music more an echo than a sound. Only a few wanderers trail this part of the beach. I lean into Tess. Her shoulder is sticky with beer or saltwater or glow paint, but it doesn't matter—everything spins less with her by my side.

After a few minutes, she says, "What the hell happened?"

My tongue doesn't feel thick anymore, but I still struggle to get out the words. "Everyone hates me."

"That didn't answer my question," Tess says. "But continue, who hates you?"

"Cassie, Marie—everyone!"

Tess snorts. Actually snorts. She's laughing at me. "Dude, you know what Marie's like. Remember the dance recital thing in seventh grade? She always flips her shit over the smallest thing."

I guess that's true. Marie tends to turn most situations into a level ten disasters. Especially if they're about Cassie. "But," I say, "Cassie's mad at me too. Or not mad, worse. Hurt. I hurt her. She's leaving for the fucking navy, and I stopped talking to her. I'm an asshole. I'm—" I gather a breath. "I'm just like *her*."

Tess drops my hand, leans forward, and grabs a thin shred of driftwood. She uses it to draw circles in the sand. When she notices me watching, she breaks the driftwood in half and hands me a piece. We sit there together with our swirls, the tide washing them away as soon as we draw them.

"You're not your mom," Tess says after the long stretch of silence. Her words surprise me. She knows I don't like to talk about her. Even if I accidentally bring her up. "You're nothing like her," Tess repeats.

Everything feels wrong—tight, loose, itchy, slick. I don't believe Tess. I can already feel my mom's infection crawling under my skin and coming out through my pores, mutating my DNA, turning me into someone who flees instead of fights, like now, when I ran away from Marie because I couldn't handle a friend telling me the truth. "Then why did I leave everyone behind?" I ask. "Why did I ignore them? Why didn't I care enough?"

"You didn't," Tess interrupts me, then pauses. "Don't you understand the fact you're asking these questions means you actually give a shit and are nothing like your mom at all?"

The words make sense, but they still don't settle. Maybe I do give a shit, but the fact is, my friend needed me, and I wasn't there. Just like my mom is never there when I need her. What if caring isn't enough to keep me from turning out like her?

I stand and smudge my toe in the sand. Then I kick the sand. Then I kick the water, stepping further and further into the ocean until it ripples around my thighs, and then I look up at the moon and scream. I scream so loud that my throat feels raw and my head light. I scream so loud that my hands shake and my eyes water. I scream loud so that—even if she's halfway across the country—my mom might hear my cry.

EIGHTEEN

I WAKE WITH a pounding headache and sand in my mouth. No, not sand. The complete absence of moisture. Another reason not to drink, besides it not mixing with surfing— hangovers are the fucking worst. Without moving any of my lifeless limbs, I pry open my eyes and look around.

Tess and Lincoln are also on my bed, sprawled on either side of me. They're fully clothed, as am I, still in our stained neon and tie-dye.

After Tess calmed me down last night, I found multiple worried texts from Lincoln on my phone. We met him back at the house, where he must have not been *that* worried about me, because he was making grilled cheese sandwiches with the remainder of the bread and cheese and dancing to a Motel/ Hotel song blasting from my computer speaker. He too assured me that my friends didn't hate me. Apparently he stayed with a few of them after he lost track of me, and they wanted to know where the hell I was so they could hang out—which should relieve me, but Marie's words keep replaying in my mind.

With the effort only an absurdly full bladder can provide, I crawl out of bed and find my way to the guest bathroom. I flick on the light and glance in the mirror, which is a mistake. My normally hassle-free hair is a tangled rat's nest, and there are dark circles under my eyes, not to mention streaked neon glitter paint. If I were to judge the success of the night by the look of my face, it must have been a pretty shitty night. I turn the water on hot and scrub my skin until it's clean. When I glance back in the mirror, I notice something, or rather, the absence of something. The note I left for my mom isn't there.

Does that mean she—

Or Dad could have—

But as the questions rush through my mind, I realize I don't need to know. I don't *want* to know. Basing my decisions off of her choices, living my life off of hers, has only led me down troubled paths. If I'd been thoroughly determined to not be her, just like she tried to not be her mom, I would've never left Santa Cruz, would've never experienced the world outside of my home, would've never met Lincoln.

I won't spend the rest of my life as a reaction to hers.

I won't spend the rest of my life wondering, *will she, what if*—

I won't spend the rest of my life trying to fill in the blanks she leaves behind.

Ten minutes later, I'm out on the deck with a clean face, empty bladder, and a steaming mug of green tea. The mellow taste makes me think of Dad. The sliding glass door opens. Tess pads outside. Her hair is pulled into a messy bun, and she's wearing one of my sweatshirts over her outfit from last night. "You look like shit," she says.

I nod. "You too."

She comes and sits down on the chair next to me. "Give me a sip of that."

I hand her my tea and then lean back, trying to get my eyes and mind to focus on the crashing of the waves. But they won't focus.

"Want to talk about it?" Tess asks as she hands my mug back to me.

"Not really." I take a sip. "Maybe." Another sip. "Yes." I look Tess in the eye. "You really don't think I'm like her?"

"You are absolutely not like her," Tess says, then covers my hand with hers and continues, "That said, you *are* a *bit* of an asshole."

"I am?"

"You are."

"I am."

Silence passes as we hand the tea back and forth.

"Look," Tess says. "It wasn't your fault you had to go to Nebraska. Everyone knows that, but we also know you have this thing called a phone, and a computer, and you used them maybe twice in the past month. I mean, you can't treat your friends like that and expect to find them in the same spot you dropped them, you know?"

I do know. And suddenly I feel sick. Really sick. Stomach gurgling, throat constricting sick. I jump up from the chair and without time to do anything else, run over to the balcony and vomit off the side into the sand. "Fuck," I say, spitting out the sour taste in my mouth. There's a hint of Dragon Berry. That makes me vomit again.

"You okay?" Tess asks. "I'll get you water."

A minute later she's handing me a glass. I take a few sips. "I'm fine," I say and collapse into my chair. "Sorry. Fine. It's—"

"Rum?"

"Yeah…"

But it's not just the rum. It's this fear that even if I'm not my mom now, I will be someday. Like I'm predestined to be a terrible person or something.

But I won't accept that. I can't accept that. Because like Tess said last night, where my mom doesn't give a shit, I do. I give a shit about my friends and their lives and how I treat them. My stomach churns with how much I give a shit. And alcohol—it's also churns with alcohol.

"You're right," I say. "I kept seeing pictures of everyone having a great summer without me, and it was hard to keep hearing about all I was missing out on."

"Which makes sense. But if you'd called us, you would have known we were hardcore missing you."

"I should probably apologize," I say.

"You probably should," Tess agrees.

"Want to come with me? Moral support and all that?"

"Hmm, how about I entertain your very attractive boyfriend instead?"

Boyfriend. Another thought I keep avoiding. Lincoln will leave soon, and "boyfriend" has a certain permanence attached to it we can never really have. For now, I'll avoid it a bit longer. One breakthrough a day seems reasonable enough.

I hesitate when I get to Eric's house. The one-story clapboard home with dozens of wind chimes dangling off the back porch is almost as familiar as my own house, yet I feel like an intruder. Normally I'd let myself in through the unlocked backdoor, but I pause. I'm not sure if I'm welcome.

I knew I had to visit Eric first. Eric who wasn't even at Marie's party last night, Eric who I kissed and then barely talked to all summer, Eric who I've been friends with since before I could spell the word friend. I pull out my phone and start to message him. Then I erase what I have and put my phone back in my pocket.

Taking a short breath, I climb the stairs to the porch and walk barefoot on the worn wood slats. The wind blows up behind me, and with the sun perching behind its nest of clouds, my skin prickles. I knock twice before letting myself in.

The house is set up much like mine, so the back porch takes me directly into the kitchen. The room is empty and cool. "Hello?" I call out tentatively.

No response.

"Hello?" I call again.

This time I hear some shuffling. A door opens and closes. Feet pad down the hallway. And then, there he is, wearing no shirt, gray drawstring sweatpants, and a band pushing back his thick blond hair. My mouth grows dry for a moment at how attractive he really is.

But when my gaze meets his, all that summer heat fades.

There's no warmth in his eyes.

He smiles anyway. Kind of. A partial smile that doesn't reach beyond the crick of his lips. "Hey, Anise."

"Hey." My voice barely comes out, so I clear my throat. "Hey. Hi." I smile. "How are you?"

"Good. Great."

It's awful standing like this, a dozen feet separating us, staring at each other like strangers. No, strangers don't look at each other like Eric is looking at me. I twist the hair tie around my wrist and then force myself to hug him. The hug is awkward and stiff, but at least he hugs me back.

"So," I say and take a small step away. "How's summer been? I missed you last night."

He stares at me and then in a short tone says, "Yeah. Wasn't in the mood."

"Right," I say. "I wanted to make sure you were okay... I mean, I wanted to make sure we were okay... I...I'm sorry."

The silence stretches between us until Eric sighs. The sigh loosens the rigidity in his stance, the firmness in his gaze. He gestures at the couch that faces the ocean. We sit down next to each other.

"Look, Anise. I'm not *mad* at you. I'm—" He pauses, thinking. "I heard about Lincoln. You had every right to go off and meet someone. We kissed once. It's not like we were dating. It's not like we'd even discussed it." Another pause. "But I'd be lying if I said I hadn't been waiting for you. I thought we had something. And it was really hard when you had to leave for the summer. But I knew you'd be back. Except then you stopped talking to me. And I couldn't—I don't—understand why."

"I know," I say. "I felt the same way, but when I got to Nebraska, it was strange." I try to figure out how to explain it. "It was like half of my world suddenly fell away, and even though I knew I'd be back in a couple of months, it didn't feel that way. And then I met Lincoln and—" I hate myself as I feel a smile flickers to my lips. "Well, I met him. I wasn't thinking about you... Oh shit. Not that I wasn't thinking about you. That sounds horrible. I just meant—it wasn't a choice between you or him because you weren't there. I wasn't here. I wanted to be back here with you guys so badly, but since I couldn't... I guess it was easier to pretend you didn't exist. Shit, that sounds bad again. That's not what—"

"Anise, it's okay." He leans back on the couch and kind of laughs. "It would've been nice to stay in touch this summer, and obviously this would have been much easier if either of us had shared our feelings with each other, but we didn't, and I get why it was hard, and we're here now. And you're with Lincoln. Whatever happens, we'll always be friends. Well, as long as you return my text messages during all future disappearances. We'll be okay."

"You sure?" As relief washes over me, I realize just how scared I was of losing one of my best friends.

"Yes, of course." He pulls the band out of his hair and plays with it. "I'm not saying it won't be a little weird at first, but you're one of my people, and I'm one of yours, and that's never going to change, even if you date a thousand guys over me."

I give a shaky laugh and wipe the few tears from my face. "A *thousand*?"

———

The rest of the apologies are less nerve-wracking but still take the majority of the afternoon. Most are a repetition of the following:

Me: I was an asshole.

Friend: You *were* an asshole.

Me: I'm sorry for being an asshole.

Friend: I forgive you for being an asshole.

Me: Want to go surf?

Friend: Yes.

I make a special apology to Cassie and Marie. I still can't believe they'll be gone so soon. Cassie accepts my apology instantly because she's a million times nicer than me. Marie accepts too, even though I have to repeat *I was an asshole* a couple extra times for her. I'm already planning care packages to send them when they leave town.

It's weird. I'm kind of glad I spent the summer in Nebraska, not only because I got to spend so much time with my family, but also because it was like a trial run for when my friends and I will all be in different places. What would've happened if I went out of touch with my friends for an entire year instead of a couple of weeks? The fix wouldn't have been as easy. It might've been impossible.

It's the last day of Surf Break now, and we're all exhausted from endless hours of surfing and dancing and watching the amazing demos from visiting athletes. Once the tension cooled, Lincoln made fast friends with everyone, especially Spinner, who insisted Lincoln teach him how to skateboard. Maybe I'll even spend some time at the skate park this year. I used to look down on skateboarders, but if they're even a quarter as great as Lincoln, those are friends I want to have.

"Dude, we so don't have enough marshmallows," Tess says, dropping about a dozen bags of marshmallows on the table we're setting up with hot dog buns, chips, and drinks.

Like I promised at the beginning of summer, I'm hosting the end of Surf Break bonfire.

"Tess, we literally have enough marshmallows for the entire festival. I think we're going to be okay."

She mumbles something, and it's hard to hear, but it sounds like, *yeah, but they're not the jumbo Kraft ones.*

Lincoln comes up behind me and wraps his arm around my shoulder, pulling me into his warm chest. I look up to smile at him, and he's already smiling at me. "Come on," he says and tugs me forward. "Let's go down to the water for a bit."

I'm hesitant to leave setup since I'm the host, but we're mostly done, and parties like this tend to take care of themselves, with everyone pitching in, so I wrap an arm around his waist and follow him down to the shore.

The beach is almost empty. All the tourists are on the road out of town, and most of the locals are inside, exhausted from the eventful weekend. Lincoln and I settle on the packed sand, and as the water laps over our toes, we watch the sun melt into the water.

"I leave tomorrow," he says.

I know that, yet my stomach still twists at the words. "You could leave the next day," I suggest, "or the next."

He shakes his head. "No can do. Promised Austin I'd be back to hang out with him for his last few days of summer."

"I kind of hate that you're a good brother."

"Sometimes I kind of hate it too."

I want to kiss Lincoln before he's no longer here to kiss, but

I can't because my eyes are damp, and I'm scared if I look at him, it'll get even worse. I don't want to say good-bye. I want to keep him here.

But I would never do that to him when there's so much of the world he wants to see.

And if he's leaving, there's only one solution. It comes to me so quickly I don't even think before speaking. "I'll go with you."

He turns to me. "What?"

"I'll go with you. I'll drive with you back to Nebraska."

"*What?*" he repeats.

"We'll have a little more time together, and I'll be able to see my cousins again, and then I'll fly back with my dad as planned."

As I say the words, I know they're right. I'd love nothing more than to spend a little more time with Lincoln, catch up with my cousins again before the end of summer, take them to the park again, play one more round of Monopoly. It'll only be a few extra days with them, but the memories will last far longer.

I see hope flicker in Lincoln's eyes, but it's also mixed with confusion. "But you just got back to Santa Cruz. You love home. You want to leave again this soon?"

It surprises me too. After spending the summer worrying about being gone, I'm ready to leave again. But it's not that scary this time. I'm not my mom. Leaving isn't running away.

"Well, that's the thing," I say, pressing into him more and taking his hand in mine. "I learned something pretty cool this summer."

"Yeah, what?"

"I love home." I lean forward and kiss Lincoln—more our two smiles touching than a kiss. "But it'll be here when I get back."

———

When Lincoln and I head back to the party, most people have gathered around the bonfire, so we settle down next to them. Marie smiles at me as I sit. It's a real smile, and I think of how much I'll miss it when she leaves for college. Spinner sits next to Lincoln and hands him a double-stacked s'more. I have a feeling they'll stay friends for a long time to come. Eric calls my name from across the fire and tosses me something. I catch the small object, then open my hand to find an almost translucent peach sea marble. "Found it in the surf this morning," he says.

I close my hand around it tight and my entire body exhales.

Tess leans forward, fire flickering shadows across her face, and says, "So, truth or dare?"

This time I'm not anxious because of the game, I'm anxious because, as I look around the fire, this might be the last time we'll all play the game together. It might be the last time we sit around this circle, stretching our surf-worn bodies as the night slips away.

But it's okay. Maybe we won't all be in the same place at the same time again, but that doesn't mean we'll lose each other. It doesn't mean I'll never hunt for sea marbles with Eric or wake up at a disgustingly early hour to surf with Spinner or run sprints down the beach with Cassie. Time doesn't vanish things; it just shifts them.

I lean forward toward the fire and grin. "I'll go first."

Hours later, dares have been done, some of which could probably land us in jail, and all I missed this summer slips out from the truths. And I discover a new passion—stories. I never used to hear them from my friends because I was always there for the events. But now they're fresh and exciting and sparkling. And I'm not jealous that I'm not a part of them. I cherish each tale almost like it's my own. One day, years from now, when these memories have blended together, I won't remember the time I missed Eric's wipeout or the time I missed Cassie's summer dance recital, I'll just remember I grew up with a group of really amazing friends.

Eventually, it's my turn again. I face Lincoln because I know what he'll pick. "Truth or dare?"

"Dare."

I smile. "I dare you to go surfing." I smile wider and turn to the entire group. "I dare you all to go surfing. *Naked.*"

—————

We line the coast, dot after dot, surfboards by our sides, clothing by our feet. The wind whips lightly around us, promising smooth, mild waves. Cassie stands on one side of me, Lincoln the other, the glowing ocean in front of us.

"Ready?" Cassie calls.

Our readies chorus down the beach. And then all at once, we scream, "One, two, three," and blast off into the ocean. My strong thighs wade into the surf, and my board accepts me as I jump on and paddle out, watching the perfect wave pulse toward me, as if it were waiting for me, as if it knew I were coming.

As I mount my board, I see Tess on the shore, dancing, twirling around as if on an invisible string, and I hear my friends holler at the moon as the ocean collects us, racing us toward shore, hurtling us toward home.

ACKNOWLEDGMENTS

No one told me writing book acknowledgments would be harder than writing a book. I'm terrible with sentimentality and memory. I'll do my best to thank everyone who supported me. If I forget to mention you, please accept this thank you and preemptive apology.

To all of my readers with disabilities, thank you for finding this book. I hope you discovered some comfort and joy in it. I'm disabled due to crippling chronic pain. Lincoln's story isn't my story, but I hope it helps spread the message that *disabled* is never a person's sole characteristic. Our disabilities are a part of us, but they are in no way our full definition.

To Mom and Dad, of course. You were there for me as a little girl who loved words, as a young adult who wanted a graduate degree in writing, and now as an adult who leans on you in countless ways so I can continue to live and create stories. I love you. And also I love you. And lastly, I love you.

To the rest of my family, thank you for your constant affection and encouragement. I love you all, but I must specifically thank my grandparents: Papa Bobby, thank you for your love and for buying me tampons at Costco. Grandma, thank you for your love and for never saying no to a movie. Bubbie, thank you for your love and for teaching me the best card games. Zayde, thank you for your love; you are no longer with us, but you are always remembered. Thank you to my older brother Phillip, who is also no longer with us, but always supported my writing dreams, even when I was a little kid with nothing more than a spiral notebook and mechanical pencil with a chewed eraser. Thank you to my cousin Lauren Sandler Rose who constantly showers me with love, and my tenacious cousin Brandon Sabin, who serves this country and taught me about skateboarding.

To all of the remarkable people I met at the New School, where I wrote the initial drafts of this book. Thank you to all of my fantastic teachers, including David Levithan and Caron Levis. Thank you to my wonderful thesis advisor, Jill Santopolo, who I will always credit with helping turn my manuscript into an actual novel. Thank you to all of my peers, especially those from the Writing for Children program, and especially Elie Lichtschein, Lauren Vassallo, and Meghan Drummond. And especially especially (not a typo because y'all are worth the extra adverb) my three closest friends from graduate school and some of the most talented writers out there: Amanda Saulsberry, Anna Meriano, and Kiki Chatzopoulou. I write better because of you and keep writing because of you.

To my best friend in the world, Elise Laplante, for always supporting me, especially on the hard path I've faced lately, and yes, I'm giving you a shout-out in my book acknowledgments for driving my things from New York City to Atlanta. No one but a true best friend would drive that many hours to bring me my books and shoes.

Elise, you're my person.

To my other best friend, Katie King, for loving my words and me, for taking my author photos, for being an exceptional college roommate, and for loving board games as much as I do. I know you're going to accomplish great things in graduate school.

To some other wonderful friends, both new and old. It's been a challenging few years, and y'all have been there for me: Nic Stone, Brittany Kane, Becky Abertalli, Tristina Wright, Marieke Nijkamp, Abbie Blizzard, Laura O'Neill, Katherine Locke, Samira Ahmed, Whitney Gardner, Katherine Menezes, Justin Waxman, Angela Thomas, Raya Siddiqi, Tehlor Kinney, Christy Michell, Misa Sugiura, Deborah Kim, all of my Twitter darlings, and so many others.

To the people who've read this book, from friends to sensitivity readers to peers: Kayla Burson, Laney Berger, Ashley Woodfolk, Jay Coles, Dave Connis, Alex Wing, Melanie

Sliker, Kayla Whaley, and again, all of my Writing for Children classmates.

To my outstanding agent Jim McCarthy. I walked into DG&B as an intern and left as your proud client. Thank you for seeing something in this book and in me. Thank you for answering midnight emails. I look forward to many more years of working together (in which I'll *try* not to send you midnight emails).

To my editor Annette Pollert-Morgan—yes, I'm using the one dash on purpose just for you. It's been an incredible pleasure working with you. Your insights have made my book the strongest version of itself. I can't thank you enough.

To the rest of my team at Sourcebooks, thank you for being passionate, hardworking, and kind. I look forward to getting to know all of you, but for now, special thanks to Katy Lynch, Cassie Gutman, Alex Yeadon, Katherine Prosswimmer, Stefani Sloma, and Todd Stocke.

To my characters, thank you for barging into my brain and demanding I tell your stories. I hope to meet you again one day.

And finally to *all* of my readers, thank you. Perhaps we'll say hello once more in the pages of my next book.

ABOUT THE AUTHOR

Laura received her MFA in writing for children from the New School. She loves books, dogs, and bubble baths—okay, and quite a few people too. She currently lives in Atlanta, Georgia. You can say hello on Twitter at @LJSilverman1.

P.S. She has never surfed before, and the one time she tried skateboarding, there was a lot of blood.